"Skye Denison is the quintessential amateur sleuth: bright, curious, and more than a little nervy."
—Earlene Fowler

PRAISE FOR DENISE SWANSON'S SCUMBLE RIVER MYSTERY SERIES

Murder of a Sleeping Beauty

"A smooth, pleasant, and ultimately satisfying book."
—*Chicago Tribune*

"It's no mystery why the first Scumble River novel was nominated for the prestigious Agatha Award. Denise Swanson knows small-town America, its secrets and its self-delusions, and she writes as if she might have been hiding behind a tree when some of the bodies were being buried. A delightful new series."—Margaret Maron

"Fast-paced and lively."—*Romantic Times* (4 stars)

"Another delightful and intriguing escapade. . . . When this book reaches your local bookseller, do yourself a favor and buy it."—*Mystery News*

Murder of a Sweet Old Lady

"Skye is a quixotic blend of vulnerability and strength. . . . Denise Swanson is on her way to the top of the genre. . . . A magnificent tale written by a wonderful author."
—BookBrowser

"Superbly written with emotion and everything a good mystery needs. . . . Shame on you if you miss anything by Denise Swanson."—*The Bookshelf*

"Swanson's writing is fresh and snappy. . . . Skye Denison [is] one of the most likable protagonists in softer-boiled mystery fiction today. *Murder of a Sweet Old Lady* is more fun than the Whirl-A-Gig at the county fair and tastier than a corndog."—The Charlotte Austin Review

continued . . .

Scumble River is not a real town. The characters and events portrayed in these pages are entirely fictional, and any resemblance to living persons is pure coincidence.

Murder of a Snake in the Grass

A Scumble River Mystery

DENISE SWANSON

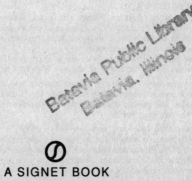

A SIGNET BOOK

SIGNET
Published by New American Library, a division of
Penguin Group (USA) Inc., 375 Hudson Street,
New York, New York 10014, USA
Penguin Group (Canada), 90 Eglinton Avenue East, Suite 700, Toronto,
Ontario M4P 2Y3, Canada (a division of Pearson Penguin Canada Inc.)
Penguin Books Ltd., 80 Strand, London WC2R 0RL, England
Penguin Ireland, 25 St. Stephen's Green, Dublin 2,
Ireland (a division of Penguin Books Ltd.)
Penguin Group (Australia), 250 Camberwell Road, Camberwell, Victoria 3124,
Australia (a division of Pearson Australia Group Pty. Ltd.)
Penguin Books India Pvt. Ltd., 11 Community Centre, Panchsheel Park,
New Delhi - 110 017, India
Penguin Group (NZ), cnr Airborne and Rosedale Roads, Albany,
Auckland 1310, New Zealand (a division of Pearson New Zealand Ltd.)
Penguin Books (South Africa) (Pty.) Ltd., 24 Sturdee Avenue,
Rosebank, Johannesburg 2196, South Africa

Penguin Books Ltd., Registered Offices:
80 Strand, London WC2R 0RL, England

First published by Signet, an imprint of New American Library,
a division of Penguin Group (USA) Inc.

First Printing, April 2003
10 9 8 7 6

Copyright © Denise Swanson Stybr, 2003
All rights reserved

REGISTERED TRADEMARK—MARCA REGISTRADA

Printed in the United States of America

To school psychologists everywhere who try every day to do the right thing for the children, especially my colleagues in Illinois

Acknowledgments

My sincere thanks to:

My paternal aunt and uncle, Pooch and Billie Swanson; my maternal aunt and uncle, Rosella and Joe Votta; my cousins Peter Bianchetta, Rich McLuckie, Phil McLuckie, and Tiffany and Justin Friddle; and the rest of my relatives and friends, who help my mother manage without my father.

Special thanks to my Personal Assistant and Der Webmeister, Dave Stybr, for supporting me in countless ways.

CHAPTER 1

The Good, the Bad, and the Ugly

Skye Denison stood in the Up A Lazy River Motor Court parking lot, slapping mosquitoes and trying to keep an eye on her godfather, Charlie Patukas. Not that he was hard to spot—at six feet, three hundred pounds, with a voice that could be heard two counties over, he was about as easy to miss as the Sears Tower in the Chicago skyline.

The problem was that he and the rest of the Scumble River Bicentennial Committee kept milling around on the grandstand. To Skye, they looked like fish in an aquarium: first they all darted to the right side of the stage; then they all charged to the left.

It was obvious that something was going on, but what? With each passing minute, the committee was getting more and more agitated. While other committee members appeared merely irritated, Charlie looked apoplectic. At seventy-three, with high blood pressure and a Type A personality, he was a stroke waiting to happen. And that was what worried Skye.

She swatted another bug and chewed on her bottom lip. Should she go up there and try to calm him down, or would that just annoy him more? There was a fine line between helping and making the situation worse. As a school psychologist, she often had to figure out when to cross that boundary. Too bad practice didn't make perfect.

While she continued to monitor the shade of red Charlie's face was turning, she dug into the pocket of her black shorts for a scrunchie to pull back her humidity-frizzed chestnut curls. The freshly-ironed white T-shirt she had put on when school got out at one o'clock now had all the crispness of a used dishtowel and stuck to her ample curves like a damp spiderweb. She felt as if she had never dried off from her morning swim.

What was she doing standing in ninety-degree heat on a Friday afternoon, waiting to hear some yahoo talk about the founding of Scumble River? She hadn't come with the intent to look out for Charlie's health. That was a bonus. Her real reason was simple. When you lived in the small town where you grew up, you were obligated to show your face at certain social events, whether you wanted to attend or not.

Even after two and a half years, Skye sometimes wondered if moving back to Scumble River had been such a good idea—not that she'd had much choice back then. But now that she'd saved a little money and could count on a decent job reference, maybe it was time to think about leaving. True, the last time she left hadn't worked out too well, but this time would be different. Wouldn't it?

She'd have to think about that later. Charlie's face had just gone from hot pink to purple. It was time to intervene. She moved closer to the platform, stepping through the dried grass, sand, and rocks that had been spread over the asphalt in an attempt to make the area look as it had two hundred years ago. Luckily, the river running alongside the motor court's parking lot had not changed, or else the committee would probably have tried to re-create it, too.

Eldon Clapp's high, whiny voice assailed her ears as she neared the grandstand. "Where is he, Fayanne? You said he'd be here a half hour before the start of the opening ceremony. For twenty years, I've done a good job as mayor of Scumble River, and now the only thing people will remember is that I ruined the bicentennial."

Fayanne Emerick, owner of the Brown Bag Liquor Store, stabbed the mayor in the chest with a dagger-like magenta fingernail, which matched the fuchsia polyester pants and shirt she had practically spray-painted on her pudgy body. "Don't you go blaming me, Eldon Clapp. I called Gabriel Scumble yesterday, just like I was supposed to. And don't think I'm eating the long-distance charges either. Why in heaven's name the great-great-grandnephew of the guy who founded Scumble River lives in Montreal is beyond me."

Obviously at least one member of the newly formed Scumble River Historical Society—or, as Skye liked to call it, the Hysterical Society—didn't know the town's past very well. Even she knew that the founder, Pierre Scumble, had been a French Canadian, a fact which might give Fayanne a hint as to why his descendant lived in Montreal.

"He's more than thirty minutes late." Mayor Clapp wrung his hands.

Miss Letitia, the only real historian on the committee, hit the mayor on his shoulder with her handbag and said, "I warned you about the Scumble family. Pierre was a rogue. It stands to reason his progeny would be untrustworthy too."

Clapp ignored the older woman—it was obvious he had tuned her out long ago—and continued to speak to the liquor store owner. "You have to do something, Fayanne."

"Me?" she screeched. "Why me?"

"Your committee was responsible for the speaker. After all, I found him for you and made the initial call. All you had to do was follow up."

"All? That man is harder to get on the telephone than the president, and his number kept changing." Fayanne bit off each word as if tearing into a strip of beef jerky.

"Don't give me excuses. We each had one thing to do.

My committee had to build the platform. Charlie's had the reenactment of the landing, Kevin's had the decorations. And Miss Letitia's prepared the historical reading."

Fayanne's small, hoglike eyes were turning from their usual muddy brown to an ox-blood red. Skye was afraid she would start punching the mayor any second. If that happened, it was a certainty that Charlie would join in the fight.

Skye had one foot on the grandstand's bottom step when a voice stopped her. "Ms. Denison, they're going to kill those kids this time."

"What?" Skye swung around, nearly losing her balance. "Where?"

Standing a little to the right of the stairs was a high school student she had seen hanging out on the fringes of several cliques. She couldn't remember the girl's name. "Who is going to kill who?"

The teen ignored Skye's question, fear evident in her eyes. "They're over behind the parked cars. You need to do something right now!"

Skye hesitated and looked back to the platform. The fracas seemed to be momentarily over. Fayanne had moved into a neutral corner and was brooding. The rest of the group was standing around at the other end of the stage. Charlie's color had faded to its normal florid state. Skye turned back to the girl, but she had disappeared.

Great. What should she do? There were hundreds of people in the parking lot; maybe she could ask one of them to go see what was wrong. No, the girl had come to her. She'd spent the last two years getting the kids at her schools to trust her, so this was not the time to ignore a plea for help.

Skye prayed Charlie would be okay and took off in the direction of the parking lot.

The sun burned down on her as she ran. Normally the seasons are very distinctive in Illinois, although occasionally spring and fall are cut a little short. This year it seemed as if summer was refusing to give way, causing the middle of September to reach a record high of ninety-five degrees.

Prolonged and intense heat often caused tempers to flare, and Skye was afraid of what she might find when she reached the parking area. She skidded around the fender of a huge black pickup, and saw that half a dozen high school bullies had cornered a group of more timid teens and were pelting them with rocks, rotten food, and verbal abuse. Skye wondered briefly which hurt the most.

She debated going for help, but leaving the trapped kids to the mercy of their tormentors was not an option. Surveying the various vehicles, she spotted one with its windows rolled down. It was an old Pinto that the owner was confident no one would steal. Skye hoped its horn worked. It would be her only way of summoning help if things went badly.

One of the bullies looked familiar. Although not as tall as many of his cohorts, he was well muscled with reddish-blond hair, blue eyes, and freckles. As she got closer, she realized he was a sophomore she had just completed a psychological assessment on the week before. In fact, she had a meeting scheduled with his parents on Tuesday. This was both good and bad news. On the one hand she had a name; on the other hand her evaluation had indicated a high likelihood that this kid had little in the way of a social conscience, despite his boyish good looks.

Skye stepped to the side of the Pinto, stood up straight, and said in a steel-edged voice, "Grady Nelson, stop that immediately!"

All action paused as the teens turned toward her. She held her ground but made sure she was in reach of the Ford's open window.

"Go away, Ms. Denison, this isn't any of your business," Grady drawled.

"I'm afraid it is, Grady. I can't let you hurt other kids."

"We aren't hurting them. We're just messing around—playing."

"But they don't seem to be having a good time."

"You just don't understand. Life's got to be fun. If it isn't fun, it has to move. If it's not moving, maybe we need to poke it a little. If we poke it, maybe we can make it mad and it'll move. I can't handle it when everything is standing still."

"How about if they come with me and you find another way to entertain yourself." She risked a peek at the kids being picked on. They seemed okay.

"Nah, that doesn't sound fun." He selected a glass bottle from a pile of debris at his feet. From his pocket he dug out a small can of lighter fluid and poured some into the container. Next, he grabbed the handkerchief from around his forehead and stuck it into the neck of the bottle.

Skye swallowed, her mouth suddenly dry. What in the world could she say to stop him from lighting that Molotov cocktail and flinging it among the teens? She glanced at Grady's gang. They seemed uneasy, too.

Hoping she had gauged their mood correctly, Skye said, "Hey, why waste your time and energy on those kids?" The words stuck in her throat. She hoped the kids she was trying to save didn't think she really felt that way about them. "How about you guys coming with me, and I'll buy you each an ice cold soda and a hot dog."

Grady glanced over his shoulder, smirking in a way that would have provoked any right-thinking adult to slap him. "Anyone want to go get a pop with the nice lady?"

The surprise on his face was priceless when most of his gang nodded, and one said, "Sure, this is getting whack."

Grady scowled, but it was clear he had lost them. Either they weren't up for setting other kids on fire, or the idea of free food and drink had won them over. Skye wished it was the former, but guessed the latter might have influenced their decision. Or at least given them a way to save face.

A small boy who looked about ten years old hung back. He scampered around Grady like a Chihuahua, begging for the bigger boy's attention, but Grady pushed him aside and stomped away. His last words trailed over his shoulder. "Hope you fags don't choke on your sody pop."

The teens hesitated, and for a moment Skye thought they'd run after Grady, but she dug a twenty out of her pocket and waved it in their direction. With much jostling and elbowing, they followed her to the refreshment stand that had been set up across the street from the reenactment area. Her last glance back revealed that the kids who had been harassed were scattering in the opposite direction.

While the boys were ordering, Skye took a look at the grandstand to see if Charlie was okay. He and the other committee members, minus Fayanne, were sitting on chairs, drinking from cans of beer. They seemed to have calmed down, at least temporarily.

As soon as the teens had wandered off, swigging from bottles of Mountain Dew and Dr Pepper, Skye went looking for one of the Scumble River police officers patrolling the event.

She spotted Roy Quirk by the Porta Potties. "Roy, I need to talk to you a minute."

He took off his uniform hat, wiping the sweat from his brow. "What's up?"

Skye quickly described her encounter with the bullies and their victims. "Is there anything we can do? Grady did have an explosive."

"I'll keep an eye out for him, but unless I catch him lighting the wick, he can claim that's the way he stores his lighter fluid."

"That's what I figured. Thanks anyway."

After Officer Quirk left, Skye collapsed under a shade tree. She was pretty sure that what she had done was not in the Illinois School Psychologists' Best Practice manual, but at least no one had gotten hurt . . . this time.

"Where have you been?" asked Simon Reid, Skye's sometimes boyfriend and the town coroner, sitting down on the ground beside her. They had gone out when she first moved back to Scumble River, but unresolved issues from her previous shattered engagement had kept them from becoming serious, and they had broken up. Then, working together on the church's youth committee during the summer had persuaded them to give it one more try. They were taking it slow and easy—no intimacy, no commitment.

She turned toward him. "Here and there. You said you had to talk to a few people, so I mingled, too."

A faint light twinkled in the depths of his golden-hazel eyes, as if to say he knew that wasn't the whole story. But instead of pursuing it, he changed the subject. Fanning himself with his hat, he said, "It's got to be close to a hundred degrees out in that sun. Tell me again why we're here."

His short auburn hair formed a fiery nimbus, and his features hinted at an elegance and refinement that were hard to find in Scumble River. Dressed in khaki shorts and a copper-colored polo shirt, he could have been on a country club patio rather than in the Up A Lazy River Motor Court parking lot.

"I could give you a bunch of reasons," Skye answered. "But the only important one is that Uncle Charlie told us to come. He wanted a big crowd to welcome Gabriel Scumble when he arrived."

"*If* he arrives. He's nearly an hour late. People will start to leave."

"No one will leave." Skye waved to her parents, who were sitting on lawn chairs in the shade of an enormous oak tree near the river's edge, her brother with them. Earlier she had chatted with her best friend, the Scumble River High School librarian, Trixie Frayne. Trixie and her husband, Owen, lived on a farm at the edge of town. "Most people are here because Uncle Charlie asked them to be."

"You make Charlie sound like a Mafia don."

"No, he's just very . . . charismatic, and he does a lot of favors for people." Skye owed her own position as school psychologist to him.

"Well, I guess it's a moot point." Simon stood and held a hand out to Skye to help her up. "It looks as if Gabriel Scumble has finally arrived."

A shiny black sedan pulled to a stop near the motor court's office. They watched as the mayor and Fayanne bolted over and flung open the door, nearly pulling the driver from the vehicle's interior. He was a compact man with curly black hair and dark eyes who seemed surprised by all the attention. Fayanne kissed him on the cheek, and the mayor pumped his hand. Talking a mile a minute, they led him up onto the platform.

People slowly resumed their seats, and voices quieted as the mayor started his speech. "In 1802, Pierre Scumble, a French Canadian fur trader, was voyaging down an un-mapped waterway when he stopped for the night. In the morning he looked around, found evidence of a rich vein of coal running through the area, and decided to establish the town of Scumble River. In a few years the population had grown to over nine hundred, a hotel and general store had been opened, and mining operations had begun."

Mayor Clapp continued to explain Scumble River's history for another half hour. Finally, he turned toward the man from the car and said, "So, it is with real pleasure that I introduce Mr. Gabriel Scumble, Pierre's great-great-great-great-great-great-great-grandnephew."

The man smiled, waved to the applauding crowd, and took the microphone from the mayor. "Allo, everyone. It's an honor to be here at your celebration. I'm sure Uncle Pierre would be proud."

Skye whispered to Simon, "I love his accent. It sounds a little like the ones in New Orleans." She started to edge her way closer to the grandstand.

"Well, that would make sense. The Cajuns were originally French Canadians," Simon murmured, following her.

The guest of honor spoke for a few more minutes, and then the mayor took over. "What we'd like to do this afternoon is get your help in reenacting Pierre's landing. If you go with Fayanne, she'll take you a little ways upstream and help you into your costume and show you the boat."

"Ah, I . . ."

Miss Letitia interrupted. "Mr. Scumble, we were so thrilled when you told Fayanne you were willing to take part in our little reenactment."

"Anything I can do to help you with your celebration," he said, kissing the older woman's hand.

Fayanne led Scumble away, and the crowd moved toward the riverbank. It was nearly twenty minutes before the canoe came into view. Skye and Simon had been swept to the shore with the rest of the assembly. She shaded her eyes, trying to get a better look. Gabriel Scumble didn't seem too happy, but who would be in this heat, paddling a canoe and wearing buckskin?

Skye turned to Simon. "Is that really what they wore back in the early eighteen hundreds?"

He shrugged. "Who knows? Remember, this is the Scumble River version of the past. Miss Letitia's the only one who actually knows the history of the town, and I'm sure they didn't listen to her if what she told them didn't fit their preconceptions."

Skye stifled a giggle and poked Simon in the ribs. "Look." One of the Scumble River citizens, dressed as an Indian Chief, had grabbed Gabriel Scumble's canoe, intending to help the man onto the shore. But the little boat swayed precariously, and both men were forced to fight to maintain their balance. Gabriel's face darkened with anger, and he used his paddle to bat the pseudo-Indian's hand away. The faux-chief teetered, did a couple of pirouettes that would have made Nijinsky jealous, and toppled into the river. He emerged seconds later, unharmed, but madder than the wet hen his feathered headdress now resembled. He muttered curses and threats as he sloshed away.

Mayor Clapp swiftly dismissed the rest of the tribe and led Gabriel Scumble up the riverbank and back to the viewing platform. Charlie stepped forward, and from behind his back he whipped out a three-quarter-size sterling silver pickax. Gabriel Scumble looked startled, but the crowd oohed and aahed.

Charlie said, "We'd like you to accept this gift on behalf of the grateful citizens of Scumble River. Without your uncle, our town wouldn't exist."

"Thank you. I'm deeply honored."

The mayor moved to the mike. "Now, we're going to let Mr. Scumble rest for a few minutes in his luxury cabin here at the Up A Lazy River Motor Court, provided free of charge by Mr. Charlie Patukas."

The crowd applauded.

Mayor Clapp continued. "This evening, between six-thirty and seven-thirty, Mr. Scumble will appear in full costume with the commemorative silver pickax for pictures. He'll be set up with the log canoe for a backdrop at the north end of the carnival, which is located in the center of the park." He paused as Fayanne whispered in his ear, then said, "The carnival rides start at seven, but the Beer Garden will open in ten minutes."

Skye and Simon had managed to work their way up to the grandstand in time to see Charlie hurry away with the guest of honor.

"Did you need to talk to Charlie?" Simon asked.

"No, just wanted to say hi before we left. I never got a chance earlier."

"We can wait. I'm sure he won't be long."

She looked at her watch and noticed it was already quarter past six. "No, we'd better get going. I've got a lot to tell you, and this took a lot longer than I thought it would." Simon had been gone all week attending a county coroners' institute in California.

He looked puzzled but led the way to his car. The interior of the Lexus was like an Easy-Bake Oven, and the seat belt buckle could have done double duty as a branding iron. Skye gingerly slid in, hoping not to leave any of her skin on the leather seats.

The drive to her cottage took less than five minutes, but then most trips within Scumble River took less then five minutes. With only three thousand in population, the town didn't cover many miles.

Skye was still trying to figure out how to break her news to Simon as she fitted her key in the front lock. Then the door swung open, and it was too late.

CHAPTER 2

The Perils of Pauline, aka Skye

Vases of yellow roses; baskets of gladioli, sweet peas, miniature orchids, and carnations; and ceramic pots of violets and lily of the valley were everywhere. They sat on tabletops, nestled on bookshelves, and crowded windowsills. The great room of Skye's cottage, which did triple duty as a living room, den, and dining area, had been turned into an indoor flower garden.

In addition to the floral offerings, boxes of chocolate candy still in their distinctive gold wrapping paper and gift baskets containing everything from fruit to perfume were piled on the sofa and chairs. The pièce de résistance was the mountain of stuffed animals in the center of the floor. If they had been real, Skye could easily have started her own zoo.

Simon stood in the foyer and surveyed the overwhelming tableau. He waited a beat, then said, "So . . . where are the dancing leprechauns?"

Skye crooked her finger for him to follow and walked all the way into the room. She reached behind the couch and picked up a two-foot-high garden gnome, which she placed at Simon's feet.

He waited another beat and said, "It's not dancing."

They both collapsed on the couch laughing. Later, while they were wiping the tears from their eyes and getting back their breath, Simon finally asked, "Where *did* you get all this stuff? Win a contest?"

"I wish." Skye bit her lip. "It's kind of hard to explain. I tried to call you a couple of times, but we never connected. It wasn't something I thought I could leave you a message about."

"No, really?"

"It's pretty complicated."

"At this point, I'd be disappointed if it were simple."

She checked her watch; she was almost out of time. How to tell him? "I need a drink. Do you want something?"

"My first choice would be an explanation, but I can tell you're still working yourself up to that, so I'll have a glass of wine."

Skye edged her way into the kitchen. The wine goblets were on the top shelf, since they didn't get a lot of use. Normally, she and Simon preferred Diet Coke. A bottle of zinfandel was pushed to the back of her fridge. It was a good thing wine got better with age, because she couldn't remember when she had purchased it. The corkscrew cooperated, and she poured the drinks with a shaky hand. She really had no choice; she had to tell Simon the whole story, and she had to tell him before eight o'clock. After that all hell would break loose.

When she returned to the great room, she found Simon sitting on the floor surrounded by a stuffed tiger, a lion, and a panther. Her nearly solid black cat, Bingo, was stalking the toys. Whenever the feline went near the fake animals, Simon would make them move or growl. It looked as if both man and beast were having a great time.

Skye hated to break up the fun. She set the glasses of wine on the coffee table and eased onto the floor next to Simon. "Okay, here's the scoop. It's been an interesting week. Late Monday night the phone rang. I kind of thought it might be you."

"You said not to call you since the time difference made it so awkward."

"I know, but I sort of thought . . . Anyway, I answered the phone, and it was my ex-fiancé."

"Luc St. Amant?"

"How many ex-fiancés do you think I have?"

"Just checking." Simon rose from the floor in one fluid motion and settled on a chair facing the sofa.

No way was she sitting at his feet like a supplicant; she also moved into a chair. "I hung up on him as soon as he identified himself."

"But that wasn't the end of it?"

"How'd you guess?" Skye jeered. "No, the next day when I got home after school, the flowers started arriving."

Simon raised an eyebrow.

"I refused to accept them." Skye got up and began to pace. "I was upset. I tried to call you. No luck. So I went over to Trixie's. I couldn't go to my parents' or Uncle Charlie's because I didn't want to tell them that Luc had contacted me."

"What did Trixie say?"

Skye felt her cheeks getting warm. "Nothing much." Trixie, her best friend, had been intrigued by Luc's reappearance in Skye's life and had encouraged her to talk to him.

"This was Monday night?"

"Yes. Tuesday morning Luc called again. This time I talked to him. I wanted to tell him not to waste his time sending me flowers. I hadn't accepted the ones he sent, and I wouldn't accept any he sent in the future. He explained that he had changed, and he had to talk to me. I said no, just leave me alone, and hung up."

Simon waved his hand, encouraging her to continue.

"I usually spend Tuesday mornings at the junior high and afternoons at the high school." She paused to see if he was following her, and he nodded. "When I got to the high

school, everyone was giggling. The secretary walked me
down to my office and swung open the door. It was full of
boxes of candy. I gave a lot away—these are what's left.
Then, to top things off, when I got home about five o'clock,
my living room was full of flowers."

"How did they get inside? You didn't leave the door unlocked, did you?"

"Of course not." She was starting to get miffed by his im-
perturbable attitude. "The delivery boy for Stybr's Florist is
related to my cousin Ginger's husband. Turns out his boss
told him the customer was offering him a fifty-dollar tip if
he could complete the delivery. He called Ginger, she called
Mom, and Mom came and unlocked the door. By the way, I
told her the flowers were from you, so prepare yourself."

"Didn't your mom and Ginger want to know why you
didn't accept the original flowers from me?"

"No, that sneaky delivery boy didn't tell Ginger there
was an original aborted delivery."

"I'm afraid to ask about Wednesday."

"I was afraid to experience Wednesday." Skye shook her
head. "Luc called again that morning. I couldn't understand
why he was calling so early, rather than at night. That's one
thing we have in common: neither one of us is a morning
person." She paused, reflecting. "Maybe he *has* changed."

Simon frowned for the first time. "You've been talking to
him?"

"A little." Skye scooped up Bingo and snuggled her face
into the black fur, suddenly cold in the air-conditioned
room. "He said that a lot had happened in the two and a half
years I'd been gone, and he needed to see me. It was urgent.
I said no, it was better to let sleeping dogs lie."

"Yeah, when you wake up those canines they tend to be
irritable and bite you in the butt."

"What I can't understand is how Luc got my school
schedule, and how he even knows where I work."

"Come on, this is Scumble River. Pick a telephone number at random. Dial and ask how to find Skye Denison, the school psychologist."

"You're probably right." Bingo started to squirm in Skye's embrace, so she put the cat on the floor. "Wednesday afternoon, I walked out of the elementary school and opened the door to my car. It was filled with gift baskets—need any cheese, crackers, bath gel, or perfume?"

Simon ignored her facetious question. "Wasn't your car locked?"

Skye tsked. "I thought you were smarter than that. You know I drive a 1957 convertible. Locking that car is like putting a chastity belt on a prostitute—it wastes your time and just annoys the thief."

"Thursday?"

"Thursday, Luc called again. This time he wanted to tell me what's happened with everyone we used to know. I listened for a bit and then begged him to stop sending me gifts."

"And?"

"I got home from school that day to find a wooden crate on my doorstep filled with stuffed animals. I plan to give them to the children's floor of the Laurel Hospital, but I haven't gotten over there yet."

"You've had quite a week." Simon got up and put an arm around her. "Did he call this morning?"

She nodded into his chest.

"But no gifts this afternoon?"

"No. But see, here's the tricky part." Skye moved slightly away from Simon and studied the carpet. She really needed to vacuum.

"Yes?"

"Well, I've decided to see Luc."

Skye watched in fascination as Simon's impassive expression became taut and derisive. "After all that man did to you? I'm beginning to wonder about your taste—that business with Kent last spring, and the way you act around Wally

Boyd. Maybe you prefer men who treat you badly. I thought you had better judgment than that."

"Good judgment comes from bad experiences, and a lot of that comes from bad judgment. Besides, Kent and I were just friends, and I don't know what you mean about Wally."

"Sure. So, you're going to give your ex another chance?"

"No, yes, I mean, I'm going to see him, not get back together with him." She turned to the bookshelves that lined three of the four walls in the great room and began to rearrange the volumes. "I need to see him."

Simon took her by the shoulders and turned her to face him. "Why? You know he's a bastard. Why do you need to reconfirm that?"

"I have two good reasons."

"Okay. Let's hear them."

"First, Luc says he's changed." She held up a hand. "Yes, I know he's probably lying. But he claims he's seen the error of his ways and wants to make up for the past by setting up a foundation for abused kids. He wants me to be on the board of directors. Think of how many kids someone with his money and connections could help."

"And this just happens to be in New Orleans, right?"

"Yes, he wants to do it in his hometown."

"I thought the root of the problem between you two was that Luc wouldn't back you up when you reported one of his friends for abusing his daughter."

"That's roughly what happened, yes."

"And now Luc plans to set up a foundation to help those kids?" Simon sounded skeptical.

"Look, I don't necessarily believe him, but I am willing to hear him out before I make up my mind. Someone from an important family like his could open up a lot of eyes down there."

"There's another reason you're seeing him."

"Yes, I need closure on our broken engagement." Skye

rested her hands on his chest. "We'll never be able to go anywhere with our relationship if I don't do this."

Simon gathered her into his arms and gave her a quick kiss. "I just want to go on record as saying that seeing Luc is a bad idea."

Before she could answer, there was a knock on the door. Simon let her go. "Are you expecting anyone?"

Skye walked to the foyer and checked the side window. She turned to Simon with a rueful smile. "Only Luc."

CHAPTER 3

Once Upon a Time in New Orleans

Skye took one look at Simon—a cold, grim expression had settled over his features—and felt the blood drain from her face. Realizing she was light-headed, she stumbled over to the hall bench, sat down, and put her head between her knees.

"Aren't you going to let him in?" Simon's voice held a challenge.

"I just need a minute."

"Shall I open the door?"

There was no sign of the warm, humorous man she had spent the afternoon with. Simon had withdrawn into a kind of cool correctness.

They stared at each other as the knocking started again.

I need to get the doorbell fixed. Skye frowned. Why had she thought of that now? Of all times, this was when she needed to stay focused.

She got up, moved toward the door, and froze. Simon stepped in front of her and opened it.

The handsome man standing with his fist raised in mid-knock put his hand down, smiled, and tipped his hat. "Bonjour, y'all." He swept past Simon into the foyer, dropped his expensive leather suitcase on the floor, and pulled Skye into his arms. "Darlin'!"

Skye closed her eyes to escape Luc's devastating grin.

Her legs felt shaky, and she drew in a deep breath before attempting to speak. "Luc, let me go." She looked around. Simon had disappeared.

Luc ignored her words, but she managed to wiggle out of his embrace, so he contented himself with grabbing both her hands. The odor of Aramis washed over her, reminding her of the hot Southern nights they had spent in their king-size bed. Oh my lord, she should never have agreed to see him. This was a gigantic mistake.

His smooth baritone was low and seductive, with just a hint of New Orleans. The uptown crowd prided itself on not having the accent most people associated with Louisiana. "When I look at your beautiful face, I feel as if we never parted. It's as if, poof, the years are gone."

Skye snatched her fingers away from his and said in a stronger voice, "Look closer. We were finished over two and a half years ago. I still remember very clearly the day you dumped me and cleaned out our apartment while I was at work being fired."

"Darlin', I was confused." He tried to get closer, but she dodged out of his reach. His touch was dangerous. "I know now I was wrong, but at the time I thought you were being unreasonable, jeopardizing everything for a lying, attention-seeking teenager. I realize now she wasn't the one lying."

"Still, you didn't believe me when I told you I was sure she was being abused."

"When she recanted, everyone thought she had been making up stories."

"I never did," she corrected him. "And you should have believed me. It was obvious she was being threatened by her all-powerful father."

"You're right, I see that now, and I've come to make it up to you—and to help children who find themselves in similar situations in the future."

Skye couldn't believe that this was the same man who had all but run her out of town on a rail. "I'm glad to hear you're going to help abused kids, but you don't have to make it up to me. It's in the past. I have a new life now."

Where was Simon? She looked around and saw that he had left through the great room's French doors and was sitting on a patio chaise lounge facing the river. He was surrounded by a gray blanket of fog that had rolled in off the water, making him almost invisible. Skye raised her voice, "Simon, come meet my *ex*-fiancé."

He got up and spoke from the open doorway. "Why don't you two settle things by yourselves first? Don't worry," he said over his shoulder as he turned back to his chair, "I'm not going anywhere."

Luc frowned. "Is that man your fiancé?"

"No, but we are dating." Skye wondered what Simon was up to, staying out on the deck. He was behaving strangely, or maybe he wasn't. Who knew in a situation like this how anyone was supposed to act?

"Ah, then I'm not too late." Luc moved close, trapping her between his body and the wall. "I've never stopped loving you."

Skye blinked back tears that suddenly formed. Her heart felt as if it had lodged in her throat and made it difficult to speak. "I don't want to hear that. You never really loved me. My middle-class background appealed to you as just another way to provoke your parents." She pushed her way free of him and ran into her bedroom. It was all too much.

She went straight to the bathroom, locked the door, and splashed cold water on her face. She had tried to erase the feeling of Luc's touch and the sensation of his kisses from her memory, but they still remained. Even now she had the strongest yearning to go back into the living room and throw herself into his arms. But a more powerful urge was to grab him by the collar of his designer shirt and demand to know why he'd broken her heart.

Skye knew she had to go back and finish things with him. But why did he have to look better now than he had in the past? His black hair, with a touch of silver at the temples, was still full and thick. His eyes were a clear indigo blue. And worst of all, the few age lines around his mouth gave him a look of strength. His youthful good looks had matured into something better, much better. Why couldn't he look like the spoiled, selfish man she knew he was?

It suddenly occurred to her to wonder how she looked to him. Should she change clothes, fix her hair, put on some makeup? No! When she'd left him, she had vowed never again to change herself for any man. Instead she dried her face and marched back to the battlefield.

Luc was seated on the sofa, trying to coax Bingo near enough to be petted. The cat sat just out of reach and stared at him with unblinking golden eyes.

"Darlin', you're back!" Luc sprang to his feet. "I see you got my gifts." He gestured around the cottage. "I hope you like them and they help you forgive me."

"I asked you to quit sending me presents." Skye stood with her back rigid and her voice like ice. "You know, for the first few months after you walked out on me, I secretly hoped you'd see the light, that you'd be miserable without me and realize your mistake. But since then I've changed."

He hung his head. "You were right. I have been miserable since you've been gone. Not a day went by that I didn't think of you. Please give me a chance to win you back."

"I don't want you back in my life. All I want is to help you with your foundation for abused kids and then once and for all say good-bye, properly this time."

Luc sat back down on the sofa and patted the cushion beside him. Skye ignored the silent invitation and seated herself across from him on the director's chair.

"Ah, but to do that, you need to hear the whole story, from when you left New Orleans to this very minute."

"Okay, then let's start with why I should believe anything you say."

"Because you still love me?"

"Buzzzz, wrong answer." Skye crossed her arms.

"Because you're a fair-minded person?"

"Strike two."

Luc opened his mouth and closed it. He repeated this several times before he spoke again. Finally he said, "Because you need closure so you can go on with your life, and until you and I really finish things, you'll never be able to have another serious relationship?"

She couldn't believe her ears. Since when did Luc St. Amant know things like that? She couldn't admit that he was right. It would give him way too much advantage. What should she say? When the answer came to her, she smiled thinly. She should say exactly what she had learned in graduate school: *Don't let him assign feelings to you; make him own his own emotions.*

Skye loved it when she could actually make use of her education. "So, you're saying you're having trouble moving on and need my help."

A strange look crossed Luc's face, but he quickly smoothed it away. "Darlin', I'll always need your succor and support."

Skye ignored the twinge in her stomach. "Okay, I'll listen to what you have to say, but I won't promise to believe it. Let's start at the beginning."

"Why don't you come sit beside me?" He patted the couch cushion again.

"No. If we're doing this, we're doing it my way. And my way is for you to keep your distance."

"You were always afraid of your own sensuality." Luc got up and sat on the coffee table facing Skye's chair. "Let yourself go, darlin'."

Skye moved her legs so her knees were not touching his. "That reminds me of one of our problems," she said. "Anytime you didn't instantly get what you wanted, you blamed a character flaw in me."

"You never used to think that way. You used to be grateful for my guidance."

"You don't want to go down that road," Skye warned. She got up and moved away from him. "It isn't one of my more pleasant memories."

"What?"

"Remembering how pitifully eager I was to fit into the mold you made for me. How I was willing to give up my own feelings, standards, even morals to be more like you and your crowd."

"When we first met," Luc said, "you told me you wanted to be more sophisticated, more uptown. You said you were sick of your small-town, naïve persona." Luc stood behind her, and put his arms around her waist. "You asked me to teach you how to behave around the 'right' people."

What he said was true, and it was a hard truth to swallow. Skye hadn't understood the rules. She had read Miss Manners, but in New Orleans things were different. It was the unspoken edicts—the social conventions, styles, trends, what-is-and-isn't-done-when—that had tripped her up. And she had desperately wanted to fit in. Now she was ashamed of how shallow she had been.

She wiggled out of Luc's embrace, unhappy with the image of her he was resurrecting. "As you said, I was naïve. It's amazing how fast you mature when you're fired, jilted, and left flat broke."

Luc refused to look her in the eye as he said, "I didn't get you fired."

"True, but you didn't stand up for me either. You didn't tell them to lay off. When your friends decided I had to be shut up to protect Mr. Big Shot, head of New Orleans society, you didn't lift a finger to help me."

"And I was wrong. I should have fought at your side, but I was weak back then, and you were accusing the most powerful man in town of sexually molesting his daughter." Luc fingered a crystal bowl on one of the bookshelves. "And she wasn't even a student in your school."

"Where she was enrolled was beside the point. I was a mandated reporter, which meant if a kid came up to me on the street and told me she was being abused, I had to tell the authorities. But that's beside the point. The point is, a child was in trouble and asked me to help her, and you didn't want me to because it might hurt your place in society."

"I know, and I recognize now how selfish that was. But at the time, especially after she took it all back and said she had lied to get her parents' attention, I . . . I took the easy way out." Luc's knuckles turned white as one hand gripped the other. "I have suffered for it."

"She had been coerced into changing her statement," Skye said. "It was obvious she was frightened of her father."

"You could see that, but I couldn't, because I didn't want to. All I could see was that you had done your duty. You made your report. The accusation was investigated and determined to be unfounded. There was nothing more you were obligated to do. You could have let it go." Luc moved to gaze into her eyes. "I wanted you to let it go."

"But I couldn't. The psychologist is the conscience of the school. We have to say the words that people don't want to hear and expose the truths that people would rather deny. We are the advocates for the children, and believe me, that is not always a very popular position."

Luc's face was sober, but he didn't respond.

"I had to try to talk the girl into telling the truth, if not for her sake then, for her younger sister's." Skye stared into his blue eyes, hoping to see compassion there.

"The sister, don't think she hasn't haunted me every day since this all happened." He looked away. "I thought there was nothing I could do. I didn't want to see what I should be doing, because it would ruin my own comfortable life."

"Oh?"

"Once you approached her again and started to stir things

back up, her father was hell-bent on seeing you crushed. If I had tried to stand by you, he would have destroyed my whole family. A St. Amant would never have danced at the Comus ball again."

"And to you that was more important than a child's welfare." Skye blinked back a tear. "More important than me."

"At the time, I told myself that this girl, who you didn't even know, was more important to you than me." Luc stared at her. "And that you would accomplish nothing by ruining our lives."

Had she pursued the matter beyond all reasonable hope for a positive outcome? Skye wondered. Maybe subconsciously she had known she would never fit into Luc's world and had sabotaged herself. Could it be that at some level she'd realized it was easier to live with being kicked out for a righteous cause than for being personally inadequate?

Suddenly Skye could almost see Luc's point. He had always talked about their daughter being queen of the Comus ball. That would have been a tough dream to give up. "I think I understand the motivation for what you did, but I still don't understand why you did it the *way* you did."

He took her hand. "I was wrong to leave without a word."

"And to take everything."

"Yes, even though it was all mine. I had paid for it all." A line formed between his eyebrows. "I should have been more generous."

"You left me completely broke, knowing I was going to be fired."

"I didn't realize you had maxed out your credit cards or spent every dime of your salary." He untangled his fingers from hers and moved a step back. "You should have told me."

"How did you think I could dress the way you wanted me to and not spend tons of money?"

"I was just thinking of you. If you went to the parties and business functions wearing clothes you had ordered from the Penney's catalog, you would have been cut dead by my friends and business associates." Luc's lip curled. "When we first met, you were wearing slacks you bought at a blue light special."

"I was in graduate school, and before that, the Peace Corps. What did you expect me to dress in, Prada originals?"

"No, just not in clothes from a store that was mainly frequented by fifty-year-old housewives who lived in trailers."

"We're obviously getting off the subject here." Skye tamped down her temper with great difficulty. "All I want to know is why, even if everything was yours, you thought it was all right to leave me with nothing?"

"I was wrong. I wasn't thinking straight." Luc turned his face from Skye. "I was so hurt you had chosen that girl over our future, I wanted to punish you."

"I literally had nothing but the clothes in my closet, a few knickknacks, and less than a hundred dollars in the bank." Skye's voice cracked as she remembered her panic when she discovered how badly off she was. "You even canceled the lease on our apartment. I had less than a week to move out. If a friend hadn't let me stay with her for the last few months of school, I would have been living in my car."

"I told you, I wasn't thinking. Besides, I knew your family wouldn't let you starve or go homeless."

"It was humiliating to have to move back here, especially as a beggar. I had to borrow money from my parents."

"I'm truly sorry."

"If it wasn't for Uncle Charlie being president of the school board, and the fact they couldn't get anyone else to work here, I probably wouldn't have found another job." Skye scooted away from him. "Your friends really did a number on my professional reputation."

"They're ruthless. That's why I warned you not to mess with them."

Skye stared at him. Had he changed, or was he feeding her a line of bull? "I need to think about what you've said."

"Sure, but remember, everyone deserves a second chance. Haven't you ever done something disgraceful and needed someone to give you a break?"

Skye closed her eyes, remembering the day she told her entire hometown in her valedictorian speech that they were small-minded people, with even smaller intellects. When she moved back, the citizens had given her a chance to make things right. They'd made her suffer, but they'd given her a second chance.

Maybe Luc deserved a second chance too. The cottage grew quiet. It seemed as if Luc was merely a photographic image and Simon hardly existed as she sorted through her feelings, trying to decide whether she should give Luc an opportunity to prove he'd changed. Suddenly the hushed contemplation was broken by a fusillade of knocking on the front door.

Skye checked her watch. It was nearly ten o'clock, extremely late for anyone in Scumble River to come visiting. It could mean only one of two things. Someone was either in jail or dead.

CHAPTER 4

A Funny Thing
Happened on the Way
to the Bathroom

At first the shadowy form on her front step looked huge. The haze from the river had increased, making it difficult to see any details. Skye flipped on the outside light and squinted into the soft gray veil. Suddenly, like an amoeba, the figure split, and she could see that she had two visitors, not the one giant person she had initially imagined.

"Who is it?" Luc asked, as he crowded next to Skye to peer out of the foyer's side window.

"Is someone at the door?" Simon asked, entering from the patio.

"All I can tell is there are two of them," Skye answered. "Guess I'd better find out."

"No." Luc put his hand over hers on the knob. "If you don't know them, maybe you shouldn't let them in."

Skye shrugged. Her house was already filled with people she didn't seem to know anymore. She did put the chain on, and she opened the door only a crack. "Who is it?"

"It's us, Ms. Denison, Justin and Frannie. Please let us in. It's real important." Justin's voice cracked.

As she freed the door and opened it, Skye said over her shoulder to Luc, "It's a couple of students from my high school." To Simon she added, "It's Frannie and Justin." Frannie's father was employed by Simon at his funeral home, and both kids had worked for him during the summer.

The teens tumbled in like puppies, then stood and stared at the three adults. Finally, Justin said, "Ms. Denison, we need to talk to you alone, right away."

"Why? What's wrong?" As soon as the words left her mouth, Skye could have kicked herself for being so stupid. It was obvious they didn't want to speak in front of Luc and Simon. "Never mind."

"Thanks, Ms. D." Frannie brushed her long, wavy brown hair from her eyes.

The good hostess in Skye kicked in, and she began introductions. "Luc, as I said, these are students from my high school, Frannie Ryan and Justin Boward. Frannie, Justin, this is . . . ah . . . my guest, Mr. St. Amant."

Frannie narrowed her brown eyes and turned to Simon. "St. Amant. Weren't you and Dad talking about Ms. Denison being engaged to a guy called Luc St. Amant? I remember because it's such a weird name."

It was clear from Simon's expression that he wasn't sure whether to deny the conversation or try to explain. The latter seemed to win. "We might have mentioned it in passing. We were probably talking about something else and it came up."

"Nope." Frannie smiled sweetly. "You and Dad were talking about how hard it is to understand women. And you said something like you'd never understand why Ms. Denison couldn't just get over that low-down skunk she'd been engaged to."

Luc shot Simon an outraged look—and Skye a triumphant one.

"I don't recall that conversation. Perhaps you didn't hear us correctly. That happens sometimes when you *eavesdrop*."

"I heard all right." Frannie frowned and turned to Luc. "So, are you Ms. Denison's fiancé?"

Luc gave Frannie the tight-jawed smile that adults give children who make them uncomfortable. Before he could answer, Skye decided it was time to step in. "How about some lemonade while we talk?"

"No!" Justin answered for them both. "I mean, no, thank you. We really need to talk to you right away."

"Sure, I understand." Skye glanced around her cottage. Where could they go? It was basically one space. The only doors were on her bedroom and the guest bathroom. It felt wrong to take the kids into either place, and she didn't want Luc and Simon in her bedroom, which would really be bizarre. Could she ask the two men to wait in the bathroom? No, better to keep them apart. Ah, she had forgotten the tiny utility room off her kitchen with its sliding pocket door. "Okay, kids, we can talk in here."

They followed her silently, and watched as she slid the door closed. Skye leaned against the washer. Frannie jumped up on the dryer, which creaked a bit under her weight. She was a solidly built girl who would never be a size two or even a twelve, a trait that continued to cause her much heartache.

Justin sat on the small built-in folding table. Skye noted how much the boy had grown since she had first started seeing him for counseling in eighth grade. He had started out close to her height—five-seven—and now was nearly six feet tall. He was still skinny with thick glasses that hid his best feature, warm brown eyes, but she bet that someday he would be a handsome man.

"So, what's up?" Skye asked, not sure she really wanted to know. Both of these kids were bright and very inquisitive—traits that had gotten them into trouble in the last year.

"Well, we were out riding around," Justin started.

"Yeah, I just got my license last week, and Dad actually let me have the car," Frannie added.

Justin scowled at Frannie, then picked up what he had been saying. "We were just buzzing the gut." He looked at Skye to see if she understood.

She nodded. "We used to call it shooting the loop or tooling."

"You did that too?" Frannie's eyes widened.

"Yes, but we used a horse and carriage."

Justin frowned at both females and cleared his throat. "So, as I was saying, we were minding our own business, just driving around downtown, when we decided to go over to the carnival."

"I'm surprised you weren't already there. There aren't many places to go on a date in Scumble River. I would have thought you'd take advantage of the carnival being in town."

"No. We aren't—we're just friends—we don't date," Frannie rushed to explain. "After all, I'm nearly a year older than Justin."

Justin stared at the floor; a dull crimson stained his cheeks. "We hang out 'cause we both like the same things."

"Oh, sure," Skye backpedaled. "Go on."

"The carnival was stupid. Mostly baby rides, and all the games were obviously rigged."

"Yeah," Frannie broke in. "This one guy got seriously bent when Justin told him that the laws of physics made it impossible for anyone to win his game. He came over the counter at us and tried to hit us with a baseball bat."

Skye shot up. "I'll call the police right away. Are you kids okay?"

"We're fine, Ms. D.," Justin said. "We're not here about that. Frannie had to use the bathroom, but all the Porta Potties had long lines and she couldn't wait, so I suggested the bathrooms over by the bandstand at the far end of the park."

Justin paused for breath, and Frannie took over. "We didn't realize it had gotten so foggy, but Justin had a flashlight on his key ring that was pretty strong, and we decided to go ahead. Once we got there I ran right into the bathroom, but when I came out, Justin grabs me by the hand and tells me to look at the bandstand."

"I thought I saw something shiny when I was messing around with the flashlight beam," the boy offered.

"At first, I thought he was trying to spook me out, but I took a look, and there *was* something shiny on the steps." Frannie leaned so far forward, she almost fell off her perch. "We decided to go take a closer look. There shouldn't be anything shiny at the bandstand."

"What did you see?" Skye asked.

"Justin went right up to the steps, but I hung back, in case there was trouble and I needed to go for help."

Skye nodded. "And what was it you saw?"

"A dead body." Justin's eyes searched Skye's face.

She fought to keep her expression neutral. "Of a person?"

"No, an alien." Justin wasn't one to pull his punches. "Of course a person. There was a man laying on the steps."

"Did you know who it was?" Skye asked.

"I didn't get a look at his face, but . . ."

"But?" Skye pressed.

"He was dressed like Daniel Boone, and I think he had a silver pickax sticking out of his chest. As soon as I saw that, I pushed Frannie back, and we got the hell out of Dodge. We drove right over here."

"Why didn't you go to the police?" Skye looked at each teen in turn.

Both rolled their eyes.

Justin snorted. "Yeah, like that's what *you'd* do."

Last spring the boy had caught Skye trying to break into the funeral home, and he loved to remind her of her folly.

She hated being hoisted on her own petard. "That is exactly what I would do . . . in most cases. Why come to me?"

Frannie answered, "We were afraid. Besides, they'll listen to you. Chief Boyd has a crush on you."

Skye ignored that last bit. "How about your parents?"

Justin hung his head. "Ms. Denison, you know my parents can't handle this. They can barely handle picking out what to order on the pizza—when they remember to get dinner."

Skye nodded reluctantly. Justin's father had a severe physical disability, and because of it his mother had sunk into a deep depression. The boy was pretty much raising himself. "Why not your dad, Frannie? He's great in a crisis."

"He went to Kankakee with a friend. It's his meeting night for the veteran's association," Frannie said. "Maybe we should go out, and you could take a look before we bother the police. We kind of thought it could be someone playing a joke on us."

"Oh, no." Skye shook her head. "Even if it was a prank, Chief Boyd would lock up all of us if we disturbed a crime scene. We have to call him right now."

"That sucks!" Justin jumped down from where he'd been sitting and headed for the door.

Skye blocked his exit and said with a straight face, "If the world didn't suck, we'd all fall off."

There was a moment of silence, then Frannie giggled and Justin snickered. The tension had been broken, and Skye felt safe leaving the kids and heading for the phone. As she dialed, she tried to remember who was dispatching tonight. Her mother, May, worked part-time as a police, fire, and emergency dispatcher. If she was on duty, the situation would take twice as long to explain.

Skye was relieved to hear another dispatcher's voice answer her call. "Hi, Thea? It's me, Skye. Is Wally there? Sure, I'll wait." She stretched the cord as far as it would go and peeked into the great room. Luc was sitting on the couch, trying once again to pet Bingo, but the feline was having none of it. Simon stood staring out the French doors at the fog-shrouded river.

A few moments later the dispatcher came back on the line. "Wally's not here, but I got a hold of him just now. Hang up. He'll call you in a second."

Skye followed the directions, wondering why she

couldn't just have telephoned him. She had his home number.

The shrill ring startled her, and she fumbled with the receiver as she answered. "Hi. No, I'm fine. Yeah, I'd say it's an emergency."

"You sure this can't wait until morning?" Wally's voice sounded garbled.

Skye frowned. Had he been drinking? "Look, if you're busy, Roy could probably handle it. I only asked for you because you get so mad if you think I'm keeping secrets."

Her relationship with Wally had always been complicated. Though they'd never been more than friends, there had always been an attraction between them. When they first met, she had been a teen and he in his early twenties. Years later, when she returned to Scumble River, he was married. Then last summer his wife had divorced him, he and Skye had resolved a long-standing argument, and a more intimate relationship had become a possibility. So far, neither of them had acted on the opportunity.

"Just tell me what's happened." Now his voice sounded resigned.

What was wrong with him? Should she ask? Skye shook her head. She had other things to deal with first. "You remember Frannie Ryan and Justin Boward from the Lorelei Ingels case, don't you?"

"Yeah. What have they done now?"

"I think they've found a dead body in the park." Skye pulled up a seat and told Wally the teens' story.

"Shit! I'll be right there to pick those kids up."

"Wait a minute." Both Frannie and Justin were trying to talk to her at the same time. "What did you guys say?"

Frannie answered for them both. "Ms. D., can't you come with us?" The girl no longer looked sixteen; her pale, frightened face could have passed for twelve.

"Sure." Skye's thoughts flew to the two adults in her living room. No way was Luc staying alone in her house.

Making up her mind, she spoke back into the phone. "Wally, we'll meet you at the police station. The kids want me to stay with them, and I have a problem I can't leave here, so I'll see you in ten minutes." She hung up before he could protest.

Next, Skye poked her head into the great room. "Simon, we've got a situation."

He came striding into the kitchen. "What is it?"

She summarized what Justin and Frannie had told her.

"Would you like me to go with you and the kids?"

"No, you'd better go get the hearse and meet us out there. This sounds like a job for the county coroner."

He nodded and kissed her on the cheek. "What will you do with him?" Simon nodded toward Luc, who had been standing in the door listening intently.

"He'll have to leave."

"But, darlin', I have nowhere to go." Luc came into the kitchen and took her hand.

Frannie and Justin were watching this drama from the doorway of the utility room with avid faces.

"Go to your motel. I'll call you tomorrow," Skye ordered.

"I don't have a hotel room. Everything within thirty miles is booked because of your blasted bicentennial."

"Okay, we can't figure this out now. I need to drive these kids to the police station, and it looks as if you can either come with me or drive around in your car." Skye herded everyone toward the front door.

Luc's expression was a cross between dread and confusion. "Why can't I wait here? This doesn't involve me."

"Because I don't want you here alone. Just come on." Skye got everyone outside and over to her car. "Kids, get in the back. Luc, take the front seat. Let's move it."

"This is your car?" Luc asked, his gaze roaming along the huge aqua '57 Bel Air's tail fins.

"Yes, and I don't want to hear any comments."

On the short drive to the police station, Skye explained

what was going on to Luc. She was thankful, though surprised, when he offered no opinion and asked no questions.
Had he really changed that much? This was not what she
would have guessed would be his reaction to the news she
had just shared.

Wally was waiting for them in the PD's parking lot. As
Luc got out of the Chevy, the chief's eyes widened. "Who's
this?"

Skye took a deep breath. "This is Luc St. Amant. He
needs to wait here."

"Why?"

"We're trying to figure out a place for him to spend the
night. The motels around here all seem to be full." Skye was
evading the real question.

"How do you know Mr. Amant?" Wally persisted.

"St. Amant. Never mind that now." Skye gestured to the
teens. No way was she explaining about Luc in front of
them. "Shouldn't we take care of this other matter first? I'll
tell you all about it later." To Luc she said, "Get on the
phone and find somewhere to stay. Try Joliet and Kankakee."

Wally lifted an eyebrow but acquiesced and escorted
Skye, Frannie, and Justin to his squad car without further
questions.

As she buckled herself into the passenger seat, Skye gave
a silent prayer of thanks. Since her mother wasn't on duty as
a dispatcher tonight, she had a little more time before having to explain Luc to her family. Now, if the gods were really kind, neither May nor Uncle Charlie would be listening
to their police scanners.

CHAPTER 5

A Hard Day's Night

Skye glanced over at Wally. He looked odd, rumpled—had they gotten him out of bed? She checked that the kids had their seat belts fastened and then stared out the windshield. They were driving west on Maryland Street. The windows of the few stores and offices lining the street were dark. There were no cars, people, or signs of life. After the recent bicentennial crowds, it was almost as if Scumble River had been evacuated.

As they neared the river, tendrils of fog began to cover the asphalt. A few yards farther they crossed the bridge by the Up A Lazy River Motor Court. Park Loop Road came immediately afterward.

Wally eased the squad car onto the dirt path and asked, "At the bandstand, correct?"

"On the steps." Justin leaned forward and spoke through the wire mesh dividing the front and back seats.

Scumble River Park was a small finger of land that extended into the river for about a half mile or so. It was accessible by car only from Maryland Street. Pedestrians could cross the footbridge that extended from the apex of the Up A Lazy River Motor Court parking lot. The park was also approachable in all directions by boat. The bandstand was located at the farthest tip of land.

The squad car crept slowly down the lane, with the river

to the left and the park to the right. The fog had thickened, reminding Skye of curdled milk. They passed the darkened carnival area where the silhouettes of tents, trailers, and thrill rides looked like the remains of an ancient civilization. Not a single light shone through the darkness. Skye frowned. It seemed early for the crew that operated the carnival to be settled for the night.

An expanse of trees and picnic tables, their contours muted like an impressionist painting, slid slowly by. Skye silently urged Wally to drive faster. She felt a sense of urgency she couldn't explain.

Finally, just before the road circled back toward Maryland Street, the outline of the bandstand slowly materialized. It was a wooden structure shaped something like a wedding cake but open on all sides. Down a short gravel walkway, the park rest rooms glowed under a vapor light.

Skye turned to look at the teens in the back. "Tell me again why you two were out here."

"We already told you. I had to use the bathroom." Frannie crossed her arms and huddled in a corner of the seat.

Skye knew they weren't telling her the whole story and didn't hide her skepticism. "This is pretty far to walk to use the rest room." If they weren't having sex or doing drugs, and she believed them when they said they weren't, what in the world would bring them so far from the carnival?

"There was a long line, and I had to go bad."

Wally stopped the squad car by the side of the road. Through the fog, the bandstand was just barely visible. "All of you, stay put. Understand?"

Three heads nodded, watching in silence as he got out of the cruiser. Skye's gaze never left him as he walked toward the open-walled building, obviously being careful where he stepped. She held her breath while he paused. All hope that the kids had seen something other than a dead body vanished when Wally grabbed his radio and started to talk.

As soon as other officers started to arrive, Wally put

Skye, Justin, and Frannie in separate vehicles. Skye had been stuck in squad cars before, while other crime scenes were being processed, and she knew it would be a long night.

At first she tried to see what was going on, but since the fog hid most of the action, there wasn't much to watch. At least she was dry and cool. The poor men—Scumble River had no female police officers or EMTs—working outside had to be sweating in the heat and humidity.

"Skye, are you all right?" The muggy caress of air from the open door and Simon's concerned voice startled her awake.

"Yes, I'm fine. Do they know who it is?"

"It looks like Gabriel Scumble. I did my duty as coroner and then let them take away the body."

"Who would want to kill a complete stranger?" Skye struggled to sit up and gather her thoughts. She'd been dreaming about her days as a Peace Corps volunteer in sunny Dominica. Luc's reappearance in her life must have stirred up her memories of the past.

"The police will have their hands full with this one," Simon said, not quite answering her question.

She opened her mouth to ask one of the thousand queries running through her mind but closed it without speaking. Considering that Simon hated it when she got involved in murder investigations, and that Luc was waiting at the police station, she decided to tread lightly.

Before she could think of a safe subject, Simon said as he closed the door, "I've got a couple of things to finish up, then I'll see you at the police station."

Oh, no, did that mean Simon would have a chance to talk to Luc before she could get there? That couldn't be a good thing. She was gnawing on her thumb, worrying about what the two men might discuss, when Justin climbed in the back seat.

Wally slid in behind the wheel and said, "I'm going to drop Justin off, then take you back to the PD."

"Where's Frannie?" Skye felt a momentary panic that something had happened to the girl.

"Her father took her home after he and Simon finished with the body."

"Oh, I didn't see Xavier. It must have been while I was dozing." Skye wondered what else she had missed.

"You fell asleep?" Justin's voice held bewilderment with a slight undertone of reproach.

"Yeah. It's one of the body's great defense systems. It helps you deny anything is happening when you're upset. After all, if you're not awake, you can't be made to face whatever you're trying to avoid." Skye inwardly cringed at her clumsy attempt to explain Psychology 101 to the teen.

The drive back into town was considerably slowed by the fog, which had continued to thicken. After taking Justin home, Wally and Skye rode in silence to the police station. A gray wall of cotton candy seemed to surround the car, and neither of them broke the eerie stillness.

As they were parking, Wally said, "I'm surprised you didn't use this time to ask me a thousand and one questions about the body."

"What?" She had been thinking about how she would handle the next few moments with Simon and Luc. "Oh, yeah, anything interesting?" Skye asked indifferently. She had a funny feeling that she was going to be far too busy figuring out her own love life to solve this murder for Wally.

"Late thirties to early forties, no identification, but Simon said it looked like Gabriel Scumble, and he was wearing a buckskin costume."

"But why would anyone want to kill a complete stranger? No one in town knew him."

"Could be robbery, since he had no wallet on him. Of course, the costume had no pockets, so he could have left his possessions at the motor court. I've got Quirk searching his room."

She nodded absently and slid out of the car. Her thoughts had already returned to brooding about what was about to happen behind door number one.

At least one of her worries was assuaged as Simon pulled in behind the cruiser. It was a relief to know he hadn't beat them to the station and had a chance to chat with Luc on his own.

Simon joined Skye and Wally as they entered the PD. Skye muttered, "I hope Luc found a hotel room while we were gone."

Before either man could answer, Luc rose from the worn vinyl sofa in the reception area and swept Skye into his arms. "Darlin', I've been so worried about you! Out in this vile weather with a dead body."

Simon and Wally looked at each other. At first each just gave a slight curl of his lips, then one of them snickered, and finally they both burst out laughing.

Skye had been trying to struggle out of Luc's embrace. Now, he abruptly let her go and said to Simon and Wally, "Messieurs, that is hardly the proper way to treat someone's concern for a lady."

"I don't think you know this lady very well, at least not anymore," Simon answered, raising an eyebrow in Skye's direction. "Does he, *darlin'*?"

Luc sniffed and turned to Wally. "What can one expect from a mortician? But you, an officer of the law, should be more of a gentleman."

Wally, it seemed, was no longer as amused by Luc's manner. He snarled, "Who the hell do you think you are?"

Luc straightened and pulled the invisible mantle of his money and position into place before answering. "I, sir, am Luc St. Amant, Skye's fiancé."

All eyes turned to Skye, who stuttered, "Are you out of

your mind? You're my *ex*-fiancé—*ex*, do you hear me? I don't have a fiancé."

With that, Luc, Simon, and Wally surrounded Skye and started to shout at each other. Since all of the men topped the six-foot mark on the tape measure, Skye at five-foot-seven felt like a bonsai shrub among the redwoods. She gazed from Simon's hazel eyes to Wally's brown ones. Both looked hurt and angry.

"Guys." She tried to get their attention, but they ignored her. "Fellows," she said more loudly. Again nothing. "Listen up!" she shouted at the top of her lungs. Finally, silence. "I do not appreciate you all discussing me like I'm not even here. None of you has any right to judge me. Is that clear?"

Three heads nodded reluctantly.

"Good. Wally, is there anything you need from me before I leave?"

Wally nodded but turned to Luc. "Mr. Amant, when did you get into town?"

"It's St. Amant." Luc shrugged. "I'm not sure, perhaps seven-thirty."

"What time did he show up your house?" Wally asked Skye.

"He was due at eight, and it was a couple of minutes past when he got there. I looked at my watch when he started knocking."

"That's right. I checked the time, too," Simon said.

"Why are you asking about my arrival time?" Luc asked.

"Just trying to get an idea of where everyone was, and at what time." Wally glanced at his notes. "So if you got to town at seven-thirty, where were you until eight o'clock when you arrived at Skye's?"

"Perhaps I was wrong. Perhaps it was nearer to eight when I arrived. I did not look at my watch, so I am not sure."

"Okay, then, when did Frannie and Justin get there?" The chief scribbled in his notebook.

"I'd say fifteen to twenty minutes before I called and

talked to Thea, so a little after ten." Skye yawned. "Anything else? I'm beat."

"One more question." Wally ran his fingers through the strands of gray and black at his temples. "Are you really engaged to this clown?"

"I already told you, no." Skye shook her head for emphasis. "Luc and I were engaged when I lived in New Orleans, but that was over two years ago." She headed to the door. "It's nearly two in the morning. I'm going home."

Luc took Skye's arm. "Yes, darlin', let's go home. I'm exhausted."

Shoot. She'd forgotten about the accommodation problem. Wally and Simon were staring at her as if she'd gone crazy. Reclaiming her arm, Skye said, "Did I mention that Charlie's cabins are full, as are all the motels in the general area, and Luc hasn't anywhere to spend the night?"

"Wasn't he supposed to be finding a hotel in Joliet or Kankakee while we were gone?" Simon reminded Skye.

"That's right. Did you call around?"

"Sorry, there is no hotel room within forty miles of Scumble River. Joliet is having some kind of car racing event and Kankakee is having some festival or such. It's really no problem." Luc moved closer to Skye. "I'll just stay with you."

"You are not spending the night with me."

Luc hung his head, the picture of dejection. "But, darlin', surely you wouldn't abandon me?"

Wally stepped into the fray. "Normally, I'd tell you to go to Chicago for a room, but since it's better for you to stick around, we do have a holding cell in the basement of the PD you could sleep in."

Luc narrowed his eyes. "You suspect me of murder?"

"As Skye will tell you, I suspect everyone, but what I meant was the fog is too bad to be driving in."

Skye shot him a glance. Was he telling the truth? His smile was all innocence.

"No St. Amant has ever spent a night behind bars, and I am not about to become the first. Don't be foolish, Skye. It's not as if we've never slept under the same roof before."

Skye and Simon looked at each other. He raised an eyebrow; she shrugged.

Simon crossed his arms. "Here's the deal. And it's for one night, and one night only. Luc can stay with me."

Skye turned to Luc. "I'll talk to you tomorrow about the foundation, and you'd better have papers to show me."

"That's it?" Luc asked. "I don't get any say in this?"

"A woman always has the last word in any argument. Anything a man says after that is the beginning of a new argument." Skye turned her back on Luc and looked at Wally.

The chief's face wore a mean scarecrow smile. What was the man up to? He walked through the steel door leading to the rest of the station before she could ask.

Simon grabbed a piece of paper and drew a map to his house. He handed it to Luc. "Here. Skye will take you back to her place so you can pick up your car. I'm locking the door and going to bed in twenty minutes. Don't bother coming over if you take longer than that."

To Luc, Skye said, "Go wait in the car. I'll be there in a minute."

As Luc left the building, Skye and Simon both sighed. They could hear the mumbled sound of the dispatcher talking behind the reception area's half-counter, half-glass partition, but otherwise there was blessed silence.

Simon put his arm around Skye. "You realize this situation has all the makings of a disaster."

She nodded. "And you haven't thought of the half of it. Wait until my mother and Uncle Charlie hear about it."

CHAPTER 6

Guess Who's Coming to Breakfast

Skye sprang into a sitting position clutching the sheet to her chest. Bingo, his tail fluffed to twice its normal size, ran under the bed. Someone was in the cottage. The distinctive squeak of the front door had nudged her from a dreamless sleep, but the sound of someone opening and closing drawers shoved her into full wakefulness. What should she do?

The baseball bat her brother had given her as a housewarming gift was propped between her nightstand and the wall. She grabbed it and eased off the mattress unto the floor. Thankful that the thick carpeting muffled her movements, she tiptoed to the bedroom door. It sounded as if the intruder was in the kitchen. Terrific, he was in there with her only phone.

Suddenly the radio blared. What kind of thief turned on the radio to work by? Skye edged the bedroom door open and snuck through the great room, hiding behind first the sofa, then a chair, and ultimately wedging herself between two bookcases. From there she could see through the archway into one corner of the kitchen.

She eyed the distance between her location and the exits. To get out the front door, she would need to pass the foyer's entrance to the kitchen. If she went out the great room's French doors, she'd either have to walk around the house, passing in front of the kitchen windows, or jump into the river and swim for it. She didn't think she'd make it much past the dam.

One of the things she had always liked about her cottage was the isolation and the idea that the backyard wasn't accessible except through her property or the water. But now the idea of neighbors was starting to have some appeal.

Shit! The French doors' deadbolt locks required a key to open, even from the inside, and hers were on the foyer table. Maybe the window in her bedroom? No, the noise of opening it would attract unwanted attention. She was trapped. Skye sagged against the wall. Okay, she needed to attack. Surprise was her only advantage.

She heard the trespasser open the fridge but couldn't see him. What in the heck was he doing, fixing himself a sandwich? It didn't matter; now was the time. His back would be to her, and if she were lucky, his hands would be full. Skye hurtled into the kitchen, bat raised . . . and skidded to a stop, the bat suspended in midair.

The figure at the refrigerator whirled around, holding four eggs in one hand and a half gallon of milk in the other. Both splattered all over the floor. "What in the world are you doing, Skye? You nearly gave me a heart attack jumping out at me like that." Skye's mother grabbed a roll of paper towels and started to wipe up the mess on the linoleum.

As Skye got her breathing back to normal, she stared at the petite woman kneeling at her feet. Not a wave was out of place in May's short salt-and-pepper hair. She was dressed in black bicycle shorts and a matching tank top, and a red sports bra peeked out from the armholes and neckline. Spotless white sneakers gleamed on her size five feet. When had her mother started dressing like someone in a Nike commercial?

May looked up from her squatting position. "Why are you holding a baseball bat?"

"Because you scared me to death! I thought you were a prowler."

"Where's the shotgun your dad gave you? That little piece of wood won't save you from a robber."

Skye ignored May's question and asked one of her own. "How did you get in here?"

"I used my key, of course. Good thing you didn't have the chain on." May jumped up holding a soggy mass of paper towels.

"I've asked you not to use your key except in an emergency."

"I came over to fix you breakfast."

Skye held her temper and focused on the red numbers on the microwave. It was only seven a.m. "What makes breakfast an emergency?"

"I heard this morning at exercise you had a rough night last night."

Skye hesitated. How much did her mother know? "You mean finding the body?"

May paused. "What else could I mean?" She carefully put down the new eggs she had been holding. "Does the other thing have anything to do with the gift shop you seem to have opened in your living room?"

Skye sank into a chair and buried her face in her hands. Great, now she would have to explain Luc.

"How do you want your eggs?" May had gone back to the important issue, cooking.

"I only want tea and toast. Real food this early makes me queasy."

May turned from the stove. "Are you pregnant?"

"Of course not! Why would you ask such a thing?"

"I thought maybe that's why Simon was showering you with gifts. That nonsense in there is from him, isn't it?"

"Not exactly." Skye looked at the expression on her mother's face, and it scared her more than when she had thought May was an intruder. "Uh, do you think I could have a cup of tea before I get into it?"

May poured and handed Skye a mug. Skye tore open two packets of Sweet'N Low and added them to the Earl Grey, then took a cautious sip. The hot liquid helped her focus.

"You sure I can't fix you some pancakes or French toast?" Skye shook her head. "Oatmeal, you should have oatmeal every morning. It sticks to your ribs."

Skye looked down at her curvy figure. "What I eat seems to stick there just fine as it is."

"So, what's going on with the stuff in there?" May gestured toward the great room.

"I guess I'd better start from the beginning." Skye explained the week of Luc's calls and gifts, and how she couldn't tell Simon until after the opening ceremony of the bicentennial. Then she told May about Luc, Frannie, and Justin showing up on her doorstep. She concluded with, "So, Luc is staying at Simon's, and it looks as if Gabriel Scumble was murdered."

May had been silent during Skye's story. As it ended, she asked, "There's only one thing I don't understand."

"What's that?"

"Why have you let that *bastard* talk his way back into your life? He near about destroyed you the last time. And how about Simon? You think he's going to wait around while you mess with an old boyfriend?" May heaved a giant sigh. "Have you considered that if you do make it up with Luc, that means leaving your family and living in New Orleans again? I'll never see my grandchildren."

Skye was stunned. She'd never heard May say "bastard" before. "I . . . uh . . . the thing is, I need closure, and I do want to help if Luc establishes that foundation he's talking about."

"Closure, my eye. You're still blinded by his money and because he's a big shot."

"That's not true. He says he's changed. Isn't it possible I could help him be a better person?"

May shook her head. "Don't imagine you can change a man unless he's wearing a diaper."

Skye had had enough. She'd been startled awake after less than five hours of sleep and scared out of her wits, and now her mother was telling her how to manage her love life. "I'm going to take a shower. Make yourself at home. Feel free to rummage through my drawers, write Luc a Dear John letter, or clean my kitchen—whatever makes you happy."

May's mouth hung open for a couple of seconds, but she recovered quickly. "Just remember I told you so, when this all blows up in your face."

Skye stalked out of the room, not dignifying her mother's last comment with a reply. She made her bed, stripped off her nightshirt, and stepped into the shower. As the hot water poured over her, she deliberately emptied her mind but still found herself humming a tune she hadn't heard in a while. What were the words?

Opening the shower door, she wasn't surprised to see Bingo sitting on the bath mat. He and May did not get along, and he generally hid whenever Skye's mother visited.

The melody in her head kept playing as she dressed in khaki shorts and a black T-shirt. Just as she finished French braiding her hair, the name of the song popped into her mind. It was an old Pam Tillis hit, "Mi Vida Loca." How appropriate. She had been humming "My Crazy Life." The tune seemed to come to her whenever she was about to make a fool of herself.

Somehow Skye wasn't surprised to find her mother still there when she came out of the bedroom. May had indeed been cleaning and polishing, which seemed to have calmed her down. Skye sat on the sofa and raised her voice above the noise of the vacuum cleaner. "Have you heard if they're shutting down the bicentennial activities?"

"The committee decided that the show must go on. All

the workers will wear black armbands, but it was just too hard to tell all the people to leave. Besides, what would they do with the food and prizes and everything?"

"True. I wonder who would want to kill Gabriel Scumble? Did he know anyone in town?"

"No. I remember Charlie saying they had a hard time tracking down a descendant of Pierre's. He would have been easy to find if anyone in town knew him." May turned off the vacuum cleaner and started rewinding the cord. "It must have been a robbery."

"Yeah, that makes the most sense. Poor guy. Quite an honor." Skye reached down to scratch Bingo, who had followed her out of the bedroom.

May tsked. "When are you going to get rid of that cat? How can you stand the dirt?"

"What do you mean? Cats are very clean; they're always washing themselves."

"Cats are not clean; they're just covered with cat spit."

"Mom, that's awful. You know what I read the other day? People who hate cats are going to come back as mice in their next life."

May grimaced. "Ew!"

Skye smiled to herself. Direct hit. "I'd better finish getting dressed. I want to check on Frannie and Justin. They seemed okay last night—I think TV, music, and video games have made kids immune to being shocked about death—but I want to make sure they're still fine this morning."

"Poor kids." May put away the vacuum cleaner and picked up her purse. "I've got to run too. I have a hair appointment at eight-thirty, and your brother better do a good job this time. Last week he made it look too round."

Skye's brother Vince was a hairstylist and owned a local salon. Everyone except May thought he was a genius with hair. For some reason, she always found something to criticize.

May paused at the door and said grudgingly, "Bring Luc to Sunday dinner."

"What?" Skye was floored that her mother would invite her ex-fiancé to a meal.

May's smile was calculating. "If he's wanting to reconcile with you, it's probably a good idea for him to meet some of your family. He never met anyone but me, Vince, and Dad when you were engaged."

Skye closed her eyes to the vision of Luc meeting her aunts, uncles, and cousins. But it would be a good test to see if he had really changed or not.

"Three o'clock. Don't be late," May ordered as she climbed into her car. "The Bicentennial Dance starts at eight, and I don't want to miss a single minute."

CHAPTER 7

A Day at the Pancake Races

Once her mom left, Skye continued to sit on the sofa appreciating her newly immaculate cottage. May had thrown away most of the flowers, stuck the boxes of candy in the freezer, and stuffed all the plush animals into several giant garbage bags. Making her mother angry was a better way to get her place cleaned than hiring a housekeeper. Everything gleamed.

Bingo climbed into her lap and started to knead her leg. Skye relaxed under his massage. Her eyelids fluttered closed, only to jerk back open at the sound of the telephone.

Great. She had a feeling the caller was either Luc, Simon, or Wally, and she didn't want to talk to any of them. Maybe she'd cheat and let the answering machine get it.

But by the third ring she couldn't stand the suspense, and snatched the receiver from its cradle. "Hello."

"Hi, did I get you up?" Simon's warm voice washed over her.

"No, Mom beat you to that hours ago."

"She heard about last night."

"The murder was the talk of her exercise class."

"So she still doesn't know about Luc?"

"Well . . ." Skye stretched the cord of the phone to the sink and ran water into her teakettle. As she set it on the stove and turned on the burner, she answered, "Yes and no.

She saw all the gifts he'd sent, so I had to tell her some of it."

"What was her reaction?" It was common knowledge how much May wanted Skye to get married and produce grandchildren.

"Strangely enough, she wasn't happy. It seems she'd rather have me single and living in town than married and living in New Orleans."

"Tough choice for her," Simon joked.

"Don't worry, you're still number one on her list of possible sons-in-law and fathers for her grandchildren."

"What a relief." His voice was a velvet murmur. "How about you? Am I still number one on your list?"

Darn, how did she get herself into spots like this? When in doubt, change the subject. "Hey, I nearly forgot. Did you see Frannie today?"

Simon let out a long, audible breath before answering, "No, but Xavier is worried. He thinks there's something on her mind. It's really a shame those two can't talk to each other."

"Sad to say, that's the situation between a lot of fathers and teenage daughters." Skye poured boiling water over the tea bag she had placed in her mug. "Anyway, I'm going to track her and Justin down this morning and try to get them to talk to me. No matter how cool they may seem, stumbling across a body can't be good for them."

"Xavier said they were going to the Pancake Races this morning. You can probably catch them there."

"Thanks, that saves me some running around." Skye hesitated, but she had to ask. "Uh, is Luc still at your house?"

"Far as I know. He was snoring like a freight train when I left. I'm over at the funeral home."

"Oh, uh, good." Skye sipped her tea and listened to the silence. She sure knew how to ruin a good phone call.

"Why? Did you want to talk to him?"

"No! Well, yes, sometime today. I want to see those foun-

dation papers he claims to have for me to sign," she said
hastily. "So, I guess I'd better get going, since I want to
catch the kids at the Pancake Race."

"Guess you'd better. Bye."

"Hey, wait. You don't know anyone who's heading over
to Laurel today, do you?"

"Xavier has to make a quick run to the Wal-Mart this
morning for some cleaning supplies. Why?"

"Could he drop off a few bags of stuffed animals at the
hospital for the children's floor?"

"Sure, put them out on your step, and he'll pick them up
within the next hour or so."

"Great," Skye said. "I really want them out of my house."

"Yeah, I really want 'the stuffed animal' out of my house,
too. See you later." Simon hung up.

Skye stirred her tea. Too bad she didn't use the loose
kind. Maybe the leaves could have told her what she should
do.

She could do nothing about Luc right now. Justin and
Frannie's welfare came first. She put her cup in the sink and
found the local newspaper. The entire front page of the
Scumble River Star was filled with the schedule of the bicentennial events. The Pancake Race Breakfast was being
held at nine o'clock in the high school parking lot.

It was already eight fifteen, too late to get to the beach for
her morning swim, but still early enough that she might snag
a decent parking spot at the Pancake Race Breakfast if she
left right away. With the school's lot being used for the
event, street spaces would be at a premium, and the Bel Air
could not be slipped into any old small opening.

She slid her feet into a pair of sandals, buckled a fanny
pack around her waist, and put on some mascara and lipstick. It was supposed to be another hot day, so any addi-
tional makeup would be a waste of time.

After putting the bags of toys on her front step, she
headed for her car. Last spring, her father and Uncle Charlie

had surprised her with the gift of a 1957 Chevy Bel Air convertible that Charlie had discovered rusting away in an old
barn. Jed had spent the winter restoring it.

The aqua monstrosity was hardly the vehicle that Skye
had envisioned herself driving around town in, but there had
been no way to turn down such a labor of love from the two
men—even if the car did lack air conditioning, required the
driver to manually raise and lower the top, and sported fins
bigger than those on the shark in *Jaws.*

People were just starting to arrive for the Pancake Race
Breakfast when Skye parked the Bel Air on the street in
front of Scumble River High. She got out, leaving the top
down. As she had pointed out to Simon, there was really no
use locking a convertible as old as this one.

The school's parking lot was set up as if for a track meet,
but within the inner circle were tables and chairs. Along the
left side, in the grass, serving stations had been set up. Each
one had a cook, a griddle, and someone to take the ticket and
hand over the plate of food.

Along the right side, on the sidewalk in front of the building, were booths where bets could be placed on the various
racing teams. There were six squads made up of four con-
testants each. The object of the competition was to carry a
pancake on a spatula around the track without dropping it. If
the racer dropped the flapjack, he had to eat it before starting over. If he made a successful circuit, the pancake was
handed over to the next team member, who repeated the
process. The first squad whose racers all completed the
course would win.

Skye shaded her eyes with her hand and inspected the
various clusters of people milling around the asphalt. She
didn't think Frannie and Justin would be members of any of
the race teams, and it surprised her to see them behind one
of the food stations. They didn't tend to be joiners.

In the few minutes it had taken her to locate the teens, the
crowd had swollen, and lines were already forming. Frannie

and Justin's station was swamped. There was no way she could talk to them until the rush died down.

The last thing she wanted was something to eat, but since she had to hang around anyway, it would probably look less conspicuous if she placed a few bets. She opened her fanny pack and took out her wallet. All she had was a five and seven singles. Spending that twenty on those bullies yesterday had used up most of her cash. She would need to stop by the bank sometime this morning before it closed at one o'clock.

"Skye, over here."

She walked toward the familiar voice. "Trixie, where are you?"

Skye's best friend, Trixie Frayne, jumped up and down at the edge of the crowd. She was short, with a cap of smooth brown hair and brown eyes that gleamed with good humor and high spirits.

When Trixie had returned to town nine months after Skye had been forced to come back home, both women had agreed it was fate. They had been best friends in high school until Trixie's family moved away her sophomore year. Being reunited nearly fifteen years later still felt like a gift.

Today Trixie wore white fringed cut-off shorts and a red tank top. She was the antithesis of the stereotypical shy, demure librarian.

"What are you doing here?" Trixie asked as Skye walked up.

"I came to see the race."

"Bullpucky! You're normally not up and around this early on a weekend, or if you are, you're out at the beach swimming." Trixie grabbed Skye's arm and whispered in her ear, "Is it about the murder last night?"

"How did you hear about that already?"

"Everybody knows. Between the people with police radios and the ones with relatives on the emergency squad, I'd say the whole town knew by midnight, two a.m. at the latest."

"Of course, what was I thinking?" Skye hit her forehead with the palm of her hand. "What's being said?"

"Mmm, let's see. The victim is Gabriel Scumble, and he was robbed. People are saying it was probably one of the carnival workers, that they steal stuff every time they're around."

"Is that all?"

"Yeah, it's still early, gossip's pretty thin on any actual details."

"I hadn't thought of the carnival people, but that might make sense. He was posing for pictures among them. Maybe he flashed a big wad of cash or something. Someone better talk to them before they leave town tomorrow night."

"So, are you investigating? Can I help?" Trixie was skipping around Skye like a hyperactive three-year-old.

"No and no. This is one Scumble River murder that has nothing to do with me."

"Sure." Trixie's look was skeptical. "But something will happen, and you'll end up in the thick of things. And when you do, I want a piece of the action."

Skye ignored her friend's comment and asked, "Did you hear that Frannie Ryan and Justin Boward were the ones who found the body?"

Trixie shook her head. "How awful. I wonder how that escaped the grapevine."

"Wally kept them out of sight to protect them from being under the microscope, so don't tell anyone." Skye paused to emphasize the importance of this point to Trixie, who silently crossed her heart. "They seemed okay last night, but I want to check with them this morning and make sure they're not feeling any post-traumatic distress."

"Good thinking. It always amazes me how well kids hide their feelings, at least at first." Trixie gestured to the crowd. "It doesn't look like you can talk to them anytime soon."

"Guess I'll just hang around until the race is over. Maybe talk to them as they clean up. What are you doing here?"

"The cheerleaders have a team competing." Trixie was the cheerleading coach.

"Oh." Skye couldn't quite picture the cheerleaders eating a pancake that had been on the ground. Or for that matter, running around a track with a spatula, looking silly.

"Stop thinking that," Trixie said, obviously reading Skye's mind. "We have a really good group of girls this season. When Zoë and her pack graduated last year, I made sure that the judges at the tryouts counted character as heavily as attractiveness. And since the money made from this event goes to the Morning Star Mission in Joliet to help the homeless, the girls were happy to help out."

"That's great. Did Frannie Ryan make the squad this time?"

Trixie's sunny smile disappeared. "No, I couldn't convince her to try out again."

Skye hugged her friend, knowing how badly Trixie felt about the outcome of Frannie's first attempt to become a cheerleader. "If you're sure her size won't be an issue this time, maybe I can convince her to give it one more chance."

"I promise. She'd be an asset. She dances like a dream." Trixie glanced at her watch. "Time to line up my team. Have you placed your bets yet?"

"No. Who else is competing?"

Trixie steered Skye over to a large white board placed between the betting booths. On it were the names of the teams and their odds printed in big black letters. "Now, not speaking as a team sponsor, here's my take," Trixie said. "The chess club isn't a good bet because they'll spend too much time trying to find the most logical way to win. The debate team might stop and try to talk the spectators into thinking they've already won. The teachers don't have any more of a chance against the kids today than they do in the classroom.

And the Future Farmers of America might stop to check the soil for nutrients or the clouds for rain."

"Your analysis sounds strangely biased. I suppose you want me to back the cheerleaders," Skye teased.

"Well, they *are* going to win. But there is one other team that has a chance. They call themselves Great Caesar's Ghost."

"Interesting. Point them out to me."

Trixie twisted around until she spotted them. "There they are, next to Justin and Frannie's food booth. I think those two are friends with them."

Skye took a step closer to see better. Interesting—one of the four kids racing as Great Caesar's Ghost had been a part of the group that Grady and his gang had been tormenting yesterday.

When a shrill whistle blew, Trixie said, "Hey, that's the warning signal. I've got to go get my girls together. See you later."

Skye waved as her friend hurried off, then moved over into the betting line. She put two dollars on the cheerleaders and two on Great Caesar's Ghost. If she won, she'd be paid in play money that she could exchange for various items that the community businesses had donated. Clutching her tickets, she looked for a place from which to watch the race.

A smallish ten-year-old boy with a red crew cut ran out of the crowd and skidded to a stop in front of her. "Miz Denison, you by your lonesome?"

Smiling, Skye squatted down to bring her to his eye-level. "Yes, I am, Junior. How about yourself?"

Junior Doozier and Skye had quite a history. He and his family always seemed to be around when something went wrong. It was never their fault; they just seemed destined to play the role of the Greek chorus and occasional rescue team.

The boy wiped his nose on the back of his arm before

answering. "Nah, Elvira's baby-sittin' me and Cletus and Bambi."

Skye quickly ran the Doozier family tree through her mind. Considering some of the unusual twists to the branches, this was no easy trick. Elvira was Junior's aunt, but only fifteen years old. Cletus was Junior's cousin, but lived with the family because his father, Hap, was in jail. And Bambi was Junior's younger sister.

Once she got everyone straight, Skye asked, "Where's your mom and dad?"

Junior shrugged bony shoulders under a grimy T-shirt. "Aw, they got loaded last night at the carnival, so this mornin' they told Elvira to get us out of the house and went back to bed."

Skye kept her face expressionless. Not that what Junior had said surprised her, but she needed a few seconds to think of an appropriate response. "Well, it's nice your aunt could bring you, then."

"They're payin' her ten bucks."

"Did you eat yet?" Skye asked, trying to gain some control over the conversation.

"Nah, I ain't got no money."

Skye knew better than to ask about Elvira buying him breakfast. "Are you hungry?"

"Sure, wanna listen to my belly talk?" He lifted his shirt and exposed his midriff.

"No, thanks." Skye handed him five dollars, which left her with three singles. Definitely time to go to the bank. "Here, I think you still have time to get a plate before the race starts."

He looked at the bill, then back to her. "Could I use this to bet instead?"

"No! Food only."

The boy rolled his eyes and scampered off. Skye found a couple of empty seats at a table and sat down.

Junior was back in a few minutes bearing a plate loaded

with pancakes, bacon, sausage, and fruit. He thrust it into her face. "See what I got. They was closin' the stand down, so they give me the rest of the food."

"Great, can you eat all that?"

"Sure, Mama says I got a hollow leg 'cause I eat so much."

Skye watched the boy attack his plate and wondered for the hundredth time if she should call DCFS about the situation at the Dooziers.

The Department of Children and Family Services was a last-ditch attempt to save children who were being abused or neglected. There were two problems in deciding whether to call them or not: What constituted abuse and neglect? And would DCFS make things better or worse?

The Dooziers seemed to skate by on the edge. Their kids came to school every day, sometimes wearing clothes a little soiled or tight but not over the line. They didn't look malnourished and she'd never heard that any of them beat the kids—except Hap, and he was in jail. It was one of those issues where she had to separate her middle-class values and morals from her decision. So far, she hadn't placed the telephone call.

"Your mama sounds like she can be pretty funny," Skye said, trying to get the boy to talk a little more about his home life.

"Dad says she's a riot, but he's usually not smiling when he says that." Junior paused from inhaling pancakes. "But they were laughin' last night when they got home."

"Oh, were you up that late?"

"Nah, but they woke me up, so I sneaked out of bed and listened to them. They was talking about a fight at the Beer Garden. The crazy old lady that owns the liquor store was using a flyswatter on a guy dressed up like Davy Crockett."

"Really, did they say anything else about the fight?" Why had Fayanne been hitting what sounded like Gabriel Scum-

ble dressed in his buckskins, and did the police know about
it?

"Said the lady just went ape-shit and started beatin' on
the poor guy for no reason. He ran out of the tent when his
nose started to bleed." Junior stuffed a whole sausage in his
mouth and mumbled something more.

"What?"

"The race is starting. Here, save this. I want to see them
run." The boy thrust his nearly empty plate in her hand and
dashed off.

Skye stayed seated, only half watching the runners with
their spatulas go round the track. Fayanne Emerick and
Gabriel Scumble. Could there have been a romance that
went wrong? Fayanne *was* the one in charge of getting him
to Scumble River.

Junior trotted back and grabbed his plate, picked up his
fork, and started shoveling fruit into his mouth. "I think the
cheerleaders are gonna win."

"Who's second?"

"Those weirdos wearin' funny glasses and fake noses."

Skye got up. "I'll be right back. I want to see this."

"Me too." Junior left his empty plate on the table and
jumped up.

"First, throw your trash away."

Junior stuck out his lip but grabbed his garbage and
tossed it in a nearby can. "We don't gotta do that at home."

"You should try it some time, surprise your mama," Skye
said over her shoulder as she hurried toward the track.

Junior had been right. There was a team wearing Grou-
cho Marx glasses and noses. She'd bet anything they were
Great Caesar's Ghost, and they had taken the lead.

The cheerleaders, dressed in short shorts and tight tank
tops, were clearly the crowd's favorites, but the other team
was picking up support. More and more people were shouting encouragement. The team had been the underdogs as far
as the odds went, so if they won, the people who bet on them

would make a tidy profit. At thirty to one, Skye would make sixty dollars on her two-dollar bet.

"Miz Denison, the weirdos won, they won!" Junior cried, tugging on Skye's arm.

"You must have brought me luck. I bet on them." Skye gave the boy a quick hug.

"Go get your money, quick."

Skye and Junior made their way to the betting booths, where the winners were already lined up.

Just before it was Skye's turn to cash in, a teenage girl walked up dressed in low-riding denim shorts and a cropped tank top. Her bleached two-tone hair fell to the middle of her back, and her navel was pierced. "Junior Doozier, where have you been? I been lookin' all over for you. We're leavin'."

"Hi, Elvira. Sorry. Junior's been with me," Skye told the teen.

"Oh, hi, Miz D., that's okay. But we gotta go."

"Sure. Bye, Junior, bye, Elvira." Skye waved them away. A truly fascinating family.

After exchanging her tickets for the fake money, she went to the prize tent where she quickly selected a couple of CDs—prices were extremely inflated—and then went in search of Frannie and Justin. It would be just her luck to hang around all this time and then miss them.

She found them taking down their food booth. "Hi, did you make a lot of money for the mission?"

Justin peered up at her from under his bangs. "Pretty much, maybe two hundred dollars."

"That's terrific. I'm really proud of you guys for volunteering."

Frannie wiped the sweat from her forehead with a napkin. "Well, some of our friends were racing so we thought, what the he—"

Skye interrupted her, not wanting to have to chastise the

girl for swearing but not able to let it pass either. "Were your friends the winners?"

"Uh huh, surprised everyone."

"Not me. I bet on them."

"Cool."

Justin broke into the girl talk. "Did you hear anything more about the dead guy?"

"Not much. Anybody saying anything to you guys?"

Both shook their heads. Frannie said, "Not to us, but we hear things. Understand?"

Skye nodded. "Anything important?"

"No, they mostly get it wrong." Frannie made a face. "It's tempting to tell them what really happened."

"But probably better if you don't," Skye said.

"Oh, we agreed not to talk about it to anyone but you, Simon, or the chief," Justin assured her.

"That's a smart decision." Skye paused. "Did you want to talk about it some more now?"

The teens looked at each other, silent communication evident in their expressions. Frannie answered for them both, "Yeah, let's get a pop and sit under the big tree with the bench. I'm zonked."

"I'll go get the drinks; you two rest," Skye offered.

After handing over her last three dollars to the soda vendor, Skye walked over to the bench, handed each teen a bottle, and sat on the end, turning so she could face them. "So, what do you think about last night?"

"We've been talking," Justin answered, "and we decided we better tell you the truth. Not that we lied last night; we just didn't tell you the whole story."

"I see." Skye nodded encouragingly.

"The thing is," Frannie joined in, "a bunch of us are trying to start a school newspaper. Mr. Knapik won't let us. He says there's nothing to write about. So we thought, if we came up with a big story, he'd have to let us."

Skye nodded again, although knowing Homer Knapik,

she doubted he'd let them start a paper even if the kids found proof of Bigfoot. He wouldn't want the fuss—he was too close to retirement. And student newspapers almost always caused controversy.

Justin stood up and paced. "Anyway, so we've been trying to get the scoop on this band of bullies that have been vandalizing property all around town. We heard that they hang out at the bandstand in the park sometimes, so we were staking it out last night."

Frannie added, "But I really did have to go to the bathroom."

"Did you see anything?" Skye asked.

"No, the rest is just like we told you. I went to the toilet, Justin spotted something shiny, we saw the body and ran."

"Well," Justin said, "I did see one thing that might be important. It was just a quick glimpse as I turned away."

"What?" Skye asked.

"We checked out the bandstand earlier that night, around six-thirty, so I know what it looked like then."

"Uh huh."

"The second time I saw it, there was something new spray-painted on the wall in some weird shiny red color."

"What?" both females asked.

"It looked like this." From his shirt pocket Justin took out a piece of paper with a drawing on it.

Skye studied the figure. It was from a test she routinely administered to measure visual-motor skills. Except this symbol was remarkably poorly reproduced. Where had she seen those unique errors before?

She let her mind drift over the last few weeks. Who had she evaluated? She ticked the students off in her mind. No, not the kindergarten girl. Not the fifth grader or the eighth grader. Grady! It was Grady Nelson who had made those exact errors on the Visual Motor Integration test. Could the killer be Grady? A random act of violence would fit his personality. And Gabriel Scumble was a stranger in town. Who else would have a reason to kill a newcomer?

Skye half rose from the bench, thinking she had to tell the police. But wait. She sat down again. Could she ethically share that information, or was it covered by confidentiality? She'd better check with the Illinois School Psychologists' ethics committee first. She only hoped she could get hold of someone on a Saturday.

CHAPTER 8

The Mark of Grady

After leaving Frannie and Justin, Skye walked across the high school's athletic field to the junior high. She used her key to unlock the outer door, entered the empty building, and headed straight for her office.

The hallway smelled of pine cleaner, with an underlying odor of something less pleasant—thirty years of chalk, sweat, and vomit. Skye's sandals tapped out an urgent rhythm on the orange linoleum as she hurried past the banks of turquoise lockers.

Her office was near the back of the building. She unlocked the door and edged her way around the desk and chair that took up most of the floor space.

This was the beginning of her third year at this school. Skye had gotten used to the smallness of her office and was grateful for the private space, even if it had originally been a janitor's closet. She had spiffed it up with bright paint and a fake window. Except for the pipe sticking out of the wall where the sink had been, no one would ever guess its origins.

Skye had considered trying to disguise the pipe, but all her attempts appeared phallic—probably not a good idea in light of her predominantly adolescent male clientele.

A file cabinet was the only other furniture in the room. She unlocked it and grabbed the Illinois School Psychologists Association Membership Directory from the bottom drawer. Flipping the pages, she found the name of the Ethics and Professional Standards chair.

Luck was still with her: The chairperson's home number was listed. Skye hated bothering someone on a Saturday, but this was an emergency. She dialed the phone. When it was picked up after a single ring, she was relieved.

Skye explained the situation to the ethics chair. After some questions and pauses, the woman said, "Since the boy in question is over twelve years old, information can only be revealed with the consent of both the child and his legal guardian, except in situations where failing to disclose information would result in a clear danger to the client or others."

"So, it comes down to my best judgment as to whether someone else might get hurt if I don't tell?"

"Sort of. You're in a murky position. You should probably consult a lawyer that specializes in school law."

"Do you have a list of names?"

"Sure, but they charge three hundred dollars or more an hour, so you'd better clear it with your district first," the woman cautioned.

"Do you think they'd be able to give me a concrete yes or no?"

"I doubt it. Like so much in special education, the answer lies in how something is interpreted. So, one lawyer may say do this and another may tell you to do the exact opposite."

"I think I understand what you're saying." Skye tapped the desktop with her nail while she tried to think if there was some other question she should ask. Nothing came to her. "Thank you so much for your time. I'm very sorry to bother you at home on a Saturday."

"No problem. I wish I could be more help. It's an interesting quandary. You might want to think about writing an article for the newsletter about it once everything gets sorted out. Good luck."

After hanging up, Skye ran everything through her head again. It wasn't a clear-cut decision by any means, but it felt like the moral thing to do would be to tell the chief. Wally was an honorable man. She could trust him to do the right thing with the information—she hoped.

Considering that there had been a murder not even twenty-four hours ago, the police station was strangely quiet. Skye parked the Bel Air next to the only other car in the lot, a dented blue Chevy Cavalier. It was nearly eleven, and the temperature had reached a humid eighty-nine degrees. She was looking forward to sitting in Wally's air-conditioned office as she told her story.

Skye pushed open the glass door and walked into the reception area. To her right was a combination chest-high counter and window. The bulletproof glass had been added last February after a gun-toting Bonnie had tried to break her Clyde out of jail. She had become quite upset when she found out that his wife had already fetched him. In a snit, the woman had started firing, and things had gotten ugly. Lucky for the dispatcher on duty, that particular Bonnie was a terrible shot.

The incident had resulted in heightened security at the police department, and Skye could no longer press the "secret" button on the underside of the counter to buzz herself in. While she understood the need for it, she found the new system irritating.

She knocked on the glass, and a grandmotherly woman hurried into the dispatch room. She smiled and rushed over to let Skye into the inner sanctum.

Thea Jones hugged Skye. "It's so good to see you. You haven't been around as much as you used to. I hear a man's been keeping you busy."

Skye panicked. Could Thea already know about Luc?

Did everyone know? No, she meant Simon. "I have been busy, but no man could keep me from visiting my friends."

"Good for you. Besides, the right guy for you works right here at the PD."

Skye wanted to run screaming from the room, but instead she forced a smile. The woman meant well. "Well, I do need to talk to the chief."

Thea grinned. "I'll tell you exactly where to find him."

Skye saw her chance to sit and chat in a nice cool office slipping away. "He's not here?"

"No, he's at the park. The Crazy Craft races start at noon, and he's the judge."

"Crazy Craft, what's that?"

"It's a little hard to describe." Thea scratched her head and wrinkled her nose. "A bunch of people who are an egg short of a full carton ride anything that floats down the river. Whoever crosses the finish line first with most of their boat still intact wins."

"So, why is Wally wasting his time judging something like that?"

"Well, the thing is, the other time we tried this race, during Chokeberry Days last year, there were some differences of opinion as to who won. A bunch of drunks started pushing and shoving each other, and a few ended up in the river. A couple nearabouts drowned. Wally's hoping that if he judges the thing, that won't happen this time."

"I suppose cancelling the race is out of the question."

Thea looked at Skye with a puzzled expression. "But everyone had so much fun last time."

"Of course, how silly of me." Skye smiled and patted the dispatcher's hand. "You said Wally was in the park. Do you know where exactly?"

"Sure, he's at the boat launch just past the bandstand."

Skye started to leave but stopped. "Near where the body was found?"

The dispatcher nodded.

"But the evidence. People will be trampling all over that area."

"Oh, Wally had the crime-scene technicians from the sheriff's office out there early this morning. They released the area about an hour ago, except for the bandstand and about fifty feet around it, and they taped that off."

"Did they find anything?"

"I haven't heard," Thea said.

"Do you know if they talked to the carnival workers yet?"

"Yep, Wally and our officers were up all night interviewing that crew. Not that they found anything out from them. They all alibi each other." The phone started ringing, and Thea turned to answer it.

Skye waved and mouthed thank you as she backed out of the room.

Although Skye had had the Bel Air for five months, she still had trouble reversing the huge vehicle. She maneuvered back and forth, trying to avoid the light pole directly behind her, and finally freed the car from its parking spot. As she drove away from the police station, she noted all the food and craft tents set up shoulder to shoulder along Maryland Street. What a difference from last night. People and cars were everywhere now.

The booths stopped abruptly just before the bridge at the Up A Lazy River Motor Court. Both the motor court and the Brown Bag Liquor Store's lots were being used for public parking, as no cars were being allowed inside the park.

Skye pulled the Bel Air into an empty spot near the Dumpster in back. It was normally not a good place, but no garbage truck would be coming through today.

A teenager hurried up to her as she got out of the car. "Lady, you can't park there."

"It's okay, I'm Charlie's goddaughter."

The boy looked skeptical. "Sure."

There was no sign of Charlie. How could she convince

this kid? She unzipped her fanny pack and pulled out her wallet. After a short search, she found what she wanted, a picture of Charlie and her hugging. She handed it over.

He inspected it and handed it back. "Okay, I guess. I better not get into trouble over this."

"It'll be fine, I promise." She reached into her wallet to tip the boy but found the bill compartment empty. Shoot! She had forgotten to stop by the bank, and it closed at one. She'd better hurry. She found four quarters in the change compartment and handed them over. "Sorry. I need to go to the bank."

The teenager shrugged and walked away.

Skye cut diagonally across the parking lot to the southwest tip and took the wooden footbridge over to the park. It was already thronged with people.

Although the carnival wouldn't open until dusk, there was plenty for people to do during the day. The odor from the Lions Club's pony ride and the Junior Chamber of Commerce's petting farm hung in the humid air. A mini golf course, set up by the Elks, had players lined up three-deep. But the biggest crowd was at the Grand Union of the Mighty Bull's bingo tent. It seemed that no matter what the other organizations did, the GUMBs managed to do it a little better. The rivalry among the groups was legendary.

Skye waved to family and friends almost continuously as she made her way down the length of the park peninsula toward the tip. It seemed that almost everyone in Scumble River was partaking of the bicentennial events.

According to her watch, it was close to noon when she finally reached the boat docks. She could see Wally sitting on a lawn chair under an awning. A table to his right held a plate and a plastic cup. Several women hovered at his elbow, poised to offer refills.

Skye had heard that Wally's official period of mourning for his divorce had been declared over by the single ladies of Scumble River and that he had been receiving a lot of attention since then, but this was the first time she had witnessed the women in action. She felt an odd twinge of jealousy but pushed it down.

This summer, while working with Simon on the church's youth group, Skye had decided that a relationship with Wally was not an option. Simon was much more her type, and her attraction to Wally was purely physical. Besides, now was hardly the time to think of another man, not when she had both Luc and Simon pursuing her.

That settled in her mind, she climbed down the roughly hewn stairs cut into the soil. The rocky shore was hard to walk on in sandals, and it took her a few minutes to make her way past the people gathered at the water's edge. Most stood with their hands shading their eyes, peering down the river. The race must be starting soon.

As she approached the chief, who was looking more and more like a sheik with his harem, she took a deep breath, determined to keep this conversation businesslike.

She reached the edge of his awning and said, "Hi, got a minute?"

Wally jumped up, nearly trampling one of his supplicants, who had been ready to pop some tasty morsel into his mouth. "Hey, Skye, what are you doing here?" He narrowed his eyes. "Thought you'd be busy showing your fiancé around."

"He is not my fiancé. How many times do I have to explain the concept of *ex* to you?"

"Oh, I understand the *ex* concept all too well." A momentary look of misery crossed his features.

Dang! How could she have forgotten his ex-wife, Darleen? "Sorry." Why did being around him make her IQ drop twenty points? "Um, anyway. I need to talk to you about something urgent."

"The race is starting, and I really have to pay attention to that. Can it wait a little while?"

"I guess." Skye turned to go. "I'll go to the bank and come back.

Wally took her arm. Her skin tingled where he touched her. He looked down and said, "Why don't you stay and watch the race with me. You could have something to eat. Some of the ladies made lunch." He seemed unaware of the dirty looks the "ladies" were throwing him.

Skye's first inclination was to decline, but when a platinum blonde glared at her, she found herself agreeing to stay. Strangely enough, none of the women offered her any food. She and the chief walked to the water's edge.

He took his walkie-talkie from his belt and said into it, "Roy, start the race." He explained to Skye that Officer Quirk was upstream with the participants.

They watched as the first entry came bobbing into sight in the distance. From where they stood, the vessel looked no bigger than a Matchbox toy. It was quickly followed by other crafts.

Skye turned from the river and said, "It looked as if you were having a great time with all those ladies fussing over you."

"Aw, that wasn't anything."

"I just wondered, because I heard you were dating Abby Fleming."

"We went out a couple of times, but it turns out that both of us were really interested in someone else."

"Oh." Skye stopped. She really didn't want to go down that road.

Wally opened his mouth, but a yell from the river distracted him. Both he and Skye looked toward the sound. The Crazy Crafts were rounding the bend. As they neared, and Skye got a better look at them, she was amazed by the variety and ingenuity of the boats. There was one made entirely of milk cartons and one made of water jugs. Another enterprising sailor had strapped Styrofoam coolers to a lawn chair. There were plastic rafts, inner tubes strung together, and homemade canoes made out of hollowed trees.

But the clear winner, at least for creativity, was the Marshmallow Man. Some guy had attached inflated white trash bags to every inch of his body. He looked like a cross between bubble wrap and an unmade bed. It really was too bad that twigs and outcroppings were popping his bags faster than he could float toward the finish line.

The homemade canoe was declared the winner, and Wally turned his attention back to Skye. "What were we talking about?"

"I don't remember," she lied. "Let's get back to why I came looking for you."

"Sure."

She asked, "Anything new on the murder?" If he had already figured out who the killer was, she wouldn't have to tell him about the graffiti matching Grady's test drawings.

Wally took her hand. "Let me see." He used her fingers as markers. "One, the Montreal police can't locate any next of kin for Gabriel Scumble. They'll search his penthouse and get back to me. Two, there was no wallet or identification in his room at the motor court. Three, his car seems to have disappeared. And, four, there are a ton of fingerprints on the weapon. Seems as if everyone on the committee held that pickax at one time or another. They've all admitted to handling it."

"Great. Only in Scumble River would a pickax be that popular." Skye reluctantly freed her hand from the warmth of his. "Did you hear about the fight between Gabriel Scumble and Fayanne at the Beer Garden last night?"

"Yep, she claims he tried to leave without paying for his drink, but no one can corroborate her story."

"Did you talk to Earl and Glenda Doozier? I heard they were there at the time."

"They said they didn't see or hear a thing."

Skye nodded. She knew the Dooziers would never talk to

the police, but they might talk to her. Maybe she'd pay them a visit and see if their story agreed with Fayanne's . . . No. What was she thinking? She had just told Trixie she wasn't investigating this murder. There really was no reason for her to get involved beyond sharing what she heard from Frannie and Justin with Wally. Besides she had enough to worry about with Luc in town. Still it was an interesting puzzle.

"Take a walk with me," she said. "It's easier to show you rather than try and explain."

"A walk in the park with a pretty woman sounds like a great way to spend a Saturday afternoon." The warmth of his smile echoed in his voice.

She tried to ignore the attractive wrinkles at the corners of his mouth and started toward the steps. "Follow me."

"To the ends of the earth." He hurried to catch up with her as she strode across the grass.

Skye rolled her eyes but was secretly flattered by his compliments. It was hard to believe this was the same guy who had been so mad at her a few months ago that he'd actually arrested her. Since then they'd both admitted their wrongdoing, apologized, and agreed to forget and forgive. Still, she wondered at his good mood.

As they approached the yellow tape surrounding the bandstand, Skye stopped. "Can we go past this? I want to show you something on the inside."

"Sure, just don't touch anything."

Once they reached the steps, she pointed. "Okay, see that graffiti on the wall to the left? The one in the metallic orange-red paint."

Wally squinted and twisted his head. "The one that looks a little like two pointy-sided rectangles bisecting each other?"

"Yes, that's the one." Skye took out a folded paper from her fanny pack. It was a photocopy of Grady's visual-motor test. She had gone over to the high school and made a copy before heading to the police station. "See how it looks exactly like this one here?"

The chief carefully compared the figure on the paper and the one on the wall. "Yes, I see. Whose paper is this?"

"I'm planning on telling you, but I need to do it my way, okay?"

"Okay."

She took another folded piece of paper from her pack, this one light green. "Look at this." She pointed to the left square of three.

He studied the one she had indicated. "It looks kind of like the other two, but the points are in the opposite direction, the number of sides of the rectangles are different, and the amount the two cut into each other is less."

"The figure on the green paper is the model that is given to people to copy from. It's called Wertheimer's Hexagons. The white paper is a photocopy of a student's attempt to reproduce that shape. And as you can see, the form on the bandstand wall is the exact duplicate of the student's drawing."

"Go on."

"This morning I went to talk to Justin Boward and Frannie Ryan. I wanted to make sure they were all right after their experiences last night. They told me they hadn't told us the whole truth. Turns out this bandstand is the occasional hangout of a gang of boys that Justin and Frannie are trying to write a story about."

"Write a story? Why?"

Skye explained about the kids wanting to start a school newspaper, and how they had been tailing this gang of boys. She concluded with "Anyway, it looks as if Justin and Frannie were at the bandstand both before and after the murder was committed. Justin swears that the graffiti wasn't there before but was after."

Wally was silent for a moment, then took out a small

notebook and started writing. Several pages later he said, "So, who is our spray-painter?"

"Although testing is usually confidential, kids are told before we start that if they tell me something that makes me think they're going to hurt themselves or others, I will have to tell someone. I called the school psych ethics chair this morning to ask about this, as it is a little outside of that warning. She couldn't give me a clear yes or no answer, so I'm counting on your treating this information as classified, unless it leads to the murderer. Do you agree?"

"You mean I can't arrest the little jerk for some lesser offense this might lead me to?"

"Exactly."

"That's asking a lot."

"I know, but my ethics mean a lot to me."

"This is what I can agree to. I won't use this information to arrest the kid for something small, but if it's a felony, I may have no choice."

"You're making it impossible for me to tell you."

"Think about it, Skye. This information could lead to our connecting some kid to rape or assault or any number of crimes where people were grievously injured. I can't turn a blind eye to that. My ethics mean a lot to me too."

"I'm trusting you, Walter Boyd." Skye took a deep breath and said, "His name is Grady Nelson. He's a sophomore. His aunt is the secretary at the junior high."

Wally wrote down what she said and tucked his notebook back in his shirt pocket. He put an arm around Skye and hugged her. "You did the right thing."

She sagged against him for a moment and prayed that was true, but already she felt guilty.

CHAPTER 9

Long Day's Journey
Into Night

Skye left Wally at the bandstand and walked over to Charlie's bungalow, which, along with the motor court's office, occupied a small building located in the middle of the parking lot. The other cabins formed a horseshoe around the perimeter. The architecture was strictly 1950s Route 66 style: gray and white fake brick siding, a flat roof, and room for one car in front of each of the twelve units' white doors.

When Charlie didn't answer her knock, she went around the corner to his office. A hand-lettered sign on a piece of lined yellow paper had been stuck to the door with duct tape. It read: "No Vacancy. Office closed. If checking out, put key in mailbox."

Since everyone was required to pay for their room when they registered, self-checkout wasn't uncommon. But where was Uncle Charlie? It wasn't like Skye's godfather to remain silent and out of sight when something big was happening in Scumble River. She had been half expecting a phone call or a visit from him since the body was discovered.

Skye was torn. It was quarter to one, and if she didn't leave immediately, the bank would close before she got there. She had twenty-three cents to her name, and as far as she knew, the only ATM was still broken. Some moron had tried to rob it last weekend by chaining it to his pickup. The machine had moved approximately a half inch from the wall. The pickup had lost its axle.

She scrawled a hasty note to Charlie, saying she'd see him the next day, and shoved it under the office door, then ran to her car. The Bel Air's interior was nearly the temperature of the planet Venus, but there was no time to wait for it to cool off. Gritting her teeth, she got in and felt her thighs scream as they came in contact with the blistering leather. The steering wheel was worse. She searched the glove compartment. Her options were slim: a hairbrush, a flashlight, and a Kotex Maxi Pad. The latter, folded lengthwise, slipped over the steering wheel like it was made for it. She just hoped no one noticed what type of protection she was using.

The bank was only a mile or so away. Normally this would be a two-minute drive, but the roads were packed with cars and people. She inched down Basin Street and lucked out when a pickup pulled out of a parking spot right in front of the bank. It was a minute to one when she pushed open the double glass doors, but there was no one in sight. The bank's interior looked like the scene of an alien abduction—everything intact but the humans missing.

Skye waited. What if they wouldn't give her any money because it was past closing time? She tried coughing, jingling her keys, and tapping the pen on the counter. Finally, she called out, "Yoo hoo, anybody here?"

"Hold your horses. I'll be right with you." The voice that answered from the back room belonged to either her cousin Ginger or her cousin Gillian. They were twins and hard to tell apart. "No hurry. It's just me, Skye." Last year she might not have admitted her identity to either cousin, but they had been getting along a lot better since last spring, when Skye had helped them out with their daughters' beauty pageant.

Ginger emerged, still adjusting her pantyhose. She was a tiny blonde with big blue eyes, wearing a cerise top with ruffled cap sleeves and a black skirt with an embroidered rose running along the slit up her thigh. "Sorry, I'm the only one working, and I had to go."

"Sure, no problem. I just need to cash a check." Skye slid the slip of paper across the counter. "I'm surprised they'd leave you here all alone."

"Well, I'm not exactly all alone. Karl's in the booth watching the security cameras." Ginger frowned. "But two tellers called in sick, and Mr. Yates' mother died this morning. The new owners still haven't hired anyone to take his old job, since he got promoted to president when Mr. Ingels left."

She paused for breath, and Skye said hastily, "I see." She did not want to rehash last April's town scandal. "You haven't seen Uncle Charlie around lately, have you?"

"His receipts from the motor court were in the drop box this morning, but I didn't see him. Why?"

"Oh, I haven't seen him since the speech yesterday, and I was wondering if he was okay."

"Why wouldn't he be?"

"You heard about the murder, right?"

"Yeah."

"Well, Charlie generally likes to be in the thick of things, but he hasn't been around."

"He'll turn up." Ginger lost interest and started counting out Skye's money.

Skye watched in fascination as the bills flicked rapidly through her cousin's fingers. "Thanks. Taking the kids to the carnival tonight?"

"Yeah, they're real excited."

"Have a good time. Maybe I'll see you there."

"We'll be in the Beer Garden after nine, once we dump the kids at Mom's." Ginger put a closed sign on the counter and walked Skye to the door. "I'm locking up behind you, and then I'm out of here."

"Bye." Skye walked back toward her car wondering what she should do next. Her stomach growled and gave her a hint. Lunch. Should she be good and go home and have something healthy? Or should she buy something yummy from one of the food tents?

She decided to take a peek at what the local organizations were offering. After all, it would be a shame to give up such a great parking spot. She strolled south toward the smell of frying chicken and found herself in front of the Catholic church.

The Altar and Rosary Society had set up picnic tables under several dark green awnings. Skye looked closer. Were those the awnings that Reid's Funeral Home usually used for the families to sit under at the cemetery during the final services? She wondered if anyone else realized what the canvas shelters were normally employed for.

"Skye, how nice to see you here. The ladies have outdone themselves."

"Father Burns, everything sure smells wonderful." Skye smiled at the tall, thin priest. He was one of the good guys, and she always felt at peace in his presence.

He pointed to a table in the far corner. "Come sit over here after you get your plate."

"Thanks, Father. Can I get you anything?"

"No, the ladies keep me well supplied. I think they're trying to fatten me up."

"That may be a lost cause. You've looked the same for the past twenty years." Skye made her way to the food line. She was behind two men who appeared to have just come in out of the fields.

One of the farmers was speaking. "Can't take this kind of thing too often. Shouldn't have stayed so long at the Beer Garden last night, but the missus was having a good time, and we don't get out much." He took off his John Deere cap and wiped his face with a red bandanna. "I'm already beat, and I gotta get that south fifty in the bin today."

"Quit your bellyaching. You left too early. Missed all the excitement."

"We was there when Fayanne threw out the Canuck."

"No, later. Fayanne and the mayor got into it."

"Can't believe that. Clapp's such a gutless wonder."

"Fayanne fed him a knuckle sandwich."

"Wonder what the deal is on that?"

Skye wondered too, but the men had made it to the head of the line and were too busy filling their plates to keep on talking.

She handed the woman behind the table a five-dollar bill and was given a pink ticket, which allowed her one pass through the food line, a drink, and a dessert. All-you-can-eat tickets were blue and cost seven-fifty.

With a roll of plastic utensils wrapped in a napkin in one hand and her plate piled with fried chicken, corn on the cob, and coleslaw in the other, she was trying to figure out how to take the glass of lemonade one of the church ladies was handing her when a voice asked, "Need some help?"

"Simon, when did you get here?"

"I walked over from the funeral home a few minutes ago." He took the plate from her. "Where are you sitting?"

"Over there with Father Burns." She led the way.

Simon put down her plate and left to go get his own lunch.

"That's a good man," Father Burns said. "I'm very glad you two are chairing the youth committee. You've both done an outstanding job. This was our best summer ever."

Skye ignored the priest's comment about Simon, not sure where he was going with that remark. "Thank you. It was fun. I'm hoping we can do something big to keep them occupied this winter."

"You and Simon seem to function well together."

Obviously the priest would not let her off the hook. "Most of the time. We do disagree on occasion."

"But you work things out."

"True, so far."

"I saw your mom this morning, and she was a little worried about you."

"She's only happy if she has something to worry about. If she has nothing to worry about, she worries that she's forgotten what she wanted to worry about." Great. May must have told Father Burns about Luc. Now what was she supposed to do? Simon returned while she was thinking.

Father Burns turned to him. "I was telling Skye how happy I am with the job you've both done with the youth group."

"Thanks. I like hanging out with the kids."

"And it doesn't hurt to have a pretty partner, does it?" Father Burns teased.

Simon took Skye's hand. "That's the best part. It really gave us a chance to get to know each other on a deeper level."

"I understand you were generous enough to take in a visitor to Scumble River who could find no other lodging," the priest said to Simon.

He shot Skye a look. She shook her head slightly and mouthed, "May."

"Yes, an old friend of Skye's showed up last night, and what with the bicentennial he couldn't find a motel room."

"Will he be staying long?" Father Burns asked.

"No." Skye paused. She wasn't prepared to lie to a priest. "I mean, I don't know. I think he just has some papers for me to sign. He's setting up a foundation in New Orleans for abused and neglected kids and has asked me to be on the board."

The priest nodded. "A very good cause, no doubt. Perhaps you and Simon can bring him to church tomorrow. I'd like to meet him."

"I'll ask him, Father."

"Then I'll see you all tomorrow." Father Burns got up, and several ladies rushed to take his plate away.

After making sure the priest was well out of earshot, Skye said, "That was awkward."

"What did your mom say to him?"

"God only knows." Skye giggled at her own joke.

"She called me this morning and invited me to Sunday dinner."

Skye raised her eyebrows. "That should be interesting. I've been ordered to show up with Luc." She pushed her half-finished plate away. "It gives me a stomachache to think what my mother might be up to."

"Speaking of Luc, he's been calling you every fifteen minutes for the last two hours. He accused me of kidnapping you."

"Sorry. He always did need immediate gratification." Skye stood up and gave her plate to a church lady, who, without asking, wrapped the leftover chicken in a square of foil and handed the packet to Skye. "If I don't run into him beforehand, I'll call when I get home."

"I was hoping to take you to the carnival tonight, but Troy Yates decided to go ahead and hold the wake for his mom. I thought maybe he'd postpone because of the activities."

"That's okay. I can understand the family not wanting to wait." Skye edged her way between picnic tables toward the street. "I thought I'd stroll around a little before going home. Want to come?"

"I'd love to, but I have to go relieve Xavier. He asked for the afternoon off."

Skye waited for him to walk away.

Instead he took her hand and pulled her behind a tree. "What are you going to do about Luc?"

Skye picked up a fallen leaf from the ground and studied it. An insect had eaten hundreds of tiny holes in it, making it look like green lace. "I don't know."

"Do you still love him?"

"No. I just feel something isn't finished between us."

"Why? It's been over two years since you two split up."

"See, that's the thing. *We* didn't split up. He walked out on me." Skye continued to examine the leaf.

"So it's a matter of pride?"

"Maybe. But I think if I can say good-bye and have some control this time, I might be able to straighten out my emotions and be ready to try another serious relationship."

Simon placed his hands gently on either side of her face. His thumbs caressed her jaw. His lips brushed against hers as he spoke. "As long as that 'serious relationship' is with me, I guess I can handle Luc being around for a few days."

Without thinking, she kissed him. What started as a soft caress deepened, leaving her weak and confused. How could she be attracted to Luc last night and Wally this morning, and still lose herself in Simon's kiss? What was happening to her?

After Simon left, Skye sank to the ground and sat with her back to the tree trunk. Wow. She tried to think, but her mind wouldn't cooperate. It was time to go home.

The coolness of her cottage greeted her as she stepped inside. Bingo looked up from a favorite patch of sunlight by the French doors, yawned, and went back to sleep.

Skye detoured into the kitchen to put the leftover chicken into the fridge and get a glass of ice water. As Simon had promised, the button on her answering machine was blinking. She pressed the play button and heard several versions of the same message from Luc. Where was she? How could she disappear like this? Call him immediately.

Skye punched in the first two numbers, but was interrupted by knocking. She hung up the receiver and peeked out the foyer window. Luc stood on the top step.

She opened the door, and he swept inside. "Darlin', where have you been? I was so worried."

"Why? This is Scumble River, not the big bad city."

"But the murder last night. Obviously a killer is on the loose."

"Probably a robbery gone bad. Nothing to do with me," Skye reassured him, not really believing what she was saying.

Luc took her hand, drew her into the great room, and sat her on the couch. "I have something important to ask you."

"Oh?" This didn't sound good. "About the foundation?"

"In a way. I would like you to give me one night. To pretend we have just met. I want to take you to a wonderful restaurant and talk as if we had no history. If at the end of the evening you can look me in the eye and say you have no feelings for me, I'll never bother you again."

"What about the foundation?" Skye got up from the sofa and walked toward the windows facing the river.

"I'll let my lawyer act as liaison. You can still be on the board, but you won't need to have anything to do with me."

She stared at the blue water, watching the heat shimmer on its surface. "One night? And you'll leave town the next day if I say so?"

"Yes." He followed her and took her hand, raising it to his lips, but instead of kissing the back, he turned it and pressed his lips to the palm.

She felt a shiver and cursed herself. When had she become a loose woman? First Luc, then Wally, then Simon, and now Luc again. Maybe it was just her hormones, and she wasn't really attracted to any of them. She'd always been a good girl, so maybe things would go better for her if she was bad this one time. Maybe she just had to get it out of her system. "Okay, let's go out tonight," she agreed.

Luc feathered kisses up her arm. "What's the best restaurant in Chicago?"

"According to what I read, that would be Charlie Trotter's. But it takes months to get a Saturday night reservation." Skye idly considered moving her arm away from his lips.

"Nonsense." He kissed her softly on the neck just below her earlobe. "May I use your phone?"

She pointed toward the kitchen, not trusting her voice, and felt bereft when he interrupted his caresses to make the call.

He was back before she had even decided whether to sit down. "Our reservation is for eight."

"How did you do that?"

A secretive smile appeared on his lips. "Connections. I'll pick you up at six-thirty."

CHAPTER 10

Cool Hand Luc

As soon as Skye persuaded Luc to leave, she ran to her closet. What in the world could she wear to Charlie Trotter's? Was there time to go to Joliet or Kankakee and buy something new? She checked the clock. No, it was already past three.

Her hair. She retraced her steps and grabbed the phone from the kitchen wall, then slowly replaced the receiver. If she asked Vince to fix her hair, she might as well take out an ad in the *Scumble River Star* announcing her date. Shoot, what was the use having a brother who was a hair stylist if you couldn't even have him fix you up for a big night on the town?

Skye chewed her lip. What should she do first? A knock on her front door answered her question. Dang, she had to get that doorbell fixed soon. She peeked out the window and was relieved to see Trixie on her steps, the one person who would help her get ready without blabbing about her date.

Skye flung open the door. "Trixie, do you have ESP?" She pulled the startled woman inside.

"Probably," Trixie said as she retucked her tank top into her shorts. "Why?"

"You're just the person I want to see. I hope you're not busy this afternoon."

"Nope, that's why I stopped by, to see if you want to take

the antique shop tour. The local experts are doing appraisals like on the *Antiques Roadshow.* Owen's at the Tractor Pull."

"A good wife would have gone with her husband to see the mighty John Deere face off against the fierce International Harvester," Skye teased.

"Right." Trixie snorted. "So, what's more important than finding out if Great Aunt Bertha's toothpick holder is worth a million dollars?"

"Promise not to tell anyone?"

"Sure, cross my heart."

"Luc is taking me to Charlie Trotter's for dinner tonight."

"Oh my gosh! Are you really thinking of making up with him?"

"No, but he asked for one nice evening, and then he'll leave me alone." Skye couldn't quite meet her friend's eyes.

"And you believe him?"

"The thing is, I need to do this. I need to be the one to say good-bye," Skye admitted. "I need for him to see me looking great and doing well in my life and have him know what he missed."

"I can understand that. But what are you going to do about Simon?"

"I'm sure he'll understand."

"If you tell him."

"He's busy tonight, and he knows I have to talk to Luc and straighten things out. He wants me to, so Luc will leave."

"Should I even mention Wally?"

"No, he and I have never even dated. He's not part of the picture at all," Skye objected. "Besides, you should have seen him with his harem today at the Crazy Craft Race. He has no right to judge me."

Trixie tilted her head and regarded Skye with a worried look. "Okay, but I predict they are both going to be ticked off, whether they have the right to be or not."

"I'm just having dinner with an old friend before he goes back home."

"Ex-fiancé."

"*Ex* being the important part of that word."

"Don't tell me, tell him."

Skye was silent. If her best friend, the one who was usually reckless and impulsive, was concerned about her going out with Luc, then maybe she shouldn't do it. But she really, really wanted to end things, this time with her as the princess and Luc as the banished peasant.

Trixie put a hand on Skye's arm. "I understand. You do what you need to, and we'll hope for the best here on the home front."

"Thank you." Skye hugged her friend. "In that case, help me pick out something to wear."

"Too bad we don't wear the same size. I just bought a great new dress."

Skye looked at her friend's size four figure, mentally comparing it to her own plus-size shape, suppressed the urge to kick her, and said, "Yep, too bad."

The two women made their way to the bedroom closet. Skye folded back the doors, and they stood looking at the contents. Trixie reached in and took out a red and black polka-dot tank dress. "How about this?"

Skye shuddered, took the garment from Trixie, and threw it across her bed. "That was a mistake. I should have taken it back. It makes me look like a pregnant ladybug. What do you think of this one?" Skye held up a layered ivory slip dress with a matching lace jacket.

"That's gorgeous."

"But?" Skye heard the reservation in her friend's voice.

"But it looks a little like a wedding dress."

It went back onto the rod, and Skye pulled out a pale pink suit.

"Pink isn't your best color." Trixie wrinkled her nose.

The suit joined the polka-dot dress on the bed. At this rate

Skye would have to have a garage sale to get rid of all the clothes she was rejecting.

As more and more garments were either shoved back into the closet or relegated to the bed, Skye began to panic. Maybe this was God's way of telling her not to go tonight. She started to pace. That was it. She'd call Luc, have him bring the papers over for her to read, and give them back to him tomorrow. There really was no reason to go out with him, except to soothe her ego, and pride was one of the seven deadly sins.

Trixie interrupted her thoughts. "This is it. The perfect dress. Why is it way in the back?" She held up a black silk sheath with a beaded vee neckline and a lace hem.

"For one, it's too short." Skye held the dress against her, and it hit her several inches above the knee.

"Wear black nylons," Trixie ordered.

"For another thing, look here." Skye turned the garment around. The back swooped nearly to the waistline. "I can't wear a bra, and I never got around to buying one of those bodybriefers you're supposed to wear with it."

Trixie pursed her mouth, tapping it with her index finger, then brightened. "No, but you can wear your black bathing suit underneath."

"Mmmm, that might work." The tank suit was almost like those all-in-one undergarments sold for this type of dress. It had built-in bra cups and a plunging back. "But how in the heck will I go to the bathroom? The bodybriefers have a crotch with snaps. My bathing suit doesn't."

"You'll have to take off the dress. Better not drink too much." Trixie grinned. "And it has one other great feature."

"What?"

"It's almost as good as a chastity belt."

Skye sputtered, "Are you nuts?"

"Think about it. You'd never get undressed and let him see you were wearing a bathing suit as underwear."

"That's not even a consideration." Skye sniffed. "This is strictly a good-bye dinner."

"Right, sure. What was I thinking?" Trixie was suddenly struck by a fit of coughing.

"Are you okay?" Skye pounded her friend on the back.

"Fine, let's get started on your hair. While it dries, I can do your nails and help with your makeup."

After Trixie left, Skye added the finishing touches—pearl earrings and a chunky bracelet. After slipping on black high-heeled sandals, she stood in front of the mirror and gazed at her reflection. She looked like a Barbie doll: a plus-size Barbie, but a Barbie nonetheless.

Bingo had followed Skye and Trixie when they first went to the closet, and he'd claimed a spot on the bed as they examined various outfits, watching them through slitted eyes. Now he got to his feet, gave a catlike snort, and turned to face the headboard, his tail twitching in disapproval. Obviously he objected to Skye's transformation.

As she heard the first knock, a twinge in the pit of her stomach told her she shouldn't go through with this date. She ignored it and answered the door.

Luc seemed to fill her foyer. He was dressed all in black, from a gorgeous designer suit to shiny wingtips. Skye recalled seeing a similar suit in a fashion magazine a month or so ago. The price tag had been twelve hundred and ninety dollars. And she'd bet that the pearl gray shirt and Italian leather shoes added another thousand to the bill. She sighed; the gulf between Scumble River farmer's daughter and New Orleans aristocrat had never seemed so wide.

"Darlin', you look ravishing." Luc followed his words with a swift kiss.

"You're pretty stunning yourself. Is this a Dior?" Skye fingered the lapel of his jacket.

He nodded approvingly. "Yes, I see you still remember what I taught you about clothes."

"Oh, I remember a lot of lessons you taught me."

Luc seemed nonplussed by her reply. He glanced discreetly at his watch. "I'm not sure how long it will take us to get to Chicago. I recall there was some construction when I drove here from the airport."

"I-55 is always being worked on. Traffic shouldn't be too bad this time on a Saturday night, but we might as well get going. Even with smooth sailing it takes seventy-five minutes to an hour and a half to get into the city from here." Skye picked up her beaded evening purse from the table and checked to make sure she had her lipstick, keys, and wallet.

Luc opened the door and they walked toward his car. She hadn't noticed it the night before, but trust Luc to find a Jaguar to rent. "Nice car."

"I'm thinking of replacing my Mercedes. This gives me a chance to see if I'd like a Jag." Luc slid into his seat and backed out of the driveway.

"You must be doing very well. Is your father finally happy with you?" One of the things that had originally drawn them together was that they both felt they hadn't lived up to their families' expectations.

Luc's expression was hard to read. "Father won't be happy until I'm governor of Louisiana."

"Are you thinking of entering politics?" Maybe that's why he suddenly wanted to form a foundation for abused and neglected children. Think of the free publicity.

He was silent, seemingly concentrating on merging with oncoming traffic as he guided the car onto the highway. Finally, he spoke. "How did we get on such a serious subject? I thought we were going to have fun this evening."

No way was he getting away that easily. She needed a lot of questions answered tonight, and he would darn well start answering them. "I do want to hear about what's happened since I left. I take it you're still with your father's law firm. Has he made you a partner yet?"

"I went out on my own. Father would never have made me a full partner." He shot her a twisted smile.

"But didn't he always say if you left the firm he would cut off your trust fund?"

Luc shrugged his shoulders. "He'll change his mind as soon as I show him how successful I am."

So, Luc had lost access to his trust fund and wasn't drawing the enormous salary he'd had in his father's firm. Still, if the money he spent was any indication, he must be doing well. Skye frowned. Something didn't add up. Ah, it must be the stock market. Luc had always been a wizard with investments. If she had had any extra money while they lived together, she would have bought whatever he did. It seemed as if he always knew when certain shares would rise, and he made thousands and thousands from that knowledge.

The Jaguar ate up the miles, and they were passing Louis Joliet Mall before she knew it. Only about thirty miles to Chicago.

A thought she couldn't quite grasp flitted through her mind, causing her to ask, "What have you heard about the murder?"

Luc gave her a startled glance. "Nothing. Why would I hear anything?"

"Well, you are staying with the county coroner. I thought Simon might have mentioned something."

"No, he doesn't say more than he has to around me." Luc relaxed back in his seat. "I don't think he likes me much."

"Probably not." Skye noted his unusual reaction to her mention of the murder. Could he be involved somehow? No, she was being silly. How would Luc know Gabriel Scumble?

Time for another change of subject. What was safe to talk about? Ah, she knew. "How's Buffy?" Skye had liked Luc's younger sister. Although she did what was expected of her—had attended McGehee's and been a Kappa at Newcomb—Skye always thought she had managed to retain her

individuality. Quite an accomplishment in New Orleans's
society.

"She's become a nun."

"You're kidding! That must have been quite a surprise.
How did your folks react?"

"Mother is crushed, and although the old man is putting
up a good front, I can tell he's disappointed. It's looking less
and less likely that there'll ever be another St. Amant queen
of the Comus Ball."

"How about your children? You always said you wanted
a son and a daughter."

His expression held a note of mockery. "I doubt if he sees
me as the best hope for the St. Amant line."

"Why?"

"That's part of what I want to talk to you about, but not
tonight. Remember, we just met, and this is supposed to be
our first date."

His tone was light, but there was a lingering sadness
around his eyes that matched Skye's own emotions. "Okay,
then tell me all about yourself. What do you do for a living?
What's your favorite color? What made you decide to establish a foundation to assist abused children?"

Luc swung his head in her direction, and the Jag followed, narrowly missing the car beside it. "You ask tough
questions for a first date."

Skye, her heart still in her throat after their near collision,
didn't respond. Instead she concentrated on watching Luc
maneuver the sleek car through Saturday night traffic.
Something was going on at McCormick Place, and all the
lanes were full.

As he tried to ease past the jam, Luc finally gave in and
responded to her questions. "I'm a lawyer. I have my own
firm that specializes in maritime law. My favorite color is
green, the exact shade of your eyes. And I want to establish
a foundation to assist abused children to make up for a
wrong in my past."

He certainly knew the right things to say, but could she believe him? She sat lost in thought until they pulled up in front of a renovated 1880s townhouse in what seemed to be a residential area. If there was a sign indicating that this was the famous Charlie Trotter's, she couldn't see it.

Skye was about to ask if they were in the right place when a valet swept open the passenger door. She slithered out of the low-slung car, trying to keep the hem of her dress nearer her knees than her waist. Now she remembered why she didn't like wearing short skirts.

Luc materialized at her side, took her elbow, and guided her up the outside steps. He murmured, "Does this remind you of our evenings out in New Orleans?"

She nodded. This was the kind of life she had wanted so badly when she had first gotten out of the Peace Corps, the life she had had with Luc. But after over two years in Scumble River, those days had all faded to a faint memory.

As they entered, they were met immediately by a maitre d' and shown to a table for two. Burgundy carpet and upholstery contrasted starkly with white linens. It was undeniably elegant. Skye fought to enjoy the experience rather than be overwhelmed by it. Some part of her from her high school days would always feel like the wallflower.

Water was immediately poured into the etched crystal stemware, and the sommelier presented Luc with the wine list. While the men conferred with all the seriousness of choosing the next U.S. president, Skye looked at the other diners. To a man, they were all wearing dark suits in shades ranging from charcoal to midnight. For the most part the women, too, were dressed in black. One or two wore a shade of red. Were they daring, ahead of the fashion curve, or hopelessly behind it?

The sommelier left, and Luc said, "I'm told the best table is in the kitchen, where you get to watch Charlie at work, but I thought this would give us more privacy. I hope you don't mind."

"Not at all." Sitting in the kitchen didn't sound like a treat to her. She did that all the time at her mother's.

Luc smiled and covered her hand with his. "You don't know how often I've thought of you like this—beautifully dressed, at a wonderful restaurant, the night stretching ahead of us."

"It is fun, isn't it?" Skye felt the tug at her heart he intended and freed her hand. "So, what's good here? I'm starved."

"Let's take a look."

She studied the menu, a line forming between her eyebrows. "Am I reading this correctly? We only have two choices?"

Luc nodded. "Yes, there are two dégustation menus: the Grand or the Vegetable. I understand the selections change nightly, depending on what Charlie is inspired to make from the ingredients available."

"I see."

"You don't seem pleased."

"I like to order what I feel like eating rather than what the chef feels like cooking."

"Many important restaurants with truly gifted chefs serve this way." Luc's tone had become condescending.

"I'll have to tell my mother that. That's exactly like dinner at her house—whatever she has in the fridge and wants to cook."

For a moment, it looked as if Luc was about to explode with anger, but instead his features sank into sadness. "I'm sorry. I thought I was bringing you to a place you'd enjoy."

Skye took a deep breath. Why was she being such a hick? This was the type of life she had always wanted, wasn't it? "I'm sure I will enjoy myself. I don't know what made me say that. Let's order."

After the wine was poured, Luc raised his glass and said, "Here's to new beginnings and forgiveness."

Skye echoed, "New beginnings."

The wine was light and somewhat sweet. Skye knew Luc preferred a drier variety. It was clear that he had chosen the bottle with her in mind. Did he do it to make a gallant gesture or to get her drunk? He knew she rarely drank.

They chatted about old friends and old times until the first course was served, along with glasses from another bottle of wine. As the appetizer—duck prosciutto breadsticks with ricotta and dried figs—was placed in front of Skye, she said jokingly, the alcohol already affecting her inhibitions, "Where's the rest of it?"

Luc frowned briefly but recovered and answered, "There are many courses. They want you to save room for dessert."

Skye caught Luc's frown and decided to push him a little, knowing what a snob he used to be. "With these prices, it should take two waiters to carry in the plates."

Luc's mouth tightened for a moment before he smiled. "Money is no object when one is wooing the woman of one's dreams."

Skye had to give it to him: The man was smooth.

The food was delicious, although half the time she wasn't sure what she was eating. Their talk drifted into more personal areas. Luc admitted to being upset over the estrangement with his father and alluded to a plan that would repair their damaged relationship.

Enjoying the wine, food, and conversation, Skye felt her mood mellow by the time dessert arrived. When the baked chocolate mousse was put in front of her, she took a spoonful without paying much attention. The minute the intense chocolate flavor interlaced with a burnt caramel sauce hit her tongue, her focus was riveted to what she was eating.

When she finally looked up, after scraping the dish clean, it was into Luc's amused blue eyes. "I love watching you eat. When you find something you really like, it's such an erotic experience. Would you like more?" He offered his untouched portion to her.

His words made her blush, and she shook her head. "No,

thanks, that was enough." She wiped her mouth with the napkin. "It was a fabulous meal. Thank you."

While Luc paid the check, Skye used the ladies' room. Quite an undertaking with her bathing suit underwear. They met by the door, where Luc's car was waiting for them. The ride back home was mostly silent, both lost in their own thoughts.

Near the Scumble River exit, Luc asked, "If we had just met, and this was our first date, would you go out with me again?"

"That's so hard to answer. We've been through too much to just forget the past."

The Jag turned right onto Basin Street, gliding silently through the intersection. "But don't you think that could mean we've made all our mistakes, and they're behind us?"

"I don't know, Luc." Skye concentrated on finding her keys. "I've started new relationships and have responsibilities. I'm sure you're dating someone and have obligations you have to fulfill too."

His face was rigid. Had she hit a nerve, or was he angry because his attempt to wine and dine her wasn't ending the way he'd envisioned?

"We all have a life," he said. "But sometimes it has to be redirected when a new opportunity presents itself."

Skye didn't understand what he was getting at. The wine was making her fuzzy. "Maybe. I can't think straight right now. I need some sleep."

"How about the foundation papers? I brought them for you to sign."

"Leave them with me. I'll read them over and sign them in the morning."

"Why don't you sign them now, and I'll send you a copy to read at your leisure?"

Skye gave him a sharp look. Did he think she was still the little fool who would do what he told her, without looking into it herself? "No, just leave them with me, and I'll give them back to you in the morning." The car turned down her street. "That reminds me, my priest has asked that you attend Mass with me tomorrow. It's at ten o'clock."

"Fine, I'll pick you up at quarter of."

"Where are the papers?"

"I'd rather go over them with you than just leave them. They're full of complicated legal terms. I'll bring them over tomorrow." He took her hand. "Or I could just stay the night."

The night had taken on an unreal air. The caress of his fingers in her palm felt wonderful. This was the life—good wine, exceptional food, and a rich, handsome man at your side. She frowned. Things were going too well. She was obviously overlooking something . . . or someone. She straightened and sobered quickly as they turned into her driveway. Damn! Simon's white Lexus gleamed in the moonlight.

CHAPTER 11

Never on Sunday

Skye looked at the microwave clock as she fixed coffee. It was one minute past midnight, and she suddenly felt like Cinderella. But who was the handsome prince? Tough question.

She had convinced Luc to leave, but Simon had insisted on having a talk . . . right now. He was furious. She had never seen him so angry. He didn't rant or rave; he just got colder and colder. Another few degrees and she'd have to put on her winter coat.

"You can't hide in the kitchen the rest of your life." Simon stood in the doorway, no trace of expression on his handsome face.

"I'm not hiding." Skye picked up the tray, carried it into the great room, and set it on the table by the sofa. She poured a cup of coffee and handed it to him. For a minute she thought he might throw it in her face.

"Are you ready to explain now?" he asked.

"Explain what?" She tasted the scalding liquid.

"If you're going to take that attitude, I might as well leave."

"Maybe that would be best." She took another sip. "What are you doing here anyway?"

"I called after the Yates wake and got your answering machine. When you hadn't called me back by eleven, I got worried. You hadn't mentioned going anywhere. With all these strangers in town and a killer on the loose, I was concerned."

"The fact that Luc hadn't returned to your house didn't make you think I might be with him?"

"The thought crossed my mind, but I was sure you were too smart to fall for his line of bull." His voice was hard.

"You knew I planned to talk to Luc."

"Talk, not date."

Skye decided there was no good comeback and ignored Simon's statement. "Well, I'm sorry you were worried, but I had no idea you'd be calling me. You usually don't after a wake."

"I'd heard something about the murder and thought you might be interested."

"Why? This murder has nothing to do with me. Any information I hear, I'm turning right over to Wally." Skye made a face. "Besides, your previous reaction to my sleuthing has not been very positive. You normally refuse to tell me anything and don't want me to get involved."

"True"—Simon drew his brows together slightly—"but you asked me to change my attitude about that. I'm trying."

"Uh-huh."

"Let's get back on track here. What in the world do you see in that Southern fried fake?"

Skye sank onto the couch, suddenly too tired to stand. "It's a long story."

"It's time I heard it." Simon sat next to her but didn't touch her.

"I'm not sure where to start." Skye began to take the pins out of her hair. Her head had begun to throb. "You know I left Scumble River the day after I graduated from high school."

Simon nodded.

"I had two goals: never return to Scumble River, and do something that would help people. Unfortunately, a BS in psychology doesn't leave you with many practical skills. One day a month or two before I finished college, I saw an ad for the Peace Corps. It seemed like an answer from God. I'd get to travel and to make a difference in someone's life."

"How does this relate to Mr. Charming?" Simon folded his arms.

"Give me a minute; I'll get to that." Skye finished taking her hair down and dug a brush from her purse. "I did two stints in the Peace Corps. I'm not sure if I signed up the second time more because I couldn't think of anything else to do or because I still hoped to find some satisfaction from helping people."

Simon took the brush from her and started easing the tangles from her hair. "Did you find it?"

"No. By the time my second tour was over, I was totally disillusioned. Nothing I had done in all those years had changed things for the better." Skye blinked back a tear.

"You were what, twenty-five years old?"

Skye nodded.

"Maybe you were too young to tell if you had made a difference."

"Maybe, but that's how I was feeling at that period in my life. And that's the point, don't you see?" She turned to face him.

"I'm trying, but I still don't understand how St. Amant fits in." Simon spoke without inflection, but there was something in his eyes that made Skye think he felt more than he showed.

"You'll see." She leaned back, and he continued brushing her hair. "One of the Peace Corps volunteers I was friends with was planning on attending graduate school to become a school psychologist. I had no idea what I was going to do with my life, and graduate school was another way of postponing the need to face the real world, so I applied to where she was going and was accepted."

"This was in New Orleans?"

"No, in Shreveport, but her family lived in New Orleans, and she and I spent nearly every weekend with them."

"Is that how you met what's-his-name?"

"Yes, and a lot of other people like him. And they were fun. They led lives that I had only read about in books. So, I decided if I couldn't change the world, I would live the good life."

"Wasn't your lack of money and family background an issue?"

"To some extent. But at the end of my service in the Peace Corps, I received a modest readjustment allowance. I used that for living expenses and took out a student loan for grad school. And since in Southern society, the girl rarely pays for anything except her clothes, I was just able to get by. As to family background, as long as I was Luc's guest, I was accepted."

"When did you two become engaged?" Simon asked.

"The summer after I finished my internship."

"And you were still enjoying the good life?"

"Yes . . . most of the time. Some of his expectations had become a little constraining." Skye's voice was taut, her fingers twisting themselves into a knot.

"Had you set a date for the wedding?"

"The next August."

"And he moved out of your apartment when?"

"April."

His voice was sympathetic. "Were you stuck with all the wedding bills?"

"No, his family was arranging everything. It was going to be in New Orleans."

"That explains why May doesn't like him." Simon turned slightly and took both her hands. "Let me see if I have this straight. When you got out of the Peace Corps, you were disenchanted with the idea of saving the world so decided instead to live the good life."

Skye nodded.

"And St. Amant represented that life?"

She nodded again. "I needed him."

"Needing someone like him is like needing a parachute. If he isn't there the first time, chances are you won't be needing him again."

"I know that. Truly, I do. I'm a different person now. When that girl came to me in New Orleans and told me her father was sexually abusing her, I knew that no matter what, I had to keep trying to make the world a better place. And even if I never got to see that I made a difference, I would have to trust God that I was helping someone."

"And the good life isn't important to you anymore?"

"Well, I still like the occasional taste, but like cotton candy, too much leaves you empty and feeling sick."

"Did you tell St. Amant this?" Simon cupped her face, and his gaze searched her face.

"I will. Tomorrow we'll take him to Mass, dinner at my parents, and then I'll tell him good-bye forever."

"Because your values have changed?"

"Yes." Skye frowned, hearing a little voice say, *Maybe Luc's values have changed too.* Before she could figure out where that little voice was coming from, she felt Simon's lips on hers. The touch started as a whisper but quickly grew into something hard and searching. She shivered as his hands slipped into the open back of her dress.

Suddenly he stopped. Skye could feel his fingers investigating the swimsuit she was wearing underneath her clothes. Soon he would ask what it was. Trixie had been right; the suit was as good as a chastity belt. No way would she let Simon see what she was wearing for underwear.

Skye twisted out of his arms and backed away. "Let's wait and finish this after I've told Luc good-bye." It was time for Simon to leave. "Too much has happened."

Simon kissed her again, lightly this time. "If you insist."

"It's for the best." Skye steered him out the front door,

walking with him down the steps to his car. "So, what did you hear about the murder?"

Simon raised his eyebrow but answered, "The Montreal police called Wally back. They searched Gabriel Scumble's penthouse. They can't find any sign of a next of kin. In fact, the place looked like he had stripped it of all personal items. The building manager won't answer their questions, so they're trying to get a warrant for his office records."

"That's odd."

Simon got into his Lexus and started the engine so he could roll down the window. He leaned through the opening. "This whole case seems pretty odd. But murder in Scumble River is rarely ordinary."

"True." Skye kissed Simon good night and watched as he backed his car out of the driveway. Sighing, she trudged inside and went to bed.

A buzzing sound insinuated itself into Skye's consciousness. She fought her way out of the sheet that had become wound around her tighter than the bandages on a mummy, and batted at the clock until the noise stopped.

She sank back on her pillows. Why had she set the alarm for five-thirty? Too early to go swimming. Shoot! The Bird Walk Breakfast! She had promised Charlie she'd help him with it.

Skye leaped out of bed and hurried into the bathroom, narrowly missing Bingo as he attempted to rub against her ankles. There was no time for a shower. A quick swab of the washcloth in the most obvious places had to do. After hurrying into a pair of denim shorts and a short-sleeve chambray shirt, she stuffed her feet into a pair of tennis shoes, scraped her hair back into a ponytail, and ran out the door.

When she pulled into the parking lot at the Up A Lazy River Motor Court, there were already a dozen people milling in front of the office. She excused herself as she plowed through them and went inside.

Charlie was on the telephone. "I don't know crap about birds. You get your butt over here right now and guide these people like you promised." He paused, and not bothering to cover the receiver, parroted to Skye, "Ursula is too upset to lead the bird walk. Wally brought her nephew Grady in for questioning yesterday and was mean to him."

Skye felt a pang of guilt. It was her fault that Grady and his family were going through this. It was bad enough if he was guilty, but what if he was innocent? "Is he in jail?" she asked.

Charlie shook his head no, then shouted into the telephone, "Don't you hang up on me, Ursula Nelson." He slammed the handset down on the cradle and shot Skye a speculative look. "This murder is really messing up town business. You better give Wally a hand in finding out who killed Gabriel Scumble. We need to put this behind us."

"No. There's no reason for me to get involved. Besides, I have enough on my plate right now."

He ran his hands through his thick white hair. "Just keep an eye out, and give Wally a heads up if you find out anything. I want this settled PDQ."

Uncle Charlie's hair now looked very much like that of the teenage boys who gelled and moussed their hair to get it to stick up in the air. Skye fought a giggle and said, "Fine, if something falls into my lap, I'll tell Wally right away. But that's all I'm doing."

"Fine."

"Did you get my note yesterday?"

"What? Oh, yeah. Sorry I missed you. I had some business in Laurel, and when I got home, it was too late to call."

What kind of business would Charlie have at the county seat on a Saturday afternoon that would keep him out until the wee hours? Skye sure hoped he wasn't gambling again. A few years ago he had almost lost the motor court when he started visiting the Joliet casino boats too often. He had promised to quit, but Skye knew gambling was an addiction, the same as alcohol, and going cold turkey was harder than most people realized.

Charlie glanced at his watch and narrowed his blue eyes. "You'll have to lead the bird brains." Charlie couldn't fathom why people wanted to get up at the crack of dawn and traipse through the trees just to see a robin, but if they were willing to pay money to do it, he was willing to have the town profit from their foolishness.

"Me? I can't tell a sparrow from a wren." Skye backed toward the door, but the big man moved quicker and blocked her exit. She tried another tack. "Who will make the coffee, set the tables, and get things ready for the breakfast?"

"I'll figure that out later. We promised those people a guided walk around the park and a chance to see the rare Cooper's hawk that's been spotted around here. They were supposed to start at sunrise, so you'd better get going."

She was all set to say no when she took a good look at Uncle Charlie. His normally pale skin was gray and hung on his face like a bathing suit that had lost its spandex. No way could she turn him down. "Okay, I'll go, but be prepared to refund their money when they return complaining."

Charlie pushed open the screen door of his office and waved Skye through. He introduced her to the crowd, explained that their original guide had become ill, and thrust a piece of paper into her hand—a diagram of the park with different birds written in each area—then disappeared back inside.

Skye stood frozen, clutching the map in her hand. After a few moments of silence people began to mumble. Finally, a woman with no-nonsense gray hair and a sharp nose confronted Skye. "You have no idea what to do, do you?"

Skye shook her head.

"Then I better take over." The woman examined the group. "Who here are experienced birders?" Three of the eleven people raised their hands. Even without their affirmation, it was obvious they were the experts. They wore

jeans, multipocketed shirts, and sensible walking shoes and
carried notepads, guidebooks, and binoculars. The others
were dressed like Skye, in shorts and sandals or tennis
shoes.

The woman who had taken charge nodded to the pros and
said, "Each of you take two of the beginners, I'll take the
other two and her." She jerked her thumb at Skye. "We'll
each start our walk in a different quarter of the park so we
don't stumble over each other and make a lot of noise."

The group started toward the footbridge that connected
the parking lot to the park. While they were crossing, Skye
told the women, "Thank you. I'll make sure your fee is re-
funded."

The woman nodded but didn't say anything. Skye persisted. "What's your name?"

"Annabel Lee." The woman pinned Skye with her stare.
"Don't say it. My mother was an Edgar Allan Poe fan."

Everyone had crossed into the park and Skye, trying to
retain a bit of her leadership role, announced loudly, "Okay,
remember to meet back here at eight o'clock, and we'll return to the motor court for breakfast."

Annabel frowned and whispered, "And from now on,
everyone keep your mouths shut and your eyes open."

An hour later, Skye trudged a few feet behind her group.
So far they had seen robins, wrens, a female cardinal, and a
million crows, but no Cooper's hawk. She hoped the others
were having better luck.

They were nearing the tip of the park, the halfway mark,
and Skye was thinking of suggesting that they take a rest and
sit on the bandstand's steps, when suddenly a shout broke
through the silence. "Miss, over here!"

Skye hurried toward the voice, which seemed to be coming from between the back of the bandstand and the road, an
area filled with dense underbrush and vines.

Both Skye and Annabel arrived at the same moment. The
older woman's lips were already in a shushing position but

re-formed into a shocked grimace when she saw what the novice birder was holding up.

It was a man's white handkerchief, half covered in what looked like dried blood. Flakes fell as a breeze fluttered through the area.

Skye swallowed hard, then asked, "Does either of you have a plastic bag?"

Annabel reached into one of her many shirt pockets and produced a Ziploc.

Skye took it from her, opened it, and held it out to the younger woman. "Put that in here. Try not to touch the sides with it." After the hanky was secured, Skye asked, "Where did you find that?"

The woman pointed to a bush. "I saw something toward the center and thought maybe it was a nest, so I pushed aside the branches, and the handkerchief was stuck down near the bottom. It looked chewed near the edge. I bet a squirrel found it somewhere else and dragged it over here. I'll bet it has something to do with that murder Friday night. Right?" She finished all in a rush.

"There's a good chance," Skye answered. "So, what we need to do is not touch anything else and get the police. Ms. Lee, could you go back to the motor court and ask Charlie to call the chief? I'll stay here and make sure nothing else is disturbed."

"How about me?" the younger woman asked.

"You'd better stay too. Wally will probably have some questions for you." Skye looked around. "Where's the other member of our group?"

Annabel answered, "She twisted her ankle, or so she claimed. I think she was just bored. She headed back to the motor court."

As Skye waited for Wally to show up, she examined the handkerchief through the plastic. One corner had the initials SI embroidered on it, and nearby was a bright magenta lipstick smear. Where had she seen that unusual color before?

Skye chewed her bottom lip. Did this mean Grady wasn't involved with the murder? His initials certainly weren't SI, and none of his gang wore lipstick. She could feel the pangs of guilt growing. Had she pointed the finger at the wrong person?

CHAPTER 12

The Longest Day

Skye wiped the sweat off her brow with the back of her hand and looked around the tent. The bird-watchers had finally left a few minutes ago after devouring eggs, bacon, sausage, hash browns, and enough toast to start their own bakery.

She heaved the tray of dirty dishes off the table and took one final scan of the area. Satisfied she had the last load of debris, she made her way into Charlie's kitchen.

Several women crowded the small room. One was wiping down the stove, another was at the sink washing dishes, and the others were boxing up borrowed items to be returned to their rightful owners. It took a lot of salt and pepper shakers, butter dishes, and platters to put on a group breakfast.

Skye handed over her tray and went in search of Charlie. He was in his office, seated behind his desk staring into space. She said, "Looks like they're just about finished up in there."

"Wally left a few minutes ago." Charlie twisted a paper clip into a question mark. "Said he'd get the county's crime scene people out to take another look around the bandstand."

"Did Annabel Lee or that other lady have anything to add about finding the handkerchief?"

"Nah. They just whined about not seeing that damn bird. I gave both of 'em their money back."

Skye's head jerked. Charlie did not refund money lightly. What was going on? She walked around the desk and put her hands on her godfather's shoulders. "Are you okay?"

He didn't look up from his paper clip sculpture. "Yeah, I'm fine."

"It seems weird that I haven't seen you the past couple of days. Are you sure you're okay?" Skye couldn't decide if she was more worried that he might be sick or that he might have taken up gambling again.

"I'm fine. I haven't been around because the woman who normally cleans the cabins has called in sick for the past three days, and I've had to do it all myself."

"You couldn't find anyone to help?"

"I haven't had time to look. This bicentennial has been a pain in the . . ." Charlie lumbered to his feet.

"True. A murder will do that." Skye put her arms around his neck and hugged. "I've got to go home to change for church. I could come back and clean cabins afterwards."

Charlie patted her on the head. "Thanks, honey, but I got it covered for now."

"Okay, but you call me if you need help later." She knew that nearly everyone currently staying at the motor court would be checking out later today. "Are you coming to Mom and Dad's for dinner?"

"Yeah." He opened the door for her. "You bringing that ass—?"

Skye quickly cut him off. "Yes, Luc will be there."

"You going to marry that son of a bee?"

"No, he'll probably be leaving tonight or tomorrow."

Charlie snorted. "It's about time."

Attending church with both Simon and Luc had been a bad idea. Between the burning stares and the acid whispers, the experience had been less than uplifting. But Skye had fulfilled her promise and introduced Luc to Father Burns. Strangely, neither man had had much to say to the other.

Now the junior high school secretary, Ursula Nelson, had Skye trapped between the holy water font and the poor box. "Grady did not murder that foreigner," she insisted. "He may be a little wild, but he's no killer."

"Well, if the police didn't put him in jail, they must agree." Skye looked around for help. Simon was deep in conversation with Father Burns, and Luc stood with his back toward her, seemingly engrossed in the pamphlet he appeared to be reading.

"They said they were letting him go, but they'd be keeping an eye on him." Ursula's beetle-brown eyes bore into Skye. "You've got to find out who really killed that man."

Guilt settled over Skye like a sackcloth gown. What if Grady really was innocent? She had been the one to point the finger of blame at him. "I'm sure the police will find out the truth."

"The police investigation wasn't good enough when it was *your* brother they were accusing of murder."

"That was different." Skye tried to edge toward the priest and Simon.

Ursula's clawlike fingers grabbed her wrist, thwarting her escape. "No, it wasn't. You did what you had to do to free your brother. I'll do whatever I have to do to see this murder isn't pinned on Grady. He's like a son to me. My sister-in-law and brother are both useless."

"I understand how you feel, but there really isn't anything I can do."

"All I'm asking is for you to snoop around some. Heaven knows you do that all the time anyway. Besides, you owe Grady that much."

Skye gulped. Did Ursula know that she had told Wally about the resemblance between Grady's test and the mark on the bandstand?

Ursula continued. "After all, aren't you school psychologists suppose to be the child's advocate?"

Skye blew out a breath of relief; Ursula hadn't found out that she had been the whistle blower. But the older woman had a point. The discovery of that handkerchief this morning with the initials SI on it put things in a whole new light. And Skye did feel she owed Grady something. She freed herself from the older woman's grasp. "I'll do what I can."

Ursula nodded. "Let me know if you need any help. I know where a lot of bodies are buried in this town. And if I find out who pointed the finger at Grady, I'll bury one myself."

Since Luc had won the coin toss that morning, Simon and Skye were riding with him in his rented Jaguar. The look on Simon's face as he climbed into the back seat sent Skye's heart pounding. She had to finish things up with Luc soon, or she would lose any chance with Simon.

The trio drove in silence for the few minutes it took them to arrive at Simon's house. As he killed the motor, Luc said, "Why don't you wait here? I'll go grab the papers, and we can take them to your place to go over."

Skye shot a glance at Simon, who said in a steely tone, "Fine, I'll pick you up to go to your folks' house at two forty-five."

Luc, halfway down the sidewalk, turned back. "No need, my good man, we'll just meet you over there."

Two pairs of male eyes turned toward Skye. "Actually," she said slowly, searching for the correct response, "after we finish with the papers, I need to run some errands by myself, so I'll meet you both at my folks at three sharp."

Neither man seemed happy with her pronouncement, but they didn't argue. Considering how things were going, she was willing to put that in the win column.

Luc continued into the house, and Simon stood leaning on the Jaguar looking down at Skye. She searched her mind for a casual topic of conversation, but the thought of what Ursula had said tore at her insides. Simon seemed to understand and remained silent.

A door slammed, and Luc hurried toward them. "They're gone! The papers are gone. What did you do with them, Reid?"

Simon moved around the car in a flash and stood in front of Luc. "What did I do with what?"

Luc seemed unaware of Simon's cold anger and pushed a finger into his chest. "The foundation papers are missing. I want them back, now."

"Don't." Simon gripped the finger poking into him, bent it backward, and then released it. "And just for the record, I don't have your papers. In fact, I doubt they even exist."

Luc's face turned crimson, and he grabbed Simon by the lapels of his suit coat. "Are you calling me a liar?"

"Yes." Simon twisted out of his grasp. "After what you did to Skye in the past, liar is one of the nicer things I'd call you."

Skye quickly slipped between the two men. "Stop it! Luc, I'm sure your lawyer can fax you another set of papers. Simon, I appreciate the sentiment, but I'll handle this myself. Okay?"

Both men's breathing was ragged, but they nodded.

Luc turned. "I'll go call him now. Where can I have them faxed to?"

Simon's voice held an undertone of cold contempt. "You can use the machine in my office at the funeral home. The number is on it."

After Luc left, Skye put her hand on Simon's sleeve and said, "Thanks."

He shook himself, as if he were coming in out of the rain. "You're welcome. I'll give you a ride home."

"You're the best."

"Remember that." Simon kissed her on the cheek as he steered her toward his Lexus.

* * *

Skye was torn between relief and impatience. On the one hand, she had wanted to sit down with Luc and go over the papers for the foundation so she could finish things up with him. On the other hand, now she could immediately talk to Wally regarding her doubts about Grady's guilt.

After calling the police department and learning that Wally was at the park keeping an eye on the bicentennial activities, she changed from the dress she had worn to church into shorts and hopped into her car. As she parked the Bel Air at Charlie's, Skye was beginning to feel like a yo-yo driving back and forth, or maybe it was more like déjà vu.

Once again the park was teeming with people. After crossing the pedestrian bridge, she stopped briefly to watch two rows of men facing each other, and throwing chunks of coal between them. With each toss the participants acquired more and more streaks of soot, until the finalists resembled chimney sweeps at the end of their shifts.

When it became evident that there was no sign of Wally at this event, Skye moved on. The next knot of people surrounded several tables.

As she wiggled through the crowd, keeping a lookout for the chief, Skye didn't notice what was going on until a woman poked her in the ribs with an elbow and said, "I think the one dressed as the black cat should win."

Skye focused on the tabletops. Chunks of coal had been costumed to look like various people, animals, and objects. There were gravestones, birds, a huge pearl in a clamshell, and even an infant in a cradle.

While the judges made their decision as to the best dressed piece of coal, Skye slipped away and followed the throngs of people until she ended up in front of the bandstand. This afternoon it was being used as a stage for the Living History Pageant, which started with the discovery of Scumble River and ended in the present.

The play was scheduled to start at noon, and at quarter to

twelve, people had already staked out their spots to watch. Skye scrutinized faces but didn't see Wally. A noise in back of the bandstand caught her attention, and she walked around the right side. The chief was talking to a man in a tan uniform. When they finished, and the deputy walked away, she took his place facing Wally. "Hi."

He smiled down at her. "Hi. Come to watch some living history?"

"No, I heard about your talk with Grady Nelson and wondered what the outcome was."

"Nothing. The kid stonewalled like a pro. Wouldn't say a word."

"Yeah, that's exactly how he was with me. Very guarded. He'd only answer test questions, nothing spontaneous at all."

"He's a tough one. With his attitude, it's hard to believe he's not quite sixteen yet."

"What are you going to do now?"

Wally took his hat off and smoothed back his hair. "I'm not giving up. He looks to be our prime suspect. At least with the drawing and Justin's testimony, we can place him at the scene, which is more than we can do with anyone else."

Skye felt her stomach tighten. They were going after this boy because of what she had told Wally. But he had the type of personality that might make him do something just *because* the police were looking at him. "Doesn't the handkerchief we found this morning point to someone else?" she asked. "Someone with the initials SI?"

"We're checking into it."

"Are you planning to lock up Grady?"

"No, just making sure he's watched most of the time. We can't do twenty-four hours with our budget, but we can stick with him a lot."

"Oh." She could feel guilt creeping up her throat.

"You don't look happy. You did the right thing."

"I hope so."

Wally took her hand and started to walk back toward the front. "Let's watch the program."

In the few minutes Skye had been talking to Wally, the crowd had swelled, but people moved aside for them, and they were able to edge their way toward the front of the bandstand. A voice blared from portable loudspeakers, announcing the first scene: Pierre Scumble's earliest sight of what would become the town of Scumble River.

The teenage boy playing Pierre was sweating and clearly uncomfortable on stage, but he stumbled through his lines and seemed to gather confidence from the applause.

After some shifting of scenery, indicating the passing years, the main street of Scumble River emerged with houses and stores and businesses. Pierre reappeared, this time accompanied by two other teenagers in the roles of Dewey Clapp and Dolly Ann Emerick. Dewey owned the general store, and the pharmacy and managed the sawmill, while Dolly ran the saloon and the hotel.

History sped up from there, touching briefly on Illinois becoming a state, Scumble River's role during the Civil War as a stop on the Underground Railroad, its contribution to the country during World War I, World War II, the Korean War, and the Vietnam War, and ending with the bicentennial celebration.

During the final curtain, Skye whispered to Wally, "I didn't know that Fayanne Emerick and Eldon Clapp were descendants of the original settlers. I feel like an outsider. My family's only been here a hundred years or so."

Wally took her arm. The crowd had begun to move, and they were caught in the motion. "Hey, think of me. I'm the first Boyd to live in Scumble River."

"That may be a good thing," Skye teased.

As they neared the pedestrian bridge, Skye checked the time. It was nearly one-thirty, and she had one other errand to run before meeting Simon and Luc for dinner at her parents'. "I need to get going. Are you sticking around here?"

"Just until the mob thins out. Most people will be leaving town soon. I'll help with traffic later this afternoon." Wally walked with her toward her car.

"You don't think they'll stick around for the dance?"

"No, that'll be mostly locals. People like to get home early on a Sunday night since tomorrow is a work day."

"Will that be a problem? Everyone leaving with a murder investigation still open?"

"It's not good, but there isn't anything I can do about it. I've gotten addresses for anyone who was reasonably near the bandstand when the murder took place, but that's about it."

Skye opened the Bel Air's door and eased inside. It wasn't as hot today, but the sun was beating down, making the leather seats uncomfortably warm. "This has been the longest weekend ever. I'm ready to get back to school and my routine."

"What's happening with your ex-fiancé?"

"I'm hoping he'll be leaving tomorrow." Skye started the motor.

"At least we've got his address and phone number."

Skye patted Wally's arm, then put the car in gear. "See you at the dance?"

He nodded and waved as she pulled away.

CHAPTER 13

The Wild Bunch

Guilt was gnawing at Skye. She still wasn't sure she should have told the police about Grady Nelson's test results, and her recent conversation with Wally hadn't been at all reassuring. Thinking it over, she decided to make good on her promise to Ursula to see if she could find out anything more about the murder.

She knew right where to start. It was time to pay a visit to the Dooziers and find out exactly what had happened at the Beer Garden the night Gabriel Scumble was killed.

Traffic was still heavy as Skye headed east on Maryland Street. After turning north on Kinsman, she adjusted her speed to exactly thirty-five miles per hour. She knew that the Scumble River police had a habit of parking among the wrecked cars in the junkyard that occupied most of the left side of that stretch of road. They'd sit there and wait for people to speed up as they approached the highway entrance, then give the hapless drivers a ticket.

She almost missed the turn for Cattail Path. The residents always removed the street signs as fast as the city could replace them. To understand the people who lived in this area, it was important to know the story of Scumble River's more recent history. Not the one shown in the Living History Pageant, but the one passed along by word of mouth.

The best recitation Skye had ever heard came from a man

who spoke to her high school class. He'd said, "The town of Scumble River was originally built in the fork between the two branches of the Scumble River. Since then it has spread along both banks. Some might say overflowed.

"Two groups of people live in an uneasy alliance along the river. A few years ago, people from Chicago discovered Scumble River and decided to build summer cottages and retirement homes along its south bank. While this 'outside' interest served to line the pockets of some citizens, it invaded the privacy of others.

"The original group of people who have always lived along the river are known to the locals as Red-Raggers. No one seems sure how this term came into being, but it is definitely disparaging. These are not folks who appreciate uninvited guests."

Cattail Path was in the heart of Red-Ragger territory, and the Dooziers were Red-Ragger royalty.

Skye had been down this road twice in the past couple of years. The first time was to obtain a reevaluation consent for Junior Doozier, and the second was when Junior and his father had fished her out of the river. She hoped that this previous acquaintance would be enough to get Earl and Glenda to talk to her more freely than they had to the police.

She pulled into the Dooziers' dirt driveway and slammed on the brakes. Shoot, what was a squad car doing here? Wally had told her that they had already questioned the Dooziers. Great, now what? Getting the heck out of there seemed to be the best choice, but before she could back the big Bel Air out of the narrow lane, Junior came running up to the side of the vehicle yelling, "Miz Denison, Miz Denison, come help us. The cops are fixing to haul away me and Cletus."

The sun glinted off his red crew cut, giving the brief illusion of a halo, and even though Skye wasn't fooled, there was no way she could leave without finding out if she could

help. Junior had certainly come to her aid on more than one
occasion. She stopped the car and got out.

As Junior led her toward the side door, she examined her
surroundings. Weeds lined the cracked sidewalk and choked
what little grass showed between the skeletons of junked
cars and old appliances littering the yard. The house might
have been white at one time, but now the siding resembled
sections of faded cardboard with the corrugated layers sliding apart. Long years of neglect made it seem about as sta-
ble as a paper dollhouse. The barking of a dog echoed from
out of sight, but the odor of the canine's recent visit to the
front lawn hovered in the humid air.

The sound of men shouting made her flinch, but she followed the boy inside. Earl Doozier, heavily tattooed and
wearing only boxer shorts, stood toe-to-toe with a uni-
formed police officer in the entryway. Cletus stood huddled
against a wall, a finger up his nose.

Spittle flew from Earl's semitoothless mouth as he
yelled, "That ain't against the law. You show me where it
says younguns can't make a little money doing favors for
people."

The officer was Otto McCabe, a Stanley County deputy
who worked for the Scumble River police department when
they needed extra help. Unfortunately, he resembled Barney
Fife from the old *Andy Griffith Show*, and not just physically.

His response confirmed this impression. "I don't have to
show you a gosh darn thing, Earl Doozier. Those hell-raisers
of yours are coming with me to the station, and we'll just see
if I can't lock 'em up."

Even though Earl was stick-thin, except for a small pot
belly that hung over the elastic waist of his shorts, Skye
feared for the officer's safety. Everyone in Scumble River
knew you didn't try to take a Doozier out of Red-Raggers'
territory against his free will. You waited until he was away

from home, isolated from the group, before hauling him off to jail. Obviously, no one had told McCabe.

Skye cleared her throat. Both men ignored her.

Junior pushed her forward. "Pa, look, Miz Denison is here. She'll fix things up."

Earl spared her only a brief glance, but McCabe seemed stunned by her presence. This was her chance. She took Earl by the arm—and immediately regretted it when her hand met his bare skin. She had forgotten how reptilelike the tattoos made his epidermis feel. Pushing her revulsion aside, she tugged him up the short flight of stairs, across the kitchen, and into a chrome and vinyl chair. McCabe followed, choosing to stand in the doorway.

Skye took a seat between the two warriors. "So, what's this all about?"

"It isn't any of your business," McCabe whined.

"Probably not," she agreed, "but I'm here, and I'm trained in conflict mediation. How about we give it a try? Who wants to go first?"

A stubborn look settled on the officer's face. "I can handle this myself."

"I'm sure you can. But why don't you humor me? After all, I am a close personal friend of the chief." Skye wondered what Wally's reaction to that last statement would be.

McCabe crossed his arms and pouted. "Fine, see if you can make this fool understand."

Skye turned to Earl. "Okay with you if I step in?"

"I'd be obliged."

"Great. Officer, you start. Tell me what happened."

"Well, you know how fast people drive down Kinsman, trying to get to Interstate 55 in such a hurry?"

Skye nodded, wondering where in the heck this was going.

"I got me a great hiding spot to watch for them."

"Right, the junkyard."

"You know about that?" McCabe's tone was full of disappointment, but he went on. "Anyway, today I'm in my spot, I got my speed gun pointed and ready, but everyone is suddenly going the exact limit."

"That's odd. Even though the locals know to slow down, there should've been tons of out-of-towners heading home after the bicentennial."

"That's what I thought. So I get out of the squad car and investigate, and what do I find?"

"What?" Skye encouraged, caught up in the story.

"These two little brats have set up a business."

Skye looked at Junior hovering uneasily behind Earl. His cousin Cletus, standing next to him, showed little expression. "A business? I don't understand."

McCabe sighed, conveying that her ignorance was nearly too much for him to bear, but explained anyway. "The little one"—he pointed to Cletus—"was stationed about a mile from the junk yard with a big sign that said SPEED TRAP AHEAD. About a hundred yards after the junk yard the redhead had a sign reading TIPS and a bucket at his feet full of money."

"Oh, my." Skye put her hand to her mouth to cover her grin. These kids were really clever.

"See Miz Skye," Earl piped up. "They ain't done nothin' wrong."

Skye chewed her lip. What to say? "Officer McCabe, although you and I know the boys shouldn't have warned oncoming cars of your speed trap, I'm sure Junior and Cletus didn't realize they were doing anything improper." She turned and motioned for them to step forward. "Right, guys?"

Both nodded their heads, innocence glowing from their dirty faces. For a moment, Skye could have sworn she saw wings sprouting from their shoulder blades. She squinted. Dang, these kids were quite the little con men. She'd need to have a talk with both of them and keep her eye on them.

"So, do you think you could let them get away with a warning this time?"

McCabe didn't answer right away, so Skye walked over and whispered in his ear, "You know that as juvenile offenders, nothing much is going to happen to them anyway. Better to let them think you're giving them a break than let them find out how weak the court system is."

He nodded reluctantly. "Okay, I'll let it go this time. But I'm writing this in my log, and all the other officers will be aware that you've had your one warning. Do not try this again."

He stared at the boys. "Understand?"

They both nodded eagerly.

McCabe turned to go but said over his shoulder, "I'll be watching you two."

Skye sank into a chair. Phew. That had been tricky.

The short silence was broken by a high-pitched voice reminiscent of someone who had sucked on a helium balloon, screaming, "Do I have to do everything myself? Somebody better come help with these groceries, or I'm giving the stuff to the dog."

Earl, Junior, and Cletus lit out of the kitchen and down the stairs like an electrical charge had gone through the room. They returned before Skye could figure out what was going on, each toting several plastic sacks of food.

Behind them, carrying only a huge red and orange purse, came Glenda Doozier, the matriarch of the family. From her dirty feet clad in stiletto sling-back sandals, to her do-it-yourself dyed blond hair and watery brown eyes heavily framed in black eyeliner and false lashes, she was the epitome of what the Red-Raggers considered an ideal woman.

She glared at Skye. "What're you doing here?"

"Actually I came to ask you and Mr. Doozier a couple of questions about what happened the other night at the carnival Beer Garden, but I ended up saving your children from going to jail." Skye could get along with Earl and the kids just fine, but there was something about this women that rubbed her the wrong way, and it seemed the feeling was mutual.

"Why should we talk to you? You ain't no cop." The woman's voice became more strident, and the coinlike bangles on her red halter top jingled in tune with her heightened emotions.

Earl and the boys pulled chairs up around the table, obviously ready to enjoy the women's fight.

Skye swallowed her instinctual dislike of Glenda and said, "That's exactly why you should talk to me. You can avoid having the police question you again."

"You saying you'll sic the cops on us?" She put her face within inches of Skye's.

Skye took a step back. "No, not at all. I'm trying to save you from that."

The woman's eyes darted rapidly around the room. "Why should you care?"

"Because I'm nosy." Skye watched Glenda process that information.

"Okay, I heard that about you. Ask your questions."

Skye frowned. People were going around saying she was nosy? Hey, that's what Ursula had said too.

"So, you gonna ask us something or what?" Tugging at the crotch of her leather jeans, she stared at Skye. "Come on. We ain't got all day."

"Sorry." Skye would worry about her sullied reputation later. "Tell me what happened at the Beer Garden Friday night."

Earl's face bunched up. "Could you be more pacific?"

Skye ignored the urge to talk about oceans and said, "I understand that Fayanne Emerick had a disagreement with the bicentennial guest of honor."

"Yeah, she was hitting on him with a flyswatter." Glenda snickered.

"Why?"

"I'm not for sure of that." Earl scratched his butt. "Maybe

she was havin' a bad day. She punched the mayor in the nose later on."

"Did she say anything while she was beating on these men?"

"Something about money," Glenda volunteered. "I moved closer so I could hear her more better, but the old witch saw me and started whispering."

"Do you think the first guy didn't pay for his drinks?"

Earl shrugged. "Maybe. I heard her say something about not paying his debts."

"Could you hear anything when she attacked the mayor?"

"Sounded like something about money and promises." Glenda lost interest in Skye and zeroed in on Junior, who had grabbed a bag of cookies and was wolfing them down. She shrieked, "You best remember, I brought you into this world, and I can take you out!"

Junior stopped with a cookie halfway in his mouth and mumbled, "Sorry, Ma, but I was starving."

Glenda grabbed the bag from his hand. "If I told you once, I told you a hundred million times, don't exaggerate."

With that insightful suggestion ringing in her ears, Skye made her excuses and hurried away.

CHAPTER 14

Tender Mercies

What could Fayanne Emerick and Mayor Clapp have to do with money and Gabriel Scumble? Skye tossed this question around as she drove toward her folks' house. As she retraced her route back down Kinsman to Maryland Street, she noticed that Deputy McCabe was back in place at the junkyard. She hoped Junior and Cletus weren't planning on returning to the scene of their crime.

Easing around the sharp curve after Webster Drive, she turned right onto County Line Road. Her parents' farm was a mile or so east off the paved road. She was a little early, but she wanted to make sure she arrived before either Luc or Simon. This meal would be enough of an inquisition for them without giving her relatives a chance at the defendants alone.

Skye caught her breath as she turned into her parent's well-tended lane. Cars completely covered the white pea gravel. May must have invited every aunt, uncle, and cousin within three hundred miles on both sides of the family. There were more people here today than at most wedding receptions.

Oh, no. Skye spotted her mother's concrete goose lawn ornament, and her hand flew to her mouth. The goose was dressed in a white gown with a veil on top of its head. Since it was usually attired in holiday garb, this couldn't be a good sign. Please, God, even May wouldn't throw a surprise wedding, would she?

Uncle Charlie, her father, and a dozen or so other male relatives were sitting on lawn chairs under the oak, near the back door of the red brick ranch-style house. Jed's brother, Skye's Uncle Wiley, was noticeably absent. His youngest son, Kenny, had passed away in August and Wiley wasn't up to attending parties yet.

Due to the summerlike weather, the trees still had their leaves and the acre of grass remained in putting green condition. Sometimes she wondered whether her dad really did cut the lawn with manicure scissors.

When Jed noticed Skye, he got up and met her by the steps near the back patio. His faded brown eyes twinkled in his tanned, leathery face. His steel gray crew cut didn't move when he scratched his head. "Your mom's waiting for you."

"Why? I'm on time. I'm even early." Anxiety crawled up Skye's neck. Her dad didn't usually move from his chair to greet her.

"She wants to talk to you before everyone gets here."

"You mean more people are coming?" Skye felt dizzy at the thought of facing even more relatives.

"Never mind that; just get inside and calm that woman down."

She pointed. "Why does Mom have a wedding dress on the goose?"

Her father wouldn't meet her eyes. "Who knows? Just go talk to her."

Skye took a deep breath and pushed open the door. The large celery-colored kitchen was cut in half by a peninsula. Usually stools edged the counter, but today women from age twenty to eighty crowded the room, scuffing the green linoleum through its fresh coat of wax. May held the place of honor at the stove, whipping mashed potatoes with an electric mixer.

The smell of cooking made Skye's mouth water, but the thought of what her mother might have to say to her made her stomach hurt. The mixed message drew her thoughts back to dinner with her parents when she had been a teenager. On the one hand May would become incredibly upset if Skye didn't clean her plate and even have seconds. On the other, she constantly nagged Skye about keeping her weight down.

Everyone looked up as Skye entered. The conversation stopped abruptly. It almost felt as if she had walked on stage during a play, and all the women were holding their breath, waiting for their cues.

May didn't look up from her potatoes. "Where's Simon?"

"He and Luc are coming separately."

"Why?" May narrowed her eyes. "Did you do something to upset Simon?"

Skye thought, *Let me count the ways*, but said aloud, "Not that I know of."

May stared at Skye, and everyone else stood silently.

Finally Grandma Denison spoke. "Sweetie, come give Grandma a hug." Cora Denison was a big woman, five-foot-ten and solidly built. At eighty-three, she had buried a husband, two children, and a grandson but was not ready to lie down and die herself. She was famous for her dinner rolls and droll sense of humor.

When she had Skye enfolded in her arms, Cora whispered, "I hear you got a couple of studs fighting over you. Go for the youngest one. You might as well have the benefit of a youthful body, since men never mature emotionally anyway."

Skye was still giggling over her grandmother's advice when her mother ordered, "Grab an apron from the drawer, and start filling the relish platters."

"Sure." Was that all May had to say about the Simon and Luc situation? It almost felt like an anticlimax.

Skye grabbed jars of pickles and beets, plastic bags of

carrots, radishes, and celery sticks, and a can of black olives from the refrigerator. Compartmentalized crystal trays were stacked on the counter, and she set to work. Conversations resumed, and she breathed a sigh of relief.

Her feeling of well-being was short-lived, however. The door slammed twice, and Luc and Simon walked into the kitchen glowering at each other. All eyes turned to the two men. The second act had obviously just begun.

Skye wiped her hands on her apron and took each of them by the arm. "Everyone, this is Luc St. Amant, an old friend of mine from New Orleans. You all know Simon Reid."

The women twittered, and Skye heard snatches of conversations containing the words *jilted* and *fiancé*. She turned to her grandmother and said, "Grandma, I'd like to introduce my friend Luc St. Amant. Luc, this is my paternal grandmother, Cora Denison."

Luc kissed the older woman's hand. "Ah, I see where Skye gets her beauty."

Cora rolled her eyes at Skye and snorted. "And I see where Southern gentlemen get their reputation."

Simon grinned and kissed Cora on the cheek. "Good one, Mrs. Denison."

May joined the group standing in the middle of her kitchen. "Simon, Luc, why don't you two boys join the men outside? Dinner should be ready in a half hour."

The men turned to leave, but Luc grabbed Skye's arm and whispered in her ear, "Do you realize your mother just poured a can of Coke over the ham? Has she gone crazy?"

"Don't worry. The Coke makes the ham juicier. It'll taste great. Trust me." The last thing she needed was Luc pulling his "I'm a gourmet" attitude today.

With the men out of the way, the final stages of dinner assembly began. This was serious business, but everyone still took the time to impart some advice to Skye or question her about her love life.

Ginger, one of her twin cousins, started things off as she

and Skye were wrapping the rolls in aluminum foil before heating them up in the oven. "When are you and Simon going to tie the knot?"

"As soon as we get the gag in your mouth," Skye replied, then smiled sweetly and crushed the piece of foil she had just torn from the cardboard cylinder.

May chose that moment to pop up and tsk, "You girls, we ask you to do one simple thing, and you do it slower than a herd of turtles stampeding through peanut butter."

Ginger stomped off in a huff, having been insulted by both mother and daughter. Skye closed her eyes and counted to ten, twice.

Tables had been set up in the garage, the only area big enough to accommodate the number of people gathered. A wide shelf stretched alongside one entire wall, and it was there that the food was placed. As head of the house, Jed lined up first, followed by Uncle Charlie, Simon, Luc, and the rest of the men roughly according to age, with oldest first. Next came children under sixteen, and finally the women who had cooked the meal.

Skye had been assigned to pour the iced tea, milk, and coffee. When Charlie paused for his glass, he said, "I been trying to talk to Luc, but there's no grain in that boy's silo."

She patted his hand. "Don't worry, he'll be gone soon."

"And you'll still be here?"

"I'm sticking around."

When it was finally her turn to fill a plate, Skye searched for a place to sit. Custom demanded that she sit with the women, not Luc and Simon, and for that she was partially thankful. The only empty seat she could find was beside her cousin Gillian, the other twin.

"Hi, anyone sitting here?" Skye asked, determined to be pleasant.

"Nope, have a seat. Did you get any of that pea salad? It's yummy. I wonder who made it?" Skye relaxed. Gillian seemed to be in a perky mood.

"No, maybe there'll be some left later."

Gillian leaned close once Skye was settled. "I've got some great news."

"Oh?" Skye eyed her warily.

"Yep, I'm going to have a baby."

"Congratulations. I didn't know you were planning on more children."

"Oh, yes, I just haven't been able to conceive."

"Well, great."

Gillian leaned even closer. "You know, you aren't getting any younger yourself. You should pick one of those guys and get pregnant right away."

Skye choked on the forkful of baked beans she had just put in her mouth. After a sip of iced tea she said, "Thanks for the advice, but if I want to hear the pitter patter of little feet, I'll put shoes on my cat, Bingo."

It was Gillian's turn to choke. She turned a lovely shade of Smurf blue. Being a good cousin, Skye ran and got a pitcher of water from the beverage table. She refilled her cousin's glass, then returned the container. Afterwards, she stopped to talk to Vince.

He smirked. "Having a good time?" His long butterscotch-blond hair was tied in a ponytail, and his emerald green eyes matched the polo shirt he was wearing.

She was always astonished at how out-of-place Vince looked in Scumble River, yet he didn't share her difficulty in fitting in with people. "Peachy keen. I love discussing my personal life with everyone and their dog."

"Hey, that's one reason it's nice to be a guy. You can be thirty-six and single, and nobody notices."

"That's so unfair. You should be the one to get married. You're older, you've dated way more, and you own your own business." Skye punched him in the arm.

"Look, I'm not afraid of commitment. I'm just monoga-mously challenged."

"Right." Skye put a hand on his arm and leaned closer.

"Hey, have you heard anything about Fayanne and the mayor and money?" As a hair stylist, Vince was one of the best sources for town gossip.

"Nothing involving the both of them. There was a rumor that Clapp Auto wasn't doing so well, but that was a while ago, and nothing seemed to come of it. Why?"

Skye explained why she had asked, and Vince said, "Maybe it has something to do with the bicentennial funding. Clapp, Fayanne, and Charlie make up the financial committee."

"Charlie wouldn't let them get away with anything."

"True, but it only takes two signatures to write a check, not all three."

"And you know this how?" Skye asked.

"The committee gave me a deposit check for the band to play tonight."

"Interesting."

Vince's comments ran through her head until she joined the women inside the house. Dishes were piled high on the counter by the sink. Skye's Aunt Minnie, her mother's sister, had claimed the privilege of washing. The other women fought to grab each piece of crockery as it emerged from the rinse water. No one would notice if Skye slipped out to see how Luc and Simon were faring.

She found Simon sitting by himself looking through a farming magazine and petting her father's dog, Chocolate. She plopped into the chair next to him and scratched behind the Lab's ears. "You must be really bored to be reading about tractors."

"It's not so bad. The food was great, and it's been fun to hear your male kinfolk grill old Luc. I'd say he's nearly well done by now." Simon took her hand. "How are you doing?"

"Ducky. All stressed out, and there's no one I can get away with choking."

"Anything I can do?"

"Yes, grab Luc and get him and yourself out of here. I'll meet you back at my cottage."

Simon kissed her cheek. "You got it."

Skye said good-bye to her dad, Charlie, and the others, then went inside to start making her good-byes to the women.

When she got to her grandmother, Cora said, "One last piece of advice. Not all men are annoying. Some are dead."

Skye blinked. Grandma had gotten even more outspoken since Grandpa died. Since there was no answer to that statement, at least not one Skye could think of, she kissed Cora and left.

It was with a renewed sense of freedom that Skye got into her car and drove away. She loved her family, but on days like this she was reminded of why she had left Scumble River in the first place.

Both Luc and Simon were sitting in their separate cars waiting for her when she got home. She unlocked the front door, and they followed her inside. Bingo greeted them in the foyer, meowing for his dinner.

After taking care of the cat, she joined the men in the living room and asked, "Luc, do you have the papers?"

"Yes."

"Great. Your lawyer was able to fax you a new set then?"

He looked sheepish. "Not exactly."

"Oh?"

Simon stared hard at Luc until he answered. "It turns out they weren't missing after all. After you left, I looked again, and there they were."

"I see." Skye's voice was cold.

"No, really." Luc tried to take her hand, but she resisted. "They really were gone when I first looked. Someone took them, then put them back."

"Why would anyone do that?"

Luc straightened. "It was obviously to harass me. To make me look bad in your eyes."

Simon sniggered.

"No matter. We have them now. Let's go over them."
Skye said to Simon, "You don't have to stick around for this.
Even after we finish, I'll still have to change for the dance."

Simon hesitated. "I still think you should have a lawyer
look at those before you sign them."

"That would cost hundreds of dollars."

"I'll pay."

"That's very nice of you, but I'm sure I can read and decide if it's okay without a lawyer."

Simon shrugged. They'd been over this before. "Fine, I'll
pick you up at quarter to eight." He reluctantly headed for
the door.

"There's no need for you to come back." Luc lounged
back on the sofa. "We could just meet you there."

"He's going to the dance?" Simon's voice had hardened.

"No, he's not." Skye shot Luc a firm look. "At least not
with us."

"You can't mean that, darlin'," Luc appealed. "It would
be so rude to leave me home alone."

"Sorry. Simon and I have had this date planned for
months, and the tickets are sold out."

Simon smiled thinly. "You could probably get a plane
back to New Orleans tonight. Then you wouldn't have to
worry about being alone."

"But . . ." Luc tried to speak.

Simon interrupted. "After all, Skye will sign the papers
this afternoon, and that's what you came for, isn't it?"

Luc turned his back on Simon and ignored his question.

After Simon left, Skye and Luc sat at the kitchen table
with the papers spread out in front of them. She read for two
hours and made it only three quarters of the way through. So
far everything was extremely straightforward. The parts that
pertained to her stated that she would serve on the board for
three years, be reimbursed for expenses, and have equal vot-
ing power with the other four members.

She stood up and stretched. "Looks like I won't have time to finish reading this today. I need to start dressing for the dance soon."

A funny expression flickered over Luc's features before he said, "You know, Simon was right. If you signed now, I could get back to New Orleans tonight."

"True, but I just said I won't be able to finish reading them."

"Right, but you could sign anyway, and I could make you a photocopy of the part you didn't get to read."

Suddenly a heavy silence descended. It would be such a relief to get him on a plane and out of Illinois. If he were gone, she wouldn't need to worry about being attracted to him or making a fool of herself again. But could she trust him? A cynical inner voice mocked, *Trust Luc? Sure. Why don't you go buy a lottery ticket? The odds are about as good.* Besides, this was the second time he had tried to get her signature without letting her read the papers.

"Sorry. I really can't sign something I haven't read. You understand."

Luc's mouth took on an unpleasant twist. "Fine. And what shall I do tonight while you and Simon go to this all-important dance?"

Suddenly she'd had enough. "I don't know, Luc. Go to Joliet to a movie, go to Chicago to a club, or maybe just go. Leave the papers, I'll read the rest when I get the chance, and mail them to you."

"I'm so sorry." Luc stood and took her hand. "I know I'm being a swine, but it makes me so jealous to see you go out with Simon."

Skye snorted, freed her fingers from his grasp, and walked toward the bedroom. "Fine. We'll finish things up after school tomorrow. I have to get dressed now. Make sure the door is locked when you leave."

CHAPTER 15

The Sound of Music

Talk about leaping from the frying pan into the fire. The Grand Union of the Mighty Bull's assembly hall was filled, and almost everyone who had been at the Denison dinner that afternoon seemed to be at the dance, too. *Great,* Skye thought, *another evening of unending questions and unwanted advice.*

She mentally called a stop to her negative thoughts—it was silly to let her well-meaning friends and family upset her. It was time to quit worrying and have some fun. She was attending the dance of the season with a fantastic guy. What more could she ask for?

She pressed Simon's arm and smiled up at him. He looked debonair in a pair of military-cut, sable-colored twill pants and a matching polished cotton shirt. The only formal occasions in Scumble River that required a tie and jacket were weddings and funerals.

He looked her over seductively. "Did I tell you how much I like your dress? What do you call that color?"

"Sea mist."

Simon ran his hand up and down her back. "Feels good too."

She felt a tingling in the pit of her stomach. "It's silk."

"Maybe we should skip the dance."

Skye swallowed hard. Maybe they should. She and

Simon had grown so close this past summer while working together with the youth group. Every day, her feelings for him had deepened, and she had found herself more and more aware of his sensual appeal. A delightful shiver of desire ran through her. Maybe it was time to spend the night together.

No, she had to finish things up with Luc first. "I think it's a little late for that. Too many people have spotted us."

"One of these days you're going to run out of excuses."

On the stage Vince and his band, The Plastic Santa, were getting ready to play, but since the music hadn't started yet, people stood in clumps on the dance floor talking and laughing. Along the outer rim, tables and chairs had been set up. A mahogany bar stretched across the back of the room. Legend had it that General U. S. Grant had had a drink at that bar.

Their progress was impeded by people stopping them to say hello. A wild waving from one of the side tables drew Skye's attention. She tugged on Simon's arm and pointed. "I can't quite see over everyone's head. Is that Trixie trying to get our attention?"

Simon looked over to where she indicated and nodded. "Want to go say hi?"

"I think we'd better, before she hurts herself."

They edged left and arrived just as Owen, Trixie's husband, was lifting her down off a metal folding chair. He looked ill at ease and kept tugging at the collar of his dress shirt.

Although Skye and Trixie were close friends, she didn't know Owen very well. He seemed far more comfortable in his tractor shed than out in public.

As soon as Trixie's feet hit the floor, she flew around the table and grabbed Skye. "We're going to the ladies'," she announced to the men, and dragged Skye off in the general direction of the rest room. The moment they were out of earshot she said, "So what happened with your big date with

Luc? Did you dump him? Is he on his way back to New Orleans? Come on, I'm dying to hear the scoop."

Trixie finally paused for breath, and Skye quickly spoke
up. "It was a great date, but Simon was at my house when
we got back."

"Oh, shoot. Was he mad?"

"Very, but after we talked, he seemed to understand."
Skye described the conversation to Trixie. "What do you
think?"

The other woman nodded. "Yeah, he sounds okay with it.
So what happened with Luc?"

"He should be gone by tomorrow night, Tuesday morning at the latest." Skye proceeded to tell Trixie about the lost
and found papers.

"Good. Things should be getting back to normal then."
Trixie pushed open the bathroom door. "And you survived
dinner at your mother's with Luc and Simon."

"More or less." Skye gave her friend a play-by-play of
the afternoon. "The concrete goose in the wedding dress still
worries me, though."

A giggle came from behind the closed door of a stall. The
toilet flushed, and Frannie Ryan walked out still adjusting
her dress. "That's too funny, Ms. D. Your mom must really
want you married to be playing dress-up with the lawn stat-
ues."

Skye didn't tell the teen that May had a goose costume
for each holiday. Some things were best left unsaid. "Frannie, it's nice to see you here. How're you doing?" She had
been meaning to check on her and Justin, but as usual, time
had gotten away from her.

"Fine. No problem."

"That's a pretty dress." Skye was dying to ask whom
Frannie had come to the dance with.

"Oh, thanks." Frannie brushed at the pearl pink lace on
the bodice. "I found it in my mom's closet. Dad never threw
out any of her stuff." She smoothed the crinkled georgette

panels of the full skirt and asked, "Does it make me look fatter?"

Trixie answered, "It makes you look like a princess."

"It sure does," Skye agreed. Her gaze traveled the length of the skirt, which ended at the teen's ankles. Poking out from beneath the frothy hem were heavy black Doc Martens. Someone needed to take this girl shopping.

"Well, we have to get back," Trixie said, checking her hair in the mirror while Frannie washed her hands.

"Right, the guys will wonder where we vanished to." Skye opened the door and gestured for Frannie to go first. "I imagine your date is looking for you too."

Frannie shook her head. "No, I'm just here with Justin. We want to write up the murder and thought we might hear something more where there are lots of people. We figure if we get a good enough story, Mr. Knapik won't be able to turn down our request for a school paper."

Skye and Trixie exchanged looks. Homer Knapik would never voluntarily let the kids have a paper. He was too stuck in his habits and too burned out to allow anything new in his school. They'd have to find a way to force him to do it.

As the women and the girl parted, Frannie said, "Something you might want to check out, Ms. Denison. Justin and I heard that Grady was bragging all over town that even though the police arrested him and beat him and threw him in jail, he didn't tell them anything he knew about the murder."

Frannie was swallowed up by the crowd before Skye could absorb the meaning of her words. "Dang, why do teens always tell you the important stuff just before they disappear?"

Trixie snickered. "Because they're teenagers. Duh!"

The music had started by the time the women returned to their table. Owen and Simon were missing, and Ginger and Gillian were sitting in their places.

As she sat, Skye said, "Hi. Where are Flip and Irvin?"

Come to think of it, she hadn't seen her twin cousins' husbands at the family dinner either.

Ginger answered, "Well, they tell us they've gone on a fishing trip."

"But you don't believe them?" Trixie asked.

"Oh, we believe them." Gillian took a swallow of her beer. "But we know what 'I'm going fishing' really means."

"Oh?"

"Yeah, it means, 'I'm going to drink myself dangerously stupid, and stand by a stream with a stick in my hand while fish swim by in complete safety,' " Ginger explained.

Skye and Trixie were still laughing at Ginger's fishing story when Simon and Owen joined them.

Skye managed to choke out a question to Simon. "Where were you?"

"Talking to your mom and dad."

"What did they have to say?"

"Oh, nothing much." Simon grinned secretively.

"Okay, what did they really say?" Skye demanded.

Simon took her hand, pulled her out of her seat, and onto the dance floor. As they whirled away, he whispered in her ear, "Your dad said to tell Luc that he has a shot gun, a shovel, and five hundred acres in back of his house. So it would be a good idea for Luc to get the hell out of town, real soon."

"What did you say?"

"I told your dad that I would be happy to pass on that message, and that considering my profession, I was pretty good with a shovel myself."

Skye let that remark go, and she and Simon danced and talked to people until the band took a break. They made their way to the stage, where Vince was accepting a bottle of beer from a blonde. He turned to them while gesturing toward her. "Quite a girl, huh?"

Skye frowned. "Girl? Is she under twenty-one?"

Vince wrinkled his brow. "Lady?"

Skye shook her head.

"So if she's not a girl or a lady, what is she?" he asked. "A Breasted American?"

"Very funny." Skye changed the subject, knowing she would never change her brother. "The band sounded good."

"Thanks. We've been practicing a lot more often since the mayor decided to let us use the bandstand in the park on weeknights. I guess now with the murder we won't be able to use it anymore."

"How long have you been doing that?" Skye asked.

"Oh, maybe six weeks or so. We tried using the salon, but it was too full of equipment. One of the guys let us use his garage, but the neighbors complained about the noise."

"You must've drawn a crowd if you were practicing in the park."

"No, you'd be surprised how deserted that place is in the evenings." Vince took a swig of beer. "We did have a slight problem with some high school kids who considered the bandstand their private clubhouse, but we took care of it."

"When's the last time you used it?"

Vince tapped the bottle with his finger as he thought. "Thursday, the night before the carnival started. Why?"

"Did you notice any new graffiti that night?"

"Nah. Same old stuff. Why?"

"Nothing important. Just checking out something one of the kids told me."

"See you later, Sis. Time to get to work." Vince joined the other band members at their instruments.

Skye and Simon started back toward their table but were waylaid by Charlie. The big man hugged them both at the same time, one under each arm. "How are two of my favorite people?"

"We're fine, Uncle Charlie. How about you? Did you find a new housekeeper?"

"Not yet." He shook his head, and his snow-white hair swayed gently. "The people staying at the motor court are driving me crazy. Used to be you provided a clean room, plenty of towels, and a TV, and they were happy. Now they want blow dryers, internet access, and microwaves."

"Tough week." Skye commiserated with him. She could see the exhaustion on his face. "But didn't most of them check out today?"

"Yeah, but now that Scumble River is on the Midwest Fall Foliage Tour, they'll be back as soon as the leaves start to change."

"That's a good thing though, isn't it? Lots of business for you."

"So Eldon Clapp keeps telling everyone," Charlie grumbled. "I just don't understand why if it's tourist season, we can't shoot them."

Some friends joined Charlie, and Skye and Simon danced off. They were enjoying themselves when Skye spotted the mayor and Fayanne Emerick dancing together. That seemed peculiar. She didn't think they'd be that friendly after their big fight in the Beer Garden a couple of nights ago.

She maneuvered Simon closer to the odd couple and was just in time to overhear Mayor Clapp wisecrack, "I haven't spoken to my wife for eighteen months." He paused, then delivered the punch line. "I don't want to interrupt her."

The mayor's braying laughter stopped abruptly when Fayanne said, "Yeah, well, I finally figured out the way to a man's heart." She waited a beat before adding, "Through his chest with a sharp knife."

Skye swung around. *Through a man's chest.* That's how Gabriel Scumble was murdered. Which was exactly why Fayanne wouldn't brag about it, right? Skye narrowed her eyes, distracted by the bizarre vision in front of her. What on earth was Fayanne wearing? The older woman had poured herself into a raspberry satin jumpsuit that laced up the back.

Something about that color nudged Skye's memory. She jerked her gaze to Fayanne's lips. She had seen that shade of lipstick before. It was the one on the handkerchief the bird-watcher had found that morning. That unique pink-purple color couldn't be mistaken, and Skye would bet no one else in town wore such an awful shade.

It was time to talk to Wally again. She'd call him from school tomorrow, or stop by after work.

Come to think of it, why wasn't he at the dance? He'd promised to be there.

CHAPTER 16

The Bad Seed

Still slightly damp from her Monday morning swim in the high school's pool, Skye hurried down the hallway, mentally running through what she needed to accomplish before going over to the elementary school. Three kids to counsel, two teachers to consult with, and a parent to call back. Gee, it almost sounded like that song "The Twelve Days of Christmas."

If there were absolutely no interruptions, she could accomplish these tasks within the three and a half hours she was scheduled to be at the high school. As soon as that thought popped into her head, she knew she had jinxed herself. The ringing of the phone before she even got her door unlocked proved her right.

As she let herself into her office, she took a moment to gloat. It had taken two long years, but she had finally convinced the principal to let her have the room for her very own.

It had previously housed the guidance records and the part-time guidance counselor, who was also the boys' PE teacher. Although he already had an office in the gym, he had fought tooth and nail to keep this one too.

Now, the file cabinets had been moved to a small cubicle within the main office area, which also housed the photocopier and coffee pot, Coach had been told to use his gym

office, and Skye had been given exclusive rights to this
room. She considered it a major coup for school psychologists everywhere.

She dropped her purse into the desk drawer, plopped into
the comfy old leather chair, and scooped the receiver from
its cradle. "Skye Denison, may I help you?"

Opal Hill, the high school secretary, sighed. "I'm so glad
you're here. Mr. Knapik wants to speak to you right now."
She always sounded as if she were single-handedly running
the school—probably because she was.

Skye tried not to add to her burden. "Right now, like as
soon as I get a cup of coffee, or right now, like as fast as I
can walk down there?"

There was a short silence while Opal calculated. "Coffee
is okay."

"Fine, see you in a couple of minutes."

Minutes later, Skye entered the main office juggling her
appointment book, legal pad, pen, and thermal mug.

Opal stood at the counter balancing a phone on her shoulder, counting out money to a student, and sorting envelopes.
She blew a strand of wispy brown hair out of her eyes and
gestured Skye into the principal's office.

"You know, Opal," Skye said, hoping to take the worried
look off the secretary's face, "Monday is an awful way to
spend one seventh of your life."

The secretary nodded quickly and turned back to work
with a small smile.

Homer Knapik had been principal of Scumble River
High when Skye and her brother Vince went to school there.
It had been awkward going from student to colleague, but
Skye always forced herself to call him by his first name and
act as if they were both adults.

Today she pushed open his door and said, "Good morning, Homer. You wanted to see me?"

"What's all this I hear about Grady Nelson?" Homer was
seated at his desk, a pencil behind his ear and papers spread

everywhere. He was a squarely built man with an overabundance of hair sprouting over most of his body.

Knowing he was not one for social niceties, Skye didn't wait for an invitation to sit down. "I imagine you've had quite an earful about that youngster. Where would you like me to begin?"

Homer scratched a hairy ear. "How about the arrest?"

"Sure, but this is secondhand. I wasn't present."

The principal nodded.

"Grady was taken into police custody for questioning regarding the murder of Gabriel Scumble. It's my understanding that he was not actually arrested, and that he refused to answer anything the police asked. I hear he is currently bragging about having outsmarted the cops."

"Just what we need, a more powerful Grady."

"Earlier in the weekend, I caught him and his gang tormenting a group of kids at the Founder's Day Speech."

"Sounds like our Grady. That boy has delusions of adequacy."

Skye grinned. Every once in a while, Homer hit the nail on the head without even realizing it.

He searched for his calendar. "When's the meeting to go over his testing with his parents? I want this kid out of here and in an alternative school as of yesterday."

"Mr. and Mrs. Nelson are supposed to come in tomorrow at seven-thirty to meet with us and the rep from the Northwest Alternative School," Skye explained. She pinned the principal with a stare. "You *are* planning to attend that meeting, right?"

"Sure. I've got it in my book." He looked back down at his paperwork, indicating Skye was dismissed.

She got up and was reaching for the door when it flew inward, knocking her back a step.

A middle-aged woman burst into the room, sobbing. "This is it. I've had it. I quit."

Skye recognized her as one of the bus drivers and tried to

sidle out of the office. She had made it as far as the front counter before Homer yelled, "Skye, get back in here!" She reluctantly retraced her path.

The bus driver sat in one of the visitors' chairs. Skye took the other. Homer was on the phone with Opal, bellowing instructions.

He hung up and turned to the woman. "Tell her what you just told me."

"I've been driving for ten years, and I've never had anything like this happen before."

Skye patted her hand. The woman was chalk white with a film of sweat above her lip. "Take your time."

"I start my route in the country, at the very edge of our district. Then I work my way back toward the school. The bus is mixed."

"Mixed?" Skye asked.

"All ages," Homer interjected. "Kindergarten through high school."

"That must make things tougher," Skye commented.

"Usually it's okay," the woman said. "Most of them are real good kids, but lately three high school boys have been giving me a hard time. I been praying for one of them to turn sixteen and start driving to school."

Skye nodded her understanding.

"I had just picked up Nanette Carroll when it started. The three boys started teasing her about something. I couldn't quite hear, but she looked real upset. So at my next stop I had her move up to the seat right behind me. Usually I put either the little ones there to keep them safe or I make the rowdier high school kids sit there to keep an eye on them. But something felt funny today."

Skye was impressed by the woman's savvy and compassion. "It's always good to go with your gut instincts." Skye wasn't sure she understood the whole picture yet, so asked, "How old is Nanette?"

"She's fourteen or fifteen." The bus driver sighed and

went on. "Anyway, moving Nanette seemed to be the answer. But then during this one stretch of curved road where there's no place to pull over, and the traffic is usually going pretty fast so I have to really concentrate, one of the boys moved into the seat next to her, and the other two took over the one behind her. She was trapped between them and the window."

Skye felt a prickle of concern at the back of her neck. "What happened?"

The bus driver looked down at her hands and picked at a hangnail. "I guess I didn't notice they had moved right away, but I heard a scream and looked in the mirror. They had her shirt pulled up and her bra open and were touching her breasts."

"How terrible! What did you do?"

"I yelled at them, and they laughed. I pulled over as soon as I could, but those were the longest couple of minutes of my life."

"Did they stop when you pulled over?" Skye was concerned; the woman almost seemed in shock.

"Yes, but I can still feel the leader's eyes burning into the back of my neck. He knew there wasn't anything I could do against the three of them. I couldn't even make them get off the bus." The woman shook her head. "Luckily, when I radioed for help there was another bus nearby, and it trailed me back to the school."

Before Skye could say more, Homer had dismissed the woman and turned back to Skye. "What do you think we should do?"

"First we need to make sure the bus driver is okay. She looked pretty shaky."

"Opal called her sister; she'll drive her home."

"Oh, good. Where are the boys and Nanette now?"

"The girl is in the health room with Opal. The boys are in with Coach."

Skye could understand why Homer had selected Coach

to watch the miscreants. He was big and tough and wouldn't hesitate to physically restrain the offenders. Unfortunately his views were trapped in the fifties, even though he'd been just a baby in that decade. She shuddered to think of what he might be saying to the teens. For all she knew, he could be congratulating them for copping a feel.

"Call the girl's parents right now," Skye suggested, "but let's talk to the boys before we call their folks." Skye made a note on her legal pad. "By the way, who are the boys?"

"Grady Nelson, Arlen Yoder, and Elvis Doozier."

"No surprises there. Arlen is Gus's younger brother, right?" The school year before last, Gus had been expelled, and his father had assaulted Skye. He'd actually picked her up out of her seat and shaken her like a dirty rug.

"Yep, we get to deal with Mr. Yoder again."

"Swell. How does Elvis fit into the Doozier clan?" Skye asked.

"He's Elvira's twin. That makes him Earl and Hap's brother."

"Then his parents are dead. Who does he live with?"

"His great-grandmother has custody, but she's about two hundred years old. We'll have to get Earl in here."

"Wonderful. The gang's all here." Skye paused. "It just occurred to me—we'd better call Wally."

"Yeah, that's a good idea," Homer said slowly. "Let the police take part of the heat."

"I'll make the call to Wally while you call the girl's parents."

Wally arrived within minutes and strode over to where Skye was sitting behind Opal's desk. "Does the girl need medical attention?"

"She seems fine in that respect."

"Where are the boys?"

"In the back room with Coach."

"Have their parents been notified?"

"The girl's have. We wanted to talk to the boys first."

"It would have been good to keep them separate."

"I know, but by the time I found out what was happening, it was too late." Skye stood. "You go ahead into Homer's office, I'll go get one of the boys. Any preference as to who we see first?"

"Save the ringleader for last."

"Gotcha." Skye walked to Coach's new room and stuck her head in the doorway. "We'd like to see Arlen Yoder now."

The Incredible Hulk rose from a chair and followed her down the short corridor to the principal's office. The resemblance between Arlen and his father, Leroy, was astonishing. Skye felt somewhat uneasy having the boy behind her, but he followed her directions without question. She seated him between Wally and herself, facing Homer.

Homer spoke first. "You know me, this is Ms. Denison, the school psychologist, and this is Chief Boyd. We understand there was some problem on the bus this morning. Tell us what happened."

The boy cleared his throat, and Skye noticed that his face was very red, and there were tears in his eyes. "Me and Grady and Elvis were just having some fun."

"Oh?" The principal stared at him impassively.

"But then Nan got all huffy and acted like she was better than us, so Grady said we had to teach her a lesson."

"So you did what?" Homer asked.

"We pulled her shirt up and touched her . . ." The boy trailed off, his face going from scarlet to cerise.

"Touched her what?" Homer's voice was still mild.

"Her boobies," Arlen whispered. "Just once, to teach her a lesson."

Homer leaned forward. "Young man, you will be the one learning the lesson. Do you realize you can be suspended, maybe even expelled, for your actions?"

Wally added, "Arlen, what you did is not only against the

school rules, it's also against the law. If charges are pressed, you could go to jail."

"It was Grady," Arlen sobbed. "He said to do it."

"Maybe next time Grady tells you to do something, you'd better run the other way," Wally advised.

Skye led the boy out of the room, back to where he had been waiting. She told Coach, "We'd like to see Elvis now."

She recognized Elvis as one of the boys who'd been with Grady last Friday. Back then, she'd thought he was around ten years old. Now she realized his short stature and the childish look in his big brown eyes had fooled her. He buzzed around Skye like a mosquito, excited by all the attention. She indicated the seat recently vacated by Arlen.

Homer again led the questioning. "What happened this morning on the bus?"

"We got ourselves some booty."

"What?" Homer roared. "What you did was wrong, and I want you to be respectful when you talk to me about it."

Elvis stared at the principal, clearly confused. "My friend Grady said it was all right. That we were men, and we had the right to do what we wanted with the girls."

Homer's jaw dropped, and Wally said quickly, "Elvis, Grady isn't your friend, and he's dead wrong about men having the right to hurt women like that."

"We didn't hurt her. Grady said she liked it."

"Grady lied, and you did hurt her," Wally explained. "Plus, you can go to jail for what you did. Not to mention you'll probably be suspended, maybe even expelled, from school."

Elvis frowned. "But that's not fair. Grady said it was okay."

"You need to listen to the grown-ups, not Grady."

Skye led the boy out of the room. She would need to pull Elvis's records. She suspected he might be mildly mentally impaired, but she didn't remember seeing his name on any of the special education class lists. What was the story there?

Grady was the last one. He swaggered into the office and flung himself into a chair.

Homer said, "What's your version of this morning's incident?"

"The bitch had it coming. She dissed me."

"And how did she do that?" Homer asked.

"She's supposed to be my lady, and she thinks she can break up with me."

"An abominable sin."

"I do the breaking up." Grady narrowed his eyes. "Hey, a man's got to do what he's got to do, or people will take advantage."

Wally joined the conversation. "So we meet again, Mr. Nelson."

"Yeah."

"The school's going to suspend you, maybe even expel you, and once the girl presses charges, you're going to jail."

"She'll never press charges against me. She's too scared of what might happen."

The conversation went downhill from there, and Homer soon sent the teen back to Coach.

After Grady left, Skye asked, "Isn't it time to call the parents?"

Homer nodded, and she went to talk to the girl. They had decided it would be best for Skye to talk to Nanette Carroll without Homer and Wally.

Nanette was resting on the cot in the health room. She sat up when Skye walked in and pulled up a chair. "Hi, Nanette. My name is Ms. Denison. I'm the school psychologist. I hear something bad happened to you this morning. Do you feel like telling me about it?"

Nanette shook her head and fine blond hair flew around her face. "Please don't make me."

"I won't. Is there anything you'd like to talk about?"

The teen hugged her knees. "Not right now. Is my mom coming?"

"She's on her way."

"Could I be alone now?" Haunted gray eyes pleaded with Skye.

"Sure. If you ever want to talk to me, ask Opal to call me, okay?"

"Okay."

Skye went back to Homer's office. "Any luck?" she asked.

Homer smoothed the hair that swirled from beneath the cuff of his shirt. "Depends on your definition of luck. I got hold of Mrs. Yoder and Grandma Doozier, but no one answers at the Nelsons—there's no work number listed on his reg-info card."

"Would you want to call Ursula and ask her how to reach them? She's the father's sister."

"Right. I forgot Ursula was Grady's aunt."

Homer got on the phone, and Skye went back to Opal's desk. The secretary was taking a well-deserved break.

In a few minutes, Mrs. Carroll arrived. She looked like her daughter, fair skin, dull blond hair, and sad gray eyes. Wally advised pressing charges, and she agreed to consider it. She explained that her ex-husband, Nanette's father, lived out of state, and she wanted to talk to him before making any decisions.

Skye suggested counseling for Nanette. Mrs. Carroll said she didn't have the money. Skye provided her with a list of low-cost and sliding-scale services in the area and said she was available to talk to Nanette at school, if Mrs. Carroll signed a consent form. Mrs. Carroll wanted to check with her ex-husband about that too.

After Nanette and her mother left, Skye said to Wally, "Can I trade this job for what's behind door number two?"

"It's probably worse."

"True. I did want to mention something to you before the Yoders get here."

"Okay." Wally remained sitting. "Go ahead."

"A year ago last spring, Arlen Yoder's older brother Gus was caught with a knife and drugs, trying to force himself on one of the senior girls. He should have been turned over to the police, but things got messed up, and the parents managed to buy off the girl and our witness. The only consequence to his actions was not being allowed to graduate with his class, although he managed to circumvent us and participate in the ceremony anyway."

Wally made a sound of disgust deep in his throat.

"Mr. Yoder was extremely unhappy with the school's decision. During a meeting he leaned over the table and grabbed me from my chair. I wasn't seriously hurt, and Homer wouldn't call the police, but the thing is, I'm afraid to tell this man that another of his sons is in trouble."

"The jerk." Wally's expression was thunderous. "There's no reason why you have to be in the room. Homer and I can handle it. If Yoder tries anything with me, I'll shoot him."

Skye studied Wally's face. She wasn't sure if he was kidding or not.

The Yoders showed up shortly thereafter. Opal had reclaimed her desk, and Skye had moved to the health room to make some calls. Within minutes of the couple's arrival she could hear Leroy Yoder shouting behind the closed door of Homer's office. She was thankful not to have to sit through another meeting with him. That man scared her. He was huge, had no impulse control, and didn't think the rules applied to him. Just the kind of guy you didn't want to enrage.

Earl Doozier appeared before the Yoder meeting was finished, and Opal sent him in to talk to Skye. "MeMa couldn't come; she's feelin' poorly," he explained

"I'm sorry to hear that," Skye said. "I didn't know Elvira had a twin. How many brothers and sisters do you have?"

He scratched his head. "Umm, two of each."

"Does your other sister live around here?"

"Yeah, she lives with MeMa and Elvis on the home place. She's done real good for herself. She works for Doc Addison."

"I'm sure you're proud of her."

"Yep. Sure am." He leaned forward and whispered, "Say, Ms. D., is it true what Knapik said Elvis done?"

"I'm afraid so. He's fallen in with some bad company."

"I knows it, and now I'm going to do something about it." Earl dusted off his hands. "No more hanging around with Grady Nelson."

"That's a good start. Also, I wanted to ask you how Elvis was doing in school."

"Not too good. He had to take all his freshman classes over again this year."

"Is he getting any special help?"

"Nope. They tested him a while back, and I think they said he was too dumb for those special classes. But I didn't catch a lot of what that man from the county said, so maybe I got it wrong."

Skye thought over what Earl had reported and decided that when Elvis had been evaluated, his IQ must have been between seventy and eighty. That would mean he would not qualify for services with a learning disability, since a child had to have average or above average intelligence to be considered LD.

Unfortunately he also would not be considered mentally impaired, as a student's IQ had to fall below sixty-nine to qualify for that handicapping condition.

Elvis fell into a gray area. He didn't qualify for any special services, but there was no way he could keep up with average students. Skye hated when this happened. There was nothing in place to help these kids make it through school, and they usually ended up dropping out.

"No, Earl, unfortunately, I think you got it right." She heard the principal's door open and held her breath.

The Yoders marched past, dragging Arlen by the arm. Skye was relieved that they hadn't noticed her.

"My turn, huh?" Earl asked.

"Want me to come in with you?"

"No, thanks, Ms. D. I can handle this."

That meeting was a lot quieter and a lot quicker. Earl and his younger brother filed silently out the door and drove off.

Homer poked his head out. "Are they gone?"

"Yes." Skye kept her face emotionless. "Elvis has left the building."

When Homer called Grady's aunt, she said that Mr. and Mrs. Nelson were in the city shopping, and there was no way to reach them. She offered to come get him herself, but they couldn't release him without parental permission. The school was stuck with Grady until his parents got home and listened to their phone messages. It was decided he would stay where he was, and a rotation of adults would supervise him.

Wally said to Skye, "I'm going back to the station. Give me a call when the Nelsons show up."

"Do you have a minute before you leave?"

He glanced at his watch. "Sure. Want to grab some lunch?"

"Why not? What more can happen?" Oh, no, she had done it again, jinxed herself twice in one day. "I'll go get my things and meet you in the parking lot."

Skye told Opal she was leaving, grabbed her purse from her office, and hurried down the front steps. Wally had pulled the squad car up to the door and left the engine running. She slipped into the passenger seat and sighed, relieved to be making a clean getaway.

He turned to her. "Where to?"

"McDonald's is all I have time for."

"Mickey D's it is."

They drove the short distance in silence. Skye didn't

want to get started and then have to stop in the middle of a thought. After parking, ordering, and getting their food, they made their way to a corner table in the back.

Skye spread a napkin on the table and poured dressing onto her McSalad. She took a swig of Diet Coke and said, "I've got some more information about the murder for you. Have you learned anything new?"

"Let's see; still no sign of Gabriel Scumble's rental car. We all saw him drive up in it, but it's gone. We called all the rental car companies, and no one has him listed as a client. The Montreal police are having trouble getting a warrant to look at the records of the building where his penthouse is located. It seems that in the past the Scumble family has been suspected of acquiring its extreme wealth through less than honest means. But Gabriel, who appears to be the last of the line, worked his whole life to make reparations."

"So it could be that the murderer came to Scumble River's Bicentennial because he or she had a grudge against his family," Skye speculated.

"With all those strangers in town, that's certainly a possibility," Wally said. "But there's no physical evidence to point in that direction. If someone came to murder him, they would have brought their own weapon, not used whatever was handy." Wally took a bite of his Big Mac.

"True. Anything else?"

"We've sent out that handkerchief the bird woman found for DNA testing, but it's probably all Gabriel Scumble's blood."

"That handkerchief had lipstick on it, too, right?"

He nodded, his mouth full.

"Well, I knew I had seen that color before. It's a really unusual shade. I finally figured out who wears it. Fayanne Emerick had it on at the dance last night." She paused, then asked, "Why weren't you at the dance?"

Wally ignored her last question. "We can't make an arrest

on lipstick color, although I'll keep that information in mind."

"How about DNA from the lipstick?" Skye leaned forward.

"Maybe, if she had just licked her lips or something."

"Can't you do something? I'm sure the colors are a match."

"I'll check it out, but she has no motive."

Skye liberated one of Wally's fries and used it as a pointer. "But she keeps popping up. First, she had a fight with Gabriel Scumble in the Beer Garden a few hours before his murder. Second, her relatives and his relatives go back to when the town was formed. Now we have the lipstick on the bloody handkerchief."

"A lot of pieces, but nothing that makes sense," Wally said. "What does the fact that their ancestors knew each other two hundred years ago have to do with a murder now?"

Skye slumped in her seat. She couldn't be mad at Wally, because she couldn't figure out how it all went together either. But—Skye straightened in her seat—she knew who *could* figure it all out. Miss Letitia North, the town historian. She would pay a call on the older women after work.

They finished lunch, and Wally dropped Skye off back at the high school. The rest of the afternoon was quiet. Homer spent the time talking to the superintendent and school board members about the hearings for Grady, Arlen, and Elvis. Skye resumed her interrupted schedule after phoning the elementary school and saying she wouldn't be there that day. Grady's parents finally showed up at the end of the day and took him home. The excitement would start up again tomorrow.

CHAPTER 17

Dead Man Walking

Skye pulled into the Up A Lazy River Motor Court parking lot at exactly three-thirty. It was hard to believe she had been able to duck out of school so early, considering everything that had happened that day, but sometimes that was how it worked. The busier the morning, the quieter the afternoon.

Her original plan had been to go straight to Miss Letitia's and question her about the town's history, but she was worried about Charlie. His gray complexion and exhausted demeanor at the dance kept popping into her thoughts.

It was a hot walk across the blacktop. She dug into her purse, pulling out a scrunchie, and gathered her hair into a thick ponytail. The sun continued to beat down with an intensity not often seen in late September. When Skye had driven past the Scumble River First National Bank after school, the thermometer read eighty-nine degrees. It was beginning to feel like fall weather would never arrive.

Coolness greeted her as she pushed open the motor court's door and went inside. The window air conditioner rattled in an attempt to keep heat and humidity from the tiny office. Scanning the room, she noted the drab brown walls, the faded posters, and the peeling linoleum. Maybe it was time to gently suggest some redecorating. A chest-high countertop ran across the back third of the area, concealing the corner which housed the desk and chair usually occupied by Charlie.

Skye peeked over and found him slumped forward with his head cradled in his arms on the desktop. With a squeak of alarm, she flung open the hatch in the counter and ran to him. "Uncle Charlie, are you all right?" She put her hand on his forehead.

He felt warm and did not respond. She tried shaking him. Finally, his eyelids fluttered, and he sat up with a strangled cough. "What—oh, Skye—what's up? I must have drifted off for a minute."

"You were zonked out. I couldn't wake you at first."

He took out a handkerchief and blew his nose. "I'm tired. It's been hectic around here this weekend. And your ma is on this new health kick." He pointed to something behind him she hadn't noticed. It was an exercise bike. "I'll give you fifty bucks if you put ten miles on that dang contraption before May makes her nightly check."

"Sorry, Uncle Charlie, Mom scares me too much." Skye just hoped there wouldn't be one of those things waiting for her at her cottage when she got home.

He grumbled, "I keep telling her: eat well, stay fit, die anyway."

"I'm sure Mom's only doing what she thinks is best for you."

"The woman should know me by now. The only reason I'd take up exercising is so that I can hear heavy breathing again."

Skye raised her eyebrows.

"Seriously, though, what with May and Homer, I haven't had a minute to myself all day. I spent most of the afternoon on the phone with him. We sure got ourselves a situation at the high school." Charlie was the school board president.

Skye was relieved to see him perk up so fast. His color was good, and he seemed like his usual self. "Too true.

Grady Nelson is going to be the death of all of us, if we don't get him in the right placement soon."

Charlie narrowed his eyes. "Homer tells me that Alternative School is going to cost us thirty thousand a year. Spending that kind of money on a little criminal like Grady Nelson really sticks in my craw."

"A small price to pay to have Grady where he can get help and be monitored."

"Too bad we can't just expel him."

"We're in an awkward position because we've started a case study. He isn't special ed yet, but he may be tomorrow, so the question arises as to whose protection he is entitled to."

"Can you say he doesn't qualify for services?" Charlie asked.

"Not with a straight face, and certainly not ethically. Besides, do you really want someone like Grady on the loose in Scumble River? We need to help him now at age fifteen, or when he hits eighteen, we'll be sorry."

"So, we have no choice." Charlie lit a cigar. "How about the other two hoodlums?"

"I pulled their records and looked them over this afternoon. Both have had some minor infractions before, but nothing like this." She waved away the smoke from Charlie's cigar. "I think if Grady goes to this other school, a suspension will scare Arlen and Elvis back onto the straight and narrow."

Charlie heaved himself out of the battered wooden swivel chair and swooped Skye into a bear hug. "I'm sure glad you're at the school to handle things. Poor Homer is so close to retirement he can taste the cake at his party, and he just isn't up to today's modern youth."

"Well, thank you."

"Have you figured out who killed Gabriel Scumble yet?"

"No. But I've talked to some people and turned over my findings to Wally."

Charlie's intense blue eyes under bushy white brows scrutinized her face. "Have you sent that Southerner packing yet?"

She tapped her fingernails on the counter and grimaced. Darn, she had forgotten her promise to meet Luc after school and finish up those papers. "Almost. Say, can I use the phone?"

"Help yourself."

She dialed Simon's number but got his machine. After the beep, she left a message for Luc, saying she'd meet him at her cottage at seven to sign the papers.

Charlie settled back down in the creaking chair. "I am really pooped. The rest of the bicentennial tourists checked out this morning."

"Have you found someone to clean for you yet?"

Charlie stubbed his cigar out in the overflowing ashtray at his elbow. "No."

"I heard that Jack Cooper is looking for a part-time job."

"I couldn't ask Jack. This is women's work."

"Oh, you mean it's dirty, difficult, and thankless?"

Charlie snorted. "Hey, I cleaned a couple of the units myself. I just can't insult old Jack."

"How about I clean a few right now? I've got some time to kill." She knew the routine, having worked for Charlie when she was in high school.

Charlie started to protest, but Skye had already grabbed his ring of keys from the desk top and opened the door to the utility closet. She wheeled out the cleaning cart. "Where should I start?"

"If you really want to, the left side units haven't been touched."

The motor court's twelve rooms were arranged in a semicircle. At the arc of the semicircle was the deluxe cabin Gabriel Scumble had been given. "How about number six?"

"Sure, if you get that far. The police released it this morning."

Skye quickly established a routine. Strip and remake the beds, gather up the used towels and put out fresh ones, empty the trash, vacuum, and clean the bathroom. Some rooms looked as if a family of ten had camped out in them for two weeks, and with others it was hard to tell that any-one had been there at all.

When she finished unit five, she checked her watch. It was nearly six o'clock. Should she stop now, and give her-self time to clean up and eat before Luc showed up at her place? Curiosity won out over her desire for a shower and a sandwich. She wanted to see where Gabriel Scumble had stayed.

She unlocked the door and stepped inside. A wave of hot, musty air rolled over her, and she quickly switched on the AC. Evidence of the police search was everywhere. The double bed, which was normally flush against the left wall, had been pulled out into the middle of the room. Its aqua chenille bedspread and starched white sheets were piled on top of the bare mattress, which was halfway off the box springs.

The two wooden nightstands had been overturned and their drawers taken out. The matching dresser had suffered the same fate, as had the desk. An aqua vinyl armchair was turned over, exposing its underside. A similar orange chair was also resting on its seat and back.

Lamps, the telephone, and the TV had been dismantled. Every towel had been shaken open and flung into a pile in the corner of the bathroom. Only the mirrors and pictures, which were screwed to the wall, were undisturbed. Even the shower curtain had been taken down and flung into a corner.

Skye shook her head. This mess would take hours to clean up. She'd give it until six-thirty, then come back to-morrow after school to finish. As she worked, she kept ask-ing herself where someone would hide their identification in a motel room like this. It was obvious the police search had been thorough. Or had the murderer stolen Gabriel Scumble's wallet?

A ceramic, urn-shaped lamp was tipped over on the desk with its bottom off. She had begun to put it together when it occurred to her that there was another compartment in this type of fixture. She had purchased a similar one when she was furnishing her cottage. It came unassembled in a box. There had been three pieces.

The police had taken apart the bottom third, unscrewing the foot from the urn, but it also came apart at the neck. And at this end there was enough room to hide something in the center of the sphere.

Skye held her breath as she twisted the large ceramic globe from the brass tubing that held the lampshade. It was too dark to see inside. She tried sticking her hand in, but the space was too small. Finally, she upended it, and shook. At first nothing happened, then something rattled and became lodged in the opening. It was a man's wallet.

She reached for it but stopped a few inches from the leather. Better not. Instead she put the phone back together and called Wally. He said he'd be right over.

While she waited, Skye ran back to the office and told Charlie what she had found. They both greeted the chief as he strolled into the motel room.

"Evening, Skye, Charlie." Wally nodded to them. "So you found a wallet?"

Skye pointed to the lamp. "There, I haven't touched it."

"Good."

Charlie leaned against the wall and crossed his arms. "Seems like Skye keeps finding evidence your boys miss."

Wally examined the light fixture intently, ignoring Charlie's comment, then turned. "Excuse me just a moment while I make a call."

"Sure." Skye was a little disconcerted by Wally's manner. Was there a little edge beneath his affability?

She exchanged looks with Charlie as Wally dialed and

said, "Hey, Betty, let me talk to the sheriff please; it's Wally Boyd." A minute or so went by, then Wally spoke again. "Otto, could you send the crime-scene technician over to the Up A Lazy River Motor Court again? No, we haven't had another murder." He gritted his teeth and growled. "What's happening is amateurs are still finding evidence your techs missed. No, the handkerchief was yesterday. Today it's the victim's wallet."

Wally banged down the phone with an expletive and took a deep breath. "Let's have a look inside that wallet."

Charlie moved over to the desk. Skye leaned over the chief's shoulder for a better view.

Using tweezers and a pen, Wally first freed the wallet from the lamp's aperture, and then emptied it of its contents without touching anything.

As he exposed the driver's license, credit cards, and car rental agreement, Skye gasped. All bore the name Snake Iazetto, not Gabriel Scumble. "Dang!" she said. "I didn't find the victim's wallet after all. But who's Snake Iazetto? That can't be someone's real name."

Wally's smile looked a lot more genuine now. "Look at the driver's license picture. Snake Iazetto is the man we know as Gabriel Scumble. And yes, it is an unusual name, but I've seen stranger ones."

"It looks like the victim's a true snake in the grass," Skye said. Wally looked at her blankly and she explained, "You know, someone you didn't expect to be what he is. That certainly opens up a lot of new possibilities."

Charlie scowled. "How could something like this happen?"

"I'll bet I know," Skye murmured, lost in thought. "Remember how late Gabriel Scumble was last Friday? When that car pulled up, Mayor Clapp and Fayanne were so relieved to see him, they pulled the man from his vehicle, hustled him up on stage, and thrust a microphone in his face. No one asked any questions. You know, I thought he looked mighty uncomfortable, especially when you guys made him take that canoe ride."

"But why," Charlie sputtered, "would anyone go along with our mistake?"

"That's a good question." Wally leaned a hip on the desk and crossed his arms.

Charlie bent over the wallet's contents for a closer examination. "This Snake guy is from New Orleans. Wonder if he has anything to do with that boyfriend of yours."

Both pairs of male eyes turned on Skye. "Let's keep an open mind about this," she said. "Innocent until proven guilty."

Charlie sneered. "If you're too open-minded, your brains will fall out."

"This explains why we couldn't find where he rented his car from," Wally said, not distracted by Charlie's wisecrack. "We were asking for the wrong name."

"I wonder what happened to the real Gabriel Scumble?" Skye asked. "Do you think this guy could have killed him and assumed his identity?"

"That's one possibility. Scumble is or was a very wealthy man. I need to tell the Montreal police about this latest development ASAP. They'll want to expand their search to include a body." Wally took Skye's arm and guided her to the door. "Charlie, lock up this room until the crime-scene tech gets here. Skye and I need to go have a talk with Mr. Amant."

Once they were in the squad car, Wally asked Skye, "Where is Amant?"

"His name is *St.* Amant. I was supposed to meet him at my cottage at seven. It's nearly eight. He might have waited, or he might have gone back to Simon's." Skye was numb. Could Luc really have something to do with Snake Iazetto?

"Let's try Simon's first. It's closer."

"Okay."

As they drove, Skye stared out the window. Her mind

was occupied with recent events, but when they passed the town's water tower, her gaze fastened on it and she snickered.

"What's so funny?" Wally asked.

She pointed at the tank. In huge red letters the words GRADY LOVES NANETTE were scrawled across its side. "I guess if you fall in love in Scumble River, you don't have to send your girl candy or flowers, just spray-paint her name on the water tower," Skye said.

"Yeah, and if she isn't appreciative of your efforts, all you have to do to prove you're a man is tear off her shirt and let your buddies fondle her."

Skye sobered up fast. Wally was right. It was no joking matter. They rode in silence to Simon's. No one answered the door at either the house or the funeral home, so they proceeded to Skye's cottage.

Luc's rented Jag was parked in the driveway, and he was sitting on the front step. He jumped up as Skye and Wally got out of the squad car. "Where have you been? I've been waiting forever."

Wally stepped between them, saying, "We'll explain everything later. Right now we need to go to the station and have a little talk."

"Why? About what?" Luc turned to Skye. "What's all this about?"

"Come on, Mr. Amant. We'll explain everything at the station. I'm sure you can clear it all up, but right now I need you to come with me." Wally edged him closer to the police car.

"I know my rights. I'm an attorney. I don't have to go with you."

"True, but why wouldn't you want to cooperate with me? Unless you have something to hide."

"Fine."

To Skye's surprise, Luc climbed into the backseat of the squad car without protest. She joined Wally in the front seat.

The drive to the police station passed in silence. Wally pushed a button, and one of the doors to the attached garage slid up. He pulled the vehicle inside.

They filed through the station, past May, who silently buzzed open the inner door.

Wally deposited Luc in the coffee/interrogation room, and said to Skye, "I don't suppose you'd agree to wait outside?"

Before she could answer, Luc announced, "I don't want her here."

Skye retraced her steps, detouring into the dispatcher's area.

May pounced as soon as Skye entered. "What's happening? Has Wally arrested Luc?"

Skye plopped into a chair and filled her mother in on the evening's activities. When she finished, she said, "What do you think? Why doesn't Luc want me in there with him? Obviously he has secrets he doesn't want me to know about, right?"

"Definitely. You aren't really surprised, are you? You knew he was a snake."

Skye sagged in her seat. "I hoped he'd changed."

"Snakes may shed their skin, but they're still vipers underneath."

Skye's stomach growled. May's motherly antenna twitched. "Have you had supper?"

"No, it's been over nine hours since my last meal. I'm starving."

"You better go get something before you faint."

"How about them?" Skye jerked her head in the direction of the coffee room.

"I'll tell them where you are."

"Okay, but I'd better call Simon and fill him in before I go."

"Help yourself." May indicated the phone. "I'll go use the potty while you call."

Simon still wasn't home, so she left a message. She vaguely remembered some meeting he had mentioned attending. Was it the Lions Club he had recently joined? No, it was the Grand Union of the Mighty Bull. Skye had been surprised at his becoming a member of the GUMBs, but Simon had said it was a good way to meet people their own age in town.

Skye had just picked up her purse and was headed for the door when Wally's voice stopped her. "Amant wants to see you."

"Oh, why?"

"Ask him."

Skye followed the chief.

Luc sat looking down at the table. He raised his head when Skye entered the room and said, "Do you know a good criminal attorney?"

"Yes, Loretta Steiner."

"Call her."

CHAPTER 18

Catch-22

The steady, reassuring roar of Skye's hair dryer stopped in mid whoosh, accompanied by a puff of smoke and a shower of sparks that convinced her the dryer was beyond resuscitation. Before she could decide what to do, the phone began shrilling, and the cat started yowling. Tuesday was already shaping into a wonderful day. She knew she shouldn't have skipped her morning swim. The exercise gods were punishing her.

The ringing stopped abruptly. Her answering machine must have picked up. She was ninety-nine percent sure the caller was either Ursula Nelson or May. There had been half a dozen messages on her tape from Grady's aunt and an equal number from Skye's mother when Skye got home yesterday evening. It had been too late to return the calls. Ursula would have to wait until Skye got to school. May would have to wait until Skye's lunch period.

Bingo's frantic caterwauls continued. He wanted breakfast. But he too would have to wait his turn. Skye had a true emergency on her hands. What was she going to do about her hair?

She pulled the plug and threw the broken handheld dryer in the trash. Did she have time to drive over to her brother's house, get a key to his salon, and use the equipment there? No. Her first appointment was at seven-thirty with Grady

Nelson's parents. It was not a meeting to which she could be late.

She stared at the wet mass of thick, chestnut hair. On its own it would take a couple of hours to dry all the way through, and would end up looking like a Brillo pad. The only thing she could do was put it into a French braid. A time-consuming style, but it allowed her mind to think about other things as she worked.

Her first concern was her dryer. Was there anywhere in town where she could get a new one? Maybe the drug store or the hardware store carried dryers. She'd have to make a couple of calls sometime during the day and go buy one after school. With any luck, she wouldn't have to drive all the way to the Wal-Mart in Laurel.

Bingo's complaints grew louder, interrupting her deliberations. Somewhere in the feline's ancestry there had to be a Siamese grandfather or grandmother. His high-pitched wail felt like a spike of glass being pounded into her eardrum. She gave in, stopped braiding, and went to feed him.

While she was in the kitchen, her gaze was drawn to the blinking light on the answering machine. Maybe that earlier call had been Loretta. Her finger hovered above the button. Did she have time to deal with it?

It had been nearly midnight last night by the time Skye reached Loretta Steiner. Loretta was Skye's sorority sister and one of the best criminal attorneys in Illinois. A couple of years ago, Loretta had defended Skye's brother against a murder charge. Skye had provided the lawyer with two other Scumble River clients since then. Pretty soon she would start asking Loretta for a commission.

This time Loretta hadn't been able to come down immediately. She'd been at a party and didn't want to drive the long distance with alcohol in her system. She was due to arrive at the police station between nine and ten, depending on the I-55 traffic and construction conditions.

Luc had elected to wait for the attorney before giving a

statement. He had thus spent the night in the Scumble River jail. So much for his prior proud claim that no St. Amant had ever been behind bars.

No, Skye decided, she had better not listen to the messages. She needed to focus all her attention on the Nelson meeting. There would be time to talk to Loretta or Luc afterward.

Skye finished braiding her hair, then stood before her closet and contemplated her wardrobe. What was the appropriate outfit in which to inform parents that they had raised the spawn of Satan? Something cool. If Grady was a son of the devil, maybe his folks were the parents from hell. In that case, things could get mighty hot.

She fingered a taupe tank dress with a matching cropped jacket. It was a blend of that new material, Tencel, and cotton and was supposed to be lightweight and wrinkle-resistant. Teamed with nude hose and bone pumps, she'd be set for anything short of a kindergarten-type, sit-on-the-floor crisis.

It was seven-fifteen when she arrived at the high school. She signed in at the front counter and hurried to her office, where she gathered Grady's file and the paperwork that the special ed co-op had sent for her to fill out.

The Scumble River School District belonged to the Stanley County Special Education Cooperative, an entity that at one time had provided school districts with actual services. Now it was more or less a watchdog to deal with the bureaucratic red tape of special education funding.

Illinois state law had recently required changes in many of the special education forms and procedures. For years this type of gathering had been called a multidisciplinary conference, but now it had become an eligibility meeting. Skye had been allowed to go to one all-day class to learn the new process, but she still felt on shaky ground.

School district policy held that the special education co-ordinator was to chair meetings when the results of a case study were shared with parents. But the coordinator was employed by the co-op and covered six or seven schools, so more often than not, Skye was the one left to moderate, do all the paperwork, and explain the results of her findings.

Skye headed back to the main office. Her first duty was to secure a space large enough to hold everyone. For that she needed the secretary's help. "Good morning, Opal."

"Morning." Opal didn't look up from her keyboard.

"I need a room for the Nelson eligibility meeting."

"Oh my, that poor family. The conference room is free."

"Anything bigger? There are going to be eight to ten people," Skye persisted.

"Well, you could use the stage, but they're having indoor PE today so it will be really noisy."

"Anything else?"

Opal bit her lip. "I'm really sorry, but I can't think of anything else."

Skye backed off. She felt sorry for the mousy secretary, who always seemed close to tears. "The conference room, then. Please let people know when they come in. I'm heading there now."

The conference room was in the center of the school, next to the teachers' lounge. Skye could smell coffee as she walked in. She would love a cup, but it seemed rude to drink in front of the parents and not be able to offer them any. The staff paid for their own coffee, and Skye didn't feel she could give it away to visitors. Someday she would remember to bring in a pot of her own and some disposable cups.

In the conference room was a rectangular table that could comfortably hold six, eight in a squeeze. Often they managed to cram in twice that number. Skye chose a chair at the narrow end of the table closest to the wall, so no one would have to climb over her. She knew she would be there for the duration.

After putting an extra pen in the center of the table—someone inevitably didn't bring one—and a box of tissues, she started filling in the forms. The co-op secretary had typed in the biographical information before sending them to the school, but Skye added the date, when the re-eval was due, and other bits of information. Most data could only be filled in while the meeting was in session.

First to arrive was Abby Fleming, school nurse. She and Skye had a good relationship, despite a rocky beginning and Abby's status as Skye's brother's ex-girlfriend.

Abby pulled up a chair near the door. "Okay if I leave as soon as I give my report? I need to get over to the junior high and start scoliosis screenings."

"Sure, as long as there are no health issues."

Two teachers came in next. According to the law, a special education and a regular education teacher had to be present. They immediately began complaining about being pulled out of their classes.

Skye sympathized but had to follow the rules. Otherwise, when the special ed files were monitored, the district would be in trouble.

The speech pathologist, Belle Whitney, edged in the door, nodded to Skye, and sat beside Abby.

Opal stuck her head in the door. "Mr. and Mrs. Grady are here, and so is the lady from the alternative school. Should I send them over?"

"Yes, please. And tell Homer everyone has arrived, and we're ready to start.

The secretary nodded.

A few minutes went by, and then five people filed into the little room. Ursula Nelson had decided to accompany her brother and his wife. Mr. and Mrs. Nelson looked a little like Tweedledum and Tweedledee. Both were oval shaped and wore brown suits. In comparison Ursula's long torso and beady eyes made her appear like a crow protecting its eggs.

As soon as they all found chairs, Skye began the introductions. "Hi, my name is Skye Denison. I'm the school psychologist for Scumble River High School, and I'll also be taking the meeting notes."

The alternative school representative, the teachers, Abby, Belle, and Homer spoke their names and positions on staff. Ursula took over after that. "I'm Grady's aunt, Ursula Nelson. This is his father and mother, Stuart and Beatrice Nelson."

Skye nodded toward that end of the table and said, "We're here today for two reasons. One is to share the results of the case study evaluation, and the other is to discuss what we can do to make Grady a more successful student. Any questions?"

Ursula asked, "When are we going to talk about this nonsense from yesterday? Grady did not bother that girl. She made the whole story up because he broke up with her."

Skye looked to Homer, but he was busy studying the hair poking through the button openings on his shirt. "We will touch briefly on that issue near the end of the meeting," Skye said. "It would be premature to talk about it now. Abby, would you start with your summary?"

Ursula scowled but didn't pursue that line of questioning, and Abby started talking. In brief, Grady was a healthy fifteen-year-old who could see and hear. All children being looked at for special education services had to have recent vision and hearing screenings. Abby concluded her summary with "Grady's pediatrician diagnosed him with Attention Deficit Hyperactivity Disorder when he was six. Parents declined ADHD medication." As soon as she was finished, Abby slipped out the door with a murmured excuse.

Mr. Nelson said, "He was just a typical boy. He liked to run around, stir things up, and have fun. We weren't going to drug him just to make things easier for the teachers."

Skye kept her face bland but thought, *Thank you. We're all refreshed and challenged by your unique point of view.* Aloud she said, "Since we don't have a social worker on staff, we contracted with one to interview Mr. and Mrs. Nelson, and do an adaptive behavior evaluation. According to her report, his parents chose to share little of his history. Is there anything you care to add now?"

Mr. and Mrs. Nelson looked at each other before he spoke. "We don't want our son being judged bad just because of a few childish pranks. They never proved he was the one who set the fires in the neighbors' mailboxes. And we bought them a new cat and dog. Anyway, he was too little to know better, and we don't want this in his permanent record."

"Okay." Skye made a note. Phew. Grady had quite a history. "Homer, how about Grady's grades, discipline, and attendance records."

"Grady is currently flunking everything but PE, is often truant, and has five solid pages of discipline referrals."

"Teachers, anything to add?" Skye looked at the two women sitting at the end of the table.

"He's a problem in all his classes," the regular ed teacher answered. "He doesn't complete his work, disrupts others, and refuses to follow directions."

"Any questions before we go on?" Skye asked.

Mr. and Mrs. Nelson looked stunned. Freckles and wrinkles made an interesting pattern on Mr. Nelson's chalk white skin. His receding rust-colored hair was combed straight back. Mrs. Nelson was hunched over, as if she expected to be slapped.

Ursula was harder to read. Her eyes were hard, and her mouth formed a straight line. She sat with her arms folded across her chest. "Why weren't Grady's parents made aware of his disciplinary problems earlier?"

"They were notified each time something was entered into his record," Homer said, and showed Ursula the paper. "See that P next to the infraction? It means a note was sent home, or a call was made."

None of the Nelsons responded to Homer's statement.

"Some kids with chronic behavioral or emotional problems routinely screen their parents' calls and mail," Skye commented.

"We do get home after he does," Mr. Nelson offered.

"Okay then, let's hear from the speech pathologist." Skye nodded to Belle.

"Grady has above average expressive and receptive language. There are no speech problems. He does not qualify for speech and language services under the Illinois guidelines."

"Thank you, Belle. If you need to, you can go now." Skye waited for the woman to leave, then glanced down at the report in front of her. She knew the contents by heart but still found it difficult to give parents upsetting news. "I met with Grady on three occasions and observed him in several different settings."

All eyes were on her. Ursula was taking notes.

"For the most part Grady was cooperative but guarded. He volunteered little information and refused to complete some of the projective tests. His responses to the interview queries were minimal."

Mrs. Nelson murmured, "He doesn't like us to question him."

Skye met the woman's gaze and said, "That must be difficult for you."

The mother dabbed at her eye with a tissue and nodded.

"In my observations, Grady generally appeared to be distractible and impulsive. As his teacher has said, he did not follow directions or complete assignments and often provoked other students." Skye turned a page. "In our first session, I gave Grady an ability test. He scored in the superior range, one twenty to one twenty-nine. There was no significant difference between verbal and nonverbal skills. He showed weaknesses in freedom from distractibility and visual-motor integration. A strength was seen in abstract reasoning.

"In the second session, I gave him an achievement test. His reading comprehension, math skills, and written language are all significantly below expectations." Skye handed the parents a sheet of paper with the exact grade equivalents and standard scores plotted on a graph.

After a moment, Ursula said, "This says that Grady's writing is at a third grade level."

"Yes. I believe the reason for that is his extremely poor visual-motor skills. He needs to start using a computer for his written assignments ASAP."

The representative from the alternative school made a note.

Skye turned another page. "In the last session, I attempted some projective tests, which Grady refused. He did fill out a self-rating scale. It is similar to the one that his parents and teachers filled out. All the raters, including Grady himself, indicated concerns at the clinical level for the areas of attention, aggression, and atypicality."

"Atypicality?" Ursula questioned.

Skye took a deep breath. This was really hard to explain to parents. " 'Atypicality' is how we describe the more unusual behaviors that often indicate significant emotional problems."

There was silence, then Grady's father asked, "So, what does all this mean?"

"According to state checklists, Grady has both a learning disability and an emotional disorder. The learning disability is suggested because, though he has above-average intelligence, there's a significant difference between his ability and his achievement, and he has processing deficits in the areas of attention and visual-motor integration."

Skye paused to see if there were any questions, then continued. "An emotional disorder is indicated by the unusual behavior that he has displayed for a long time and to an extreme degree, even after assistance has been offered."

"What are you going to do about all this?" Ursula asked. "Just kick him out of school?"

"No, we're offering an alternative school experience for him. One with a therapeutic component." Skye indicated the woman sitting next to Homer. "Mrs. Bennett, the representative from the Northeast Alternative School, will tell you about their program and arrange for you to go visit it. It is located in Laurel and we'll provide transportation."

While Mrs. Bennett spoke, Skye hurriedly filled in the remaining paperwork. When the woman finished, Skye asked, "Any questions?" Silence. "Okay, then I'll send these papers around for signatures. Everyone signs the attendance sheet. Mr. and Mrs. Nelson sign both the attendance and the consent for initial placement."

The eligibility meeting was over. The alternative school would hold a meeting to complete the Individual Education Plan. Skye started to separate the forms into four reports. One stayed in the child's school folder, one went to the person providing the special education service, another went to the parents, and the last went to the special education administrator.

After a while she noticed that the consent for initial placement was still in front of the Nelsons. "Do you have some questions?"

"No, the thing is, we don't think we can sign." Mr. Nelson pushed the paper toward Skye.

"You don't agree with our results and our recommendation that Grady needs an alternative education setting?"

"No, uh, we don't know." Mr. Nelson wiped his brow with a tissue. "But Grady doesn't want to go to another school. And we feel it is his decision."

"Do you let him decide his own curfew?" Skye asked.

"Why, yes. We want him to be independent," Grady's father answered.

Skye just barely kept from rolling her eyes, thinking, *Cats are certainly independent. And when they are allowed to roam outside at night unsupervised sometimes they return at two a.m. and deposit a dead animal in your living room. This teenager is not above that sort of behavior.*

"How about you and your son come look at our program before you decide?" Mrs. Bennett suggested.

Mr. Nelson and Ursula exchanged glances. "Okay, we could try that."

Skye gathered all the papers together, not sure what she should do. It was the first time a parent hadn't signed at the time of the staffing. "I guess I'll hold these until you make a decision."

Mrs. Bennett made arrangements for the Nelsons to visit her school on Thursday and got up and left. Skye also dismissed the teachers. The meeting was down to Homer, the parents, Ursula, and Skye.

Ursula spoke first. "The girl's parents aren't pressing charges, so there is no reason to continue the suspension."

"That is an entirely separate issue," Homer said. "The suspension stands. We may still ask for an expulsion."

Grady's aunt smiled thinly. "I thought you couldn't suspend a special education kid unless you could prove his behavior was not a part of his handicap. From what she said" —Ursula jerked her thumb in Skye's direction—"you can't say that."

"He's not a special ed student yet."

"I see. So if my brother signs that consent paper, the suspension is lifted."

"Yes, and in that case, Grady could begin attending the alternative school as soon as transportation was arranged," Skye explained.

"We'll get back to you Thursday with our decision," Mr. Nelson said as the three of them walked out of the room.

Skye glanced at her watch. The meeting had taken over two hours. A normal eligibility conference took half that time.

Once the Nelsons left, Homer leaned toward Skye and

whispered, "Don't push those parents to sign. If they don't, we can just keep kicking Grady out of school, and it won't cost us a dime."

"Didn't you tell me yesterday to get him out of Scumble River High, no matter what?"

Homer shrugged. "Hey, back then I didn't realize how much this was going to cost. The school board is not going to be happy with me if I spend that kind of money on a kid like Grady Nelson."

Skye stared at the principal, thinking, *Homer gives automobile accident victims new hope for recovery. He walks, talks, and performs rudimentary tasks, all without the benefit of a spine.*

Luckily, before Skye had a chance to blurt out her opinion of Homer, Opal poked her head around the conference room door. "Skye, you've got a phone call from a Loretta Steiner. She says it's important."

CHAPTER 19

Crimes and
Misdemeanors

Loretta was leaning against her shiny red Mercedes when Skye pulled into the police station a little after ten o'-clock. The attorney had her face turned up toward the sun and her eyes closed. Six feet tall, with coal black hair and dark brown skin, she looked like an Egyptian queen from ancient times.

Skye got out of her car and walked up to Loretta. "Nap time?"

Loretta massaged her temples. "I should know better than to drink champagne. I have a splitting headache."

"Want some Nuprin?"

"I took something before I left home. It still hurts."

"Why were you out partying on a Monday night?"

"My brother got appointed to the bench. He's going to be a judge." Loretta grinned.

"Wow! Tell him congratulations for me."

"Will do."

"Your parents must be so proud of you two."

Loretta shook her head. "Proud, but not satisfied. They want him on the Supreme Court and me in the White House."

"Gee, all May wants is a son-in-law and grandchildren. I guess I should count my blessings."

Loretta tsked. "Speaking of that, this ex-fiancé of yours is a real piece of work. You sure know how to pick them."

"Yeah," Skye agreed. "I'm like flypaper for dysfunctional men."

"He wants to talk to you before he speaks to the police."

"Why?"

"I have no idea. He wouldn't tell me anything. He's decided you have to hear it first."

"I have a feeling this is not an honor." Skye started toward the station's door. "Did you talk to the chief? Any news about the victim?"

"Yep." Loretta chortled. "Snake Iazetto was a member of a New Orleans crime family."

"Oh my God." Skye realized Loretta was grinning. "What's so funny about that? We could be in trouble. The 'family' could seek revenge. I don't want to wake up with a chopped-off horse's head in my bed."

"Why not? You seem to enjoy dating the other end of the animal."

"That was just plain mean." Skye narrowed her eyes and shook her finger at her friend. "I'll chalk it up to your hangover—this time."

"Thanks. You're right, it was nasty." Loretta gave Skye a one-armed hug. "Anyway, I don't think you'll have to worry about the New Orleans mob invading Scumble River. While Snake was definitely part of 'the family,' he was a lowly, bumbling member. They're probably glad to get rid of him."

"Really?" Skye pulled herself together. "How lowly? How bumbling?"

"My New Orleans connection described Snake by saying if he were any more stupid, he'd have to be watered twice a week."

"So, maybe you're right and his relatives won't be too upset."

Loretta snickered. "My connection also said that his

uncle, the head of the family, claims Snake got into the gene pool when the life guard wasn't watching."

The women entered the police station. Skye pushed the button, and the dispatcher popped up into view. "Hi, Thea. I'm supposed to talk to Luc St. Amant."

"Hi, honey. Sure. He's in the coffee room. Go right in." Thea unlocked the door and swung it open.

Skye turned back to Loretta, who hadn't moved. "Coming?"

"He wants to talk to you alone. I'll sit right here and concentrate on making my head stop pounding."

Luc was sitting with his back to the door when Skye entered. She caught her breath. He looked awful. His usually immaculately styled hair stuck straight up in the front and was woven like a basket in the back. The red lines in the whites of his eyes were as large as the stripes on the flag. And his trousers and shirt were creased and soiled.

He looked at her, shuddered, and buried his head in his arms. "I'm so sorry."

"Did you do it?"

He looked confused for a moment, then said, "No, I didn't kill Snake Iazetto. But I did know him."

Skye sat, keeping the table between them and fighting the urge to comfort him. "Tell me what happened. How did you come to know a common gangster?"

"My life fell apart on me."

"Maybe you'd better start at the beginning and be a little more specific." Skye could feel her sympathy ebbing away. Luc still wasn't taking responsibility for his actions.

"Okay. I'll try. It started soon after you left town. My parents were thrilled that I had chosen my place in society over you. Almost immediately, they started to take control of little bits and pieces of my life."

"And you let them?"

"I had moved back home after leaving our apartment. At

that point, I didn't care anymore. It was easier to let them make the choices."

"That's pretty pathetic, but it doesn't explain how you got involved with the mob."

"That happened later, but as a result of my father trying to run my life."

"I see, not your fault."

"Yes and no." Luc closed his eyes. "Do you remember the charity ball my mother was planning before you left?"

"Vaguely. What's that got to do with it?"

"My mother insisted that I not only attend but also escort the daughter of an old friend of hers."

"So?"

"I ended up marrying her six months later."

"You're married!" Skye stood up so fast that the chair she had been sitting in toppled over with a crash.

Thea immediately poked her head into the room. "Everything okay in here? Wally's in his office. Should I call him?"

"We're fine," Skye reassured the dispatcher. "No need for Wally." She shot Luc a dirty look. "Yet."

After Thea closed the door behind her, Luc spoke. "No, I'm not married anymore, but I learned a hard lesson. Love is grand, but divorce is five hundred grand, each and every year."

Skye whistled. "Boy, I could have been a rich divorcée instead of a poor ex-fiancée. Any children?"

"No, we were only married eleven months."

"I still don't understand. Five hundred thousand a year is a lot of money for most people, but for your family that's a bar bill. What's the problem?"

"You're exaggerating, but nonetheless the real issue was that about the time the divorce became final, I quit my job at my father's law firm and opened up my own practice."

"I remember your mentioning that. You said you lost both your salary and your trust fund."

Luc nodded, then leaned back in his chair and stared at

the ceiling. "At first it wasn't so bad. You remember I've always been good at the stock market?"

"Yes."

"But that went sour, too. So suddenly my ex-wife is hounding me for money, my creditors have just found out my dad has cut me off so they want to be paid off, and none of my old buddies are returning my phone calls."

Realization hit Skye like the steering wheel in a car accident. "You borrowed money from Iazetto."

"That's right. The friendly neighborhood loan shark just happened to be swimming past my office one night."

"Shit. Does Wally know?"

"I don't think so." Luc sank deeper in his chair.

"Are you going to tell him?"

"I'll see what my lawyer has to say."

"So, where did you get all the money you were throwing around here the past week?" Skye asked.

"I sold my Mercedes just before I left New Orleans."

"Oh." Skye paused to process what she had heard, then continued. She still had lots of questions. "I understand how you know Iazetto, but what was he doing in Scumble River?"

"I didn't know he was here."

Skye raised an eyebrow. "Really?"

"Well, I did tell him I needed to see you before I could pay him his money. He must have followed me to keep an eye on things. He wasn't a trustful sort."

"I see. So the idea that he might come after you did cross your mind." Skye folded her arms. "And since I'm not a rich heiress and marrying me wouldn't solve your money problems, I take it your reason for coming here, the 'I want to make up with you' routine, was phony?"

Luc had the grace to look ashamed. "I must admit at first my motive for coming to see you wasn't what I claimed. But after we talked and spent time together, I realized how much I still loved you."

"But before you recognized this love, why did you need to see me so badly?"

The lines in Luc's face noticeably deepened, and he grew paler. "This is the worst part. Promise you won't hate me."

She sighed. "Just tell me. What more can you have done to me than you already did two and a half years ago?"

"Do you remember a piece of property I bought while we were engaged?"

"You bought and sold lots of property during that time."

"Well, this is the one I put in your name."

"I don't remember that." She frowned. "Wait a minute, something about doing it for tax reasons?"

"Right. I was planning on reselling it fairly quickly and since you earned so little money, you could afford the capital gains and I couldn't."

"Right. Society pays the people who care for and educate their children less than they pay garbage collectors."

He ignored her criticism. "But the sale fell through, and I let the property sit. I hadn't paid much for it, and it wasn't worth much to anyone at the time."

"But . . ."

"But after Iazetto started to demand I repay the money he loaned me or he'd kill me, I got desperate. I cleaned out my safety deposit box, looking for anything valuable to hold him off with, and I found the deed for that property. I put it on the market, and what do you know? Someone offered me nearly a million dollars for it."

Skye gasped. "Why?"

"New Orleans is growing, and what was once too far away to commute to is now just fine." Luc paused. "I thought my troubles were over. Then I realized the property was in your name."

"You needed my signature to sell it."

"Exactly."

"So you came to Scumble River to charm me out of a million dollars. There is no foundation for abused children.

You stuck the deed in among all those phony foundation papers and hoped I'd sign it without ever realizing what I had done. That's why you kept trying to make me sign those papers without reading them first. You are truly despicable."

Luc's face darkened. "The property is rightfully mine. I paid for it."

"True, and that's why I would have signed it over to you, had you asked." Skye shook her head. "You don't know me at all, do you? I would never keep what I haven't earned and don't deserve."

He gave her a startled look. "No one would just give back a million dollars."

"Maybe not in your world, but plenty of people in mine would." Skye thought about that statement. There really was a lot to be said for living in a place like Scumble River. "Give me the deed. I'll sign it right now."

"The police have it. They found it and the purchase offer when they searched me."

"The papers that briefly disappeared from Simon's house were never really taken, were they? You were just stalling, weren't you?"

"Yes, I wanted to spend more time with you."

"Right." Skye narrowed her eyes. "This explains your odd reaction the night you arrived at my cottage, too."

"I was a little on edge, and you flinging open your door before finding out who was there and then dragging me to the police station didn't help matters."

"I didn't know you had a loan shark nipping at your heels." Skye paused. An unwelcome thought suddenly intruded. "Does this mean that the New Orleans mob will send someone else to collect its money?"

Luc shrugged. "No. Maybe. Hell, I don't know."

"You'd better get the word to them that I'm ready to sign the deed as soon as you get it back from the police."

"I can't do that until I get out of jail. So you'd better be careful in the meantime."

"One more thing. Where were you between the time you arrived in Scumble River and the time you got to my place?"

"I just rode around, trying to get up my courage to see you again."

"Oh." Skye wasn't entirely convinced he was telling the truth but found she didn't really care. "At least that solves the mystery as to why anyone would want to impersonate Gabriel Scumble. Once Iazetto realized the mayor and Fayanne had mistaken him for the honored guest, all he had to do was play along, and he had the perfect cover for hanging around Scumble River."

"I'm surprised he figured that out so fast. I never thought he was very smart."

"It's time for you to talk to Loretta and let her get working on your defense. There seems to be a lot of evidence against you." Skye heard herself talking calmly and wondered why she wasn't angrier. Luc had tried to use her, and now because of him, the mob could be after her. He had betrayed her once again. She should be furious or hurt or both. Could she be growing up, or at least growing immune to Luc's charm?

Suddenly, Luc got up and walked around the table. He dropped to one knee and grabbed her hand. "I know this isn't the time or place. And you probably hate me because of the deed thing. But I love you. Even more than I did when we first met. Will you marry me?"

For a moment Skye stared into his eyes, then she jerked her hand from his grasp and ran out of the room. She was ready to deal with the New Orleans mob but not a proposal from Luc St. Amant.

Loretta popped up from the waiting room sofa and followed Skye as she ran out the police station door. Skye finally stopped when she got to her car. She opened the door and sat sideways in the driver's seat with her feet still outside the vehicle.

"What happened?" Loretta asked. "Are you all right?"

"Yes. No. I don't know." Skye took a deep breath and told her friend everything Luc had said, concluding with "Then he asked me to marry him."

"Say what? That boy must be going for an insanity plea to think you'd marry him after everything he's done to you." Skye didn't answer, and Loretta narrowed her eyes. "You aren't thinking about it, are you?"

"Of course not. I'd have to be a idiot to even consider it."

"Right." Loretta squeezed Skye's hand. "I'd better go talk to my client. That cute chief of yours is getting impatient."

"Are you going to advise Luc to tell the police the whole story?"

"Probably not. Confession is good for the soul but usually bad for your case."

CHAPTER 20

Grand Illusion

It was nearly one o'clock when Skye left the police station. She did not go back to school. She did not visit Miss Letitia, the town historian, as she had planned. Instead she stopped at the drug store, bought a new hair dryer, and went home.

Bingo greeted her, as did more messages from May. Skye kicked off her shoes and threw herself on the sofa. She knew she had better talk to May before her mother showed up on her doorstep, but she didn't feel confident she could have that conversation without her mother detecting how upset she was.

Skye forced herself over to the phone and punched in her parents' number.

It was answered in half a ring. "Skye, are you all right?"

"I'm fine. How did you know it was me?" For a second she thought her mom had gotten caller ID.

"I just hung up from Thea, and she said you left the station about ten minutes ago."

"Oh."

"I hear Loretta showed up, but he wanted to talk to you first. What did he say?"

Skye chewed her lip. How much to tell? It was a delicate balance. She needed to tell May enough to satisfy her but nothing she didn't want the whole town to hear. "He didn't kill anyone, if that's what you mean."

"So, why is he still in jail?"

"Why did Vince spend time in jail?"

"Oh." May was silent for a moment. "So, what's the story, then?"

"Well, you know about the murder victim not being Gabriel Scumble, but instead being a guy named Snake Iazetto from New Orleans. And since Luc is the only other person in town from there, Wally wanted to question him. And you know Luc asked for an attorney. You heard me call Loretta and her say she couldn't come down until this morning, right?"

"Right. Plus Wally insisted Luc stay in custody until he answered questions," May added. "But why is he still in jail now that Loretta's here?"

"As we speak, he is probably answering Wally's questions, so I'm guessing he'll be out of jail soon." Skye held her breath, hoping her mom wouldn't pursue the matter.

May pounced. "But why did he want to talk to you?"

"There were a few things he wanted me to know before he told the police and they became public knowledge."

"What?"

"That's private, Mom."

"He's already married, isn't he?"

"Divorced." Skye sank into a kitchen chair. "But how could you possibly know that?"

"Men who have been married act different than those who are bachelors."

"How?"

"I can't explain. Just watch from now on, and you'll see," May ordered.

"Fine. Don't tell me. Can I go now?"

"No. You haven't told me what Luc is really doing in Scumble River, what this Snake Iazetto has to do with anything, and what's going on."

Skye gave up. As soon as her mother reported for her three-to-eleven dispatch shift, she'd know everything. "Okay, you win. Here's the whole story." The only thing she omitted was Luc's proposal of marriage and the fact that the New Orleans mob might or might not be coming after her. There was silence when she finished.

Finally May said, "Well, that proves it."

"Proves what?"

"Men are like commercials. You can't believe a word they say."

"Which TV talk show did you hear that on?" Skye asked.

"I'm not sure. I think I read it somewhere."

"I need to get going. I'll talk to you later."

Just as Skye was hanging up she heard a muffled, "Call me if you need anything." Once again May had managed to get in the last word.

Skye took off her jacket as she headed toward the bathroom. She threw her dress across the bed and stuffed her bra, panties, and slip into the hamper. After she turned on the bathtub faucet, tuned the radio to an oldies station, and lit a couple of candles, she switched off the lights and sank into the tub. She closed her eyes and resolved to let her mind go blank.

Five minutes later, her eyes opened. Not only had her mind refused to go blank, it was crawling with conflicting images. Okay, fine, she would sort through her options and make a decision. Wait a minute, there was no decision to make, was there? Could she really even be considering Luc's proposal? No. She just had to sort things out.

First, why had she ever fallen in love with this man? That was easy. She had fallen for Luc because he represented everything she had missed by growing up in Scumble River and spending all those years in the Peace Corps. He was handsome, rich, and witty. Too bad he had also turned out to be shallow, mean, and dishonest.

If that were true, why was she still attracted to him?

Maybe she wasn't, at least not on a serious level. Any red-blooded woman would find him attractive and probably have some physical reaction to his charm. Was there anything more than that for her?

Skye examined her feelings for Luc. He was amazing to look at. He was charming. He held a certain sexual pull for her. But that was all. They had nothing in common. Nothing you could build the next fifty years on. For the life of her, she couldn't picture them growing old together. Every time she tried, a young blond bimbo popped into her vision and pushed Skye away from Luc's side.

That was the true test. She could never trust him. Without trust, there was no way they could ever have a life together. Now, she just had to turn down Luc's proposal and find out who had really killed Snake Iazetto so Luc could get his deed back. Then she could sign it, thus paying off the mob, and he could leave town. At which time she could get back to her normal life. Piece of cake.

Skye was cleaning out her linen closet as she waited for Loretta to call. They had agreed that she would let Skye know what happened with Luc's questioning and whether he was still being held at the police station.

After her not-so-relaxing bath, Skye had decided to work off her nervous energy. So far she had cleaned out her kitchen cupboards, tidied the bookshelves, and done three loads of laundry.

When she heard knocking, her heart stopped. Could the mob be after her already? No, she was being silly. They wouldn't knock. Skye ran to the foyer and looked out the window. It was Simon. She flung open the door. "Oh, Simon, you scared me."

"Why would someone knocking on your door in the middle of the day scare you?"

"That's a long story. Come inside, and I'll fill you in.

How much have you heard?" Skye figured she might as well clear things up with Simon as soon as possible.

"Let's see. You discovered Gabriel Scumble is really Snake Iazetto from New Orleans. St. Amant is being held by the police for questioning. With your help, he's hired your friend Loretta to represent him. And he spoke to you for a long time this morning before talking to Wally. Am I missing anything?"

"No, that about does it." Could she be that lucky? Was Simon not going to demand to know what Luc had said?

"So, that only leaves what he said to you."

She thought for a moment. It was now or never. Come clean with Simon, or lose him forever. "We'd better sit down."

"That bad?"

"Just complicated."

They sat on the sofa, and Skye took Simon's hand. "You were right all along. He didn't come back because he loved me. He was just trying to use me again."

"How?"

Skye told him everything, stopping just before the marriage proposal and concluding with "His plan was for me to endorse the deed without ever knowing what I signed."

"He's an idiot."

"And now the New Orleans mob may be after me."

Simon made a sound in his throat that might have been a growl. "You'd better come and stay with me."

"I can't do that. There would be too much talk. I'll be careful."

"You could go stay at your folks'."

Skye frowned. "I'm not putting them in danger."

"I wish you weren't so isolated here."

"Me too." Skye shivered. "But I'm not running away. Too bad Luc didn't just phone and ask me to sign the deed."

"He sees everything and everybody as having an angle. It

would never occur to him that you wouldn't try to keep the land or get a piece of the money."

"That's true. In his world, there is no such thing as integrity."

Simon put an arm around her and drew her to his side. She let her head rest in that comfy space men have on their shoulders that's perfect for snuggling.

He spoke so quietly at first, she thought she heard him wrong. "Are you going to marry him?"

She shot straight up off the sofa. "What? Who? Are you kidding? How did you know he asked?"

He stood also, towering over her. "It was obvious that even though his main purpose was to get your signature, he still cared for you. He knows you're the type of woman who would work hard and help him rebuild his life. How many of those society debutantes would do that?"

"Oh." Sometimes Simon's insight scared her. "Then you should also be able to figure out that I would never marry him. I told you how I fell for him and that I've changed from that superficial person."

"True, but you also can't resist the underdog. Which he sure is at this point."

"I spent this afternoon sorting things out in my mind. Do I still find him attractive? Yes. Is he a sexy man? Yes. Is there any future with him? No."

"Is there any future with me?" Simon put his finger under her chin and gently forced her to look him in the eye.

"I hope so. I hope you'll give me the chance to find out."

His hands slipped down her arms, bringing her closer, and his lips parted hers in a soul-searching journey. His fingers were exploring the soft lines of her back, her waist, and her hips when the knocking started.

Both tried to ignore the intrusion, but Loretta's strong alto voice called out, "I know you're in there. Get your butt over here and open this door."

Simon and Skye exchanged looks of mutual frustration,

and she moved out of his arms, straightened her clothes, and let Loretta inside.

The attorney took in the situation and said to Simon, "You've got lipstick on your chin."

He reached up and rubbed the pink smear away.

Skye ignored this exchange and asked, "What happened at the station after I left?"

"Wally questioned Luc. Luc answered. Wally still thinks he did it but couldn't hold him without more evidence. So Luc was released but can't leave town, and Wally kept the deed to the property."

"Can he do that?" Skye asked.

"It's his town." Loretta shrugged. "By the time I get a judge to order him to hand it over, he'll have either given it back or arrested Luc. Anyway, for now Luc's checked into Charlie's motor court."

Skye groaned. "That does it. If he's ever going to be out of my hair and take the threat of the mob off my back, we have to figure out who really killed Snake Iazetto."

Simon nodded. "Let's go someplace nice for dinner and figure out a plan."

"Really?" Skye was amazed. "Let me get this straight. You are not only saying it's all right with you if I investigate, you're going to help me?"

"I've realized you're never going to change. And even if you did, I wouldn't like you as much because you'd be a different person."

Skye felt something catch in her throat. "Thank you." This was the side of Simon she was learning to trust.

Once again Loretta broke the mood. "Dinner sounds great. I'm starved."

Simon looked at his watch. "It's five before five. I thought we'd go to Joliet or Kankakee—better food, more privacy."

"Sounds like a plan." Loretta headed for the door.

"Wait." Skye stopped her. "Don't you think I'd better

change?" She pointed to her clothes: cut-off shorts and an old University of Illinois T-shirt.

Loretta frowned. "Five minutes, Denison, or we leave without you."

It actually took Skye closer to ten minutes. Luckily she had reapplied her makeup after her bath. Loretta and Simon were waiting for her next to his Lexus. She slid into the passenger seat and said, "Where shall we go?"

"Somewhere in the direction of Chicago," Loretta answered. "I'll follow you two. That way I can head home after we eat." She paused, then added, "And make it somewhere we won't have to wait to be seated. I haven't had anything to eat since a bagel this morning."

"Well, I was thinking of Branmor's in Bolingbrook, but there might be a wait." Simon reached in his pocket and tossed a cell phone to Skye. "Call and make reservations on the way."

"When did you get a cell phone?"

"Yesterday. This way Xavier and I aren't tied to the office, waiting for calls."

The twentieth century was creeping into Scumble River. Too bad the twenty-first century had already arrived everywhere else.

As if by mutual agreement, they didn't talk about Luc or the murder on the drive to the restaurant. Instead, they drove in silence, holding hands and listening to the oldies station.

Once they arrived at the restaurant, they were shown to a quiet corner table. Crisp white linen, low-key lighting, and the subdued clink of silver and crystal provided a relaxing background. Loretta immediately got into a conversation with the server about wine.

As Skye studied the extensive menu, she caught herself thinking about her last dinner date. The highly impressive and highly expensive Charlie Trotter's with Luc seemed not only a million years ago, but as if it had happened on a planet far, far away. She looked around. This was a very nice restaurant, and certainly not cheap, but she felt a lot more relaxed here.

After they had ordered and the wine had been poured, Skye asked Loretta, "Did Luc add anything to what he told me when he talked to Wally?"

"You know I can't tell you anything he says to me—client privilege. But, no, he told Wally exactly what he told you. Although there were a few details I advised him not to disclose."

"Such as the fact that he owed Iazetto money?"

Loretta shook her head. "I can't discuss it."

Simon took a small notebook from his pocket. "Let's assume St. Amant is telling the truth. To me, the first question isn't who killed Iazetto. It's who was the real intended victim?"

"That's a good point." Skye took out her own pad of paper and pen. "We have to investigate it both ways—one, as if it were Iazetto and the other, as if it were the real Gabriel Scumble."

Loretta joined in. "Let's take one at a time. Say the killer knew he or she was killing Iazetto. Who in Scumble River would want him dead?"

"Besides Luc, there's Grady and his gang." Skye explained to Loretta about the graffiti and the bandstand hangout.

Loretta sliced a piece of bread from the warm loaf they had just been served. "He sounds like a good suspect, no matter who the victim is. I've dealt with kids like that before. They have little remorse to begin with, and being with their gang only makes it worse."

"The other thing we can't forget is the hanky with the blood and lipstick on it," Skye elaborated. "Iazetto is just the type Fayanne would take up with." She filled Loretta in on the liquor store owner's fight with the victim just hours before his death.

"The only thing I can think of is maybe someone followed him into town, murdered him, and left." Skye made a wry face. "And if that's the case, we haven't got a chance in heck of finding him."

"Now let's assume the intended victim was Gabriel Scumble," Simon suggested. He moved his notepad aside to allow the server to place a plate of mixed greens topped with a lacy swirl of french fried onions in front of him.

All discussion was put on hold until they had finished their salads.

Once they were served their entrees, Skye raised her fork and said, "Okay, if the killer thought he was murdering Gabriel Scumble, both Grady and Fayanne are still suspects. And there's something funny going on between the mayor and Fayanne, too. Something about money. And don't forget the Montreal police told Wally that Gabriel Scumble's family had a reputation as robber barons."

"But Gabriel was trying to change that reputation and was a beloved philanthropist, right?" Simon looked up from the steak he was cutting into.

"As far as we know, but . . ." Skye trailed off.

Simon nodded. "True, people can fool you."

"I'll talk to Miss Letitia and see if there's any dirt from the past we should know about," Skye volunteered.

"Okay, then I'll check on Fayanne and Mayor Clapp's financial situations," Simon offered.

Loretta loaded a fork full of pasta and shrimp. "Give me a call if you two come up with anything."

"Will do," Skye answered. "And you let me know if anything changes."

They had exhausted the subject of the murder, so over dessert, Loretta regaled them with stories about her brother's party to celebrate his judgeship and the Chicago big shots who had attended. As they walked toward their cars, they were laughing about an alderman who had showed up with a woman other than his wife and was outraged that no one believed she was his niece.

Skye couldn't resist one last question. "If we can't find out who really killed Iazetto, do you think Wally will arrest Luc?"

Loretta nodded. "If he finds one piece of physical evidence or a single witness, Luc may have to stand trial."

"Maybe that wouldn't be so bad," Skye speculated. "I'm sure he'd be found innocent."

"Not necessarily," Loretta said. "When you go to court, you're putting yourself in the hands of twelve people who weren't even smart enough to get out of jury duty." With that last bit of wisdom, she kissed Skye on the cheek, Simon on the mouth, hopped into her car, and drove off.

The combination of a full stomach, two glasses of wine, and several late nights and early mornings finally caught up with Skye. She dozed most of the way home, not waking until Simon gently shook her shoulder once they were parked in her driveway. "We're home."

"Okay." She didn't open her eyes. She had been dreaming about Simon. He had been about to make love to her. Now the real man trying to wake her up and the dream man trying to seduce her blended into one.

"Your nice comfy bed is waiting."

"Uh-huh." She struggled to become fully awake. She wanted Simon to join her in that comfy bed, but she couldn't quite fight her way out of the heavy haze of sleep to tell him that.

Skye was dimly aware of Simon taking her purse and digging out her keys, then being led toward her bedroom before the darkness descended.

CHAPTER 21

The Rules of the Game

Skye woke up alone Wednesday morning with a vague sense of disappointment. Then she realized that she wanted the first time with Simon to be special, and being fully awake was an integral requirement.

The note she found as she was leaving for work confirmed that thought. Simon wrote:

> Good morning, sleepyhead. I spent the night on your couch. The idea of the New Orleans mob thinking you stand between them and their money scares me. I threw a tarp over my car last night, so I don't think the gossips will be a problem. If anyone asks, tell them Loretta spent the night. I had an early appointment, so I left at five. I've got a funeral tonight. Call me if you want me to come over afterwards. Be careful.
>
> Simon

As Skye did her morning laps in the high school pool, she thought about her love life. She had sorted out her feelings for Luc, but what about Wally? During the long, hot summer, she and Simon had become closer and closer. Now she had all but decided to spend the night with him. So, where did that leave her attraction to Wally?

Nowhere, she decided. A relationship with Wally would be a disaster. They were too different. His world was confined to Scumble River, and he had no desire to expand its boundaries. They didn't have the same interests or the same goals in life. He was divorced, he was older, he just wasn't the right man for her. They would always be friends, but they had no future together. At least she had figured out that much.

Wednesdays she was scheduled to spend seven-thirty to noon at the elementary school. She arrived on time feeling refreshed by both her swim and her decision about Wally. Things went well, and she was able to complete an evaluation, consult with a teacher about a behavior strategy, and still make it to the high school by twelve-thirty.

The first hint that her day was about to deteriorate was the two-inch stack of messages in her box. They were all from Luc and all said the same thing. He needed to talk to her urgently. She threw them into the trash. He would have to wait until after school.

The next sign of trouble was the two girls leaning against the wall next to her office door.

Frannie Ryan spotted Skye first. "Ms. D., Nan needs to talk to you right away."

Nanette Carroll stood slumped next to Frannie.

Skye quickly unlocked her office door and ushered the girls inside. "Nanette, shall we let Frannie go to class, or would you feel better with her here?"

"She can leave," the girl barely whispered.

"Make yourself comfortable. I'll be right back." Skye followed Frannie back into the hall. "Are you and Nanette friends?"

"We know each other. We don't hang out or anything. But I found her crying in the girls' rest room after lunch. Her mom insisted she come to school today, and some of the creeps have been hassling her."

"Physically?"

"No, just, you know, saying stuff, calling her names."

"I suppose the bus story is all over the school?" Skye asked.

"Well, yeah." Frannie shifted her books from one arm to the other. "There are some morons who hang with Grady once in a while, and they've been making sure everyone hears his side of it."

"Which is?"

"Oh, it was all in fun, and she deserved it, and the girl just can't take a joke."

"Wonderful. Anyone sticking up for her?"

Frannie studied the wall next to Skye's right shoulder. "A few of us, the ones who want to start the newspaper. We're working on the real story."

"Any luck getting Mr. Knapik to agree to the paper?"

"No. He won't even look at the sample we've put together."

Skye knew she shouldn't do this, but she said, "Give it to me when you're finished. I'll make sure he reads it."

"Wow! Thanks." Frannie started to hug Skye but backed away. "Oh, one other thing. There's a rumor going around that if he's forced to go to that other school, Grady has some sort of grand finale planned."

"Thanks for letting me know." Skye scribbled on the small yellow pad she had grabbed from her desk. "Here's a pass so you won't be counted tardy. Thanks for bringing Nanette to me."

"Who else?" Frannie trudged away.

When Skye returned, Nanette was still huddled in the chair, the curtain of her blond hair shielding her face.

Skye sat in the chair next to her and turned slightly. "It must have been hard to come back to school today."

The girl nodded.

"Which part did you dread the most?"

"All of it."

"Did you take the bus?"

A quick nod.

"How was that?" Skye was looking for an opening to explore the continued harassment the girl was receiving.

"Not too bad. The driver let me sit with the little kids up front."

"That was nice of her. Are the older kids being nice to you?"

"Some of them."

"But not all?"

"No, some of the boys are calling me names, and some of the girls say I deserve what happened to me for ever going out with Grady."

"How does that make you feel?"

"Like they're right." Nanette twirled her hair. "I did do something bad. Now I'm being punished."

"What those boys did to you is not your fault."

"Yes, it is." Nanette buried her head in her hands and sobbed. "I should have never dated Grady. Everyone told me not to."

"Sometimes the only way we learn what's bad for us is by trying it out."

Nanette frowned. "I thought I was so cool to be going out with Grady. People treated me different. I liked it. But then something happened, and now I hate myself."

"Your conscience is what hurts when everything else feels good." Skye leaned toward the girl. "What happened to stir up your conscience?"

"I can't tell you. Please don't try and make me."

Skye rubbed the spot between her eyebrows that was beginning to ache. "It's really better if you do tell me."

"No, he'd kill me and my mother."

"Who, Grady?"

"I can't say. Don't you understand? I did something bad, too, so I can't press charges against Grady." Nanette blew her nose.

"You made some poor judgments, but that doesn't give Grady—or anyone else—the right to treat you like they did."

"Really?" At first the girl looked hopeful, but then the light died in her eyes. "Even so, there's nothing I can do about it. He always wins."

"Not always. Sometimes it just takes a while for the power to even out."

Nanette shook her head and didn't answer. Finally, Skye asked, "Is there anything else I or anyone at school can do to help you feel more comfortable?"

"The worst times are in the halls and the cafeteria and the gym."

"Would it be okay with you if Frannie walked with you between classes? And maybe instead of having PE, for a while you could help Mrs. Frayne in the library?"

Nanette chewed the ends of her hair. "That would be good. How about the cafeteria?"

"Do you bring your lunch?"

Nanette nodded.

"Then you can eat in the library until you're ready to return to the cafeteria." Skye examined the girl closely. "Feeling a little better?"

She shrugged.

The bell rang while Skye was trying to think of something to say that would persuade the girl to tell her what was really wrong. She settled for walking Nanette to her seventh period class and talking to Frannie, who agreed to be Nanette's hall buddy.

Skye hurried to the front office and knocked on Homer's door. The principal yelled for her to come in. She entered and took a chair.

Homer hung up the phone and said, "Anything on the Nelson boy?"

"Just who I came to talk to you about. I haven't heard anything from his parents, but according to the teen rumor machine, Grady is threatening to go out with a bang if he has to leave Scumble River High."

Homer waved his hand. "Oh, stories like that always get told when one of the tough guys gets caught. Nothing ever really happens."

"I think we have to take all threats seriously. Look at how many students have brought guns to school and shot up their classmates in the last few years."

Homer moaned. "What are we supposed to do? Search everyone at the door?"

"If you really want to do something, give me a budget."

"Tell me what you need, and I'll tell you how to get along without it."

"We can't close our eyes and hope bad things won't happen." She frowned. "The least we can do is notify his parents. Then we should get together a list of all Grady's known associates and check them when they arrive in the morning. Also, ask Wally to watch the school more closely. Although we should hire our own security guards."

Homer snorted. "Like we have the money for that."

"I'm warning you. The school board better think about getting a budget for it. Things are only going to get worse. The world has changed."

"You're probably right." Homer scowled. "It's time for me to retire. I remember when having a weapon at school meant getting caught with a slingshot."

Skye felt sorry for the older man. She could barely keep up, and she was trained for this sort of thing, so what could she really expect from someone like Homer? "You call Wally and the Nelsons. I'll get that list together."

"Fine."

The final bell rang while Skye was in the hall. She hated that. It seemed as if all four hundred kids were racing in one direction, while she was the lone salmon trying to go the opposite way.

With a sigh of relief she spotted the Instructional Material Center, known affectionately as the IMC, and escaped through its doors. She needed to talk to Trixie. The librarian usually had a pretty good idea of which kids hung together. She also wanted to tell her about her new assistant, Nanette.

Trixie was busy repairing books but shot Skye a concerned look. "Are you all right? You seem a little frazzled."

Skye glanced at her clothing. Her daffodil silk blouse had become untucked on one side, and her blue and yellow crepe skirt looked as if she had never ironed it. She straightened herself out and tucked back a stray chestnut curl before answering, "It's trying to deal with Homer. He doesn't suffer from stress. He's a carrier."

Trixie grinned. "Sounds like you'd better fill me in."

Skye told her friend everything that had happened since she had seen her at the dance, concluding with Frannie and Nanette's visit that afternoon and her talk with Homer.

"Of course Nanette is welcome to help around the library anytime she wants," Trixie said. "And she can eat lunch in my workroom, even bring a friend if she cares to."

Skye gave Trixie a quick hug. "Thanks."

"Not a problem."

"I need to make a list of the boys I've seen with Grady, either at school or when I caught him tormenting kids on Founder's Day. Tell me if I missed someone."

Trixie examined the names as Skye wrote them down. "No, I think you got them all."

"Then I'll give a copy to Wally and Homer and hope they do something about it. I certainly can't pat down these boys every morning."

"And yet you know what Homer's philosophy will be if something bad does occur."

Skye shook her head. "What?"

"Errors have been made. Others will be blamed."

"True. That, along with his famous speech to the faculty about contract negotiations—this is guaranteed to work, unless it doesn't."

*   *   *

Miss Letitia North lived in the center of Scumble River on the top floor of an old Victorian house. The bottom floor was occupied by the Historical Society and all the records of the town for the past two hundred years. No one was allowed to touch those papers except Miss Letitia and her assistant.

Skye pulled her Bel Air into the small parking lot on one side of the house, grateful that she didn't need to attempt to street park the huge car. She walked along the sidewalk, admiring the late blooming flowers. It had finally turned a little cooler, and it was once again a pleasure to be outdoors.

She rang the old-fashioned bell, as per the instructions typed on a three by five index card taped to the window. After several minutes a small face pressed itself to the glass, withdrew and the door was inched open the length of its chain.

The woman pointed to the index card and said, "We're open the first Wednesday of every month. Come back then."

"I'd like to see Miss Letitia. My name's Skye Denison. I'm May and Jed's daughter." Skye knew the protocol. In Scumble River one introduced oneself by one's parents or sometimes grandparents.

"Miss Letitia is visiting her sister in Springfield. She will be back Friday."

"Perhaps I could talk to you. Are you her assistant?" Skye couldn't figure out who else the woman could be.

"Only on the first Wednesday of every month. Today I'm just here as a friend to water her plants."

"Oh, so on days other than the first Wednesday of every month, you can't talk about the town history?"

"That is correct." The door closed in Skye's face.

Now what was she supposed to do? She'd just have to wait until Friday. Unless maybe Charlie had some insight. Simon had to work at a funeral tonight, so she'd take Uncle Charlie to dinner and pick his brain.

On the short drive to Charlie's, Skye went back and forth
with herself. Should she find Luc and tell him once and for
all that she wasn't interested in him anymore? Or should she
try to solve the murder and get him off the hook before she
turned him down?

She pulled her car in front of the motor court and cut
the engine. If she ran into Luc, she would tell him, but she
wouldn't seek him out.

Having made that decision, she bounced out of the car
and pushed open the screen door of the office. "Yoo hoo,
Uncle Charlie?" No one answered. She knocked on the connecting door to his cabin. Again nothing. Worry was beginning to creep up her neck when she heard a familiar voice
swearing a blue streak.

Skye found Charlie half in and half out of cabin number
nine. "Uncle Charlie, want to go grab a bite to eat with me?"

He leaned heavily on the cleaning cart and got to his feet,
wiping his hands on a rag. "Why have supper yourself when
you can clean up somebody else's?" He pointed to the half
cleaned pool of vomit near his feet.

"Oh, yech. Thanks for sharing."

"You're welcome." Charlie's grin was devilish. "So, why
do you want to take an old man out to eat? You've got your
hands full with a couple of young studs."

"I thought maybe you could help me with some town history, since you're a member of the Historical Society."

"Oh, that. That was just to get the bicentennial going. I
really don't know much."

"Anything about Pierre Scumble?" Skye asked.

"Nothing the mayor didn't cover in his speech last
Friday."

"Dang, I guess I'll have to wait for Miss Letitia to get
back."

"I suppose all this is about the murder? You trying to
clear that no-good ex-fiancé of yours?" Charlie gave her a
dark look.

"Yes, but only so he can leave town, and I can get on with my life."

"Okay, then. Let's go get something to eat."

Over dinner at the Feed Bag she filled him in on the situation with Grady at school. He agreed to light a fire under the school board in support of better security.

It was nearly seven when Skye pulled into her driveway and found Luc sitting in his Jag. She briefly considered reversing the car and leaving but instead cut the motor and got out. Luc met her on the front steps and watched silently as she opened the door.

Bingo greeted her in the foyer, and Skye picked him up, hoping that the warm, furry body would make it easier to say what she had to say. "Luc, have a seat. Can I get you something to drink?"

He shook his head and sat on the couch.

"I'll be right back." She walked into the kitchen and punched in Simon's number.

Funerals usually took place from six to eight, so she knew he wouldn't answer, but she left a message saying she was okay and she'd talk to him tomorrow.

Skye returned to the living room and took the chair across from Luc. "I'm glad Wally didn't keep you in jail."

"Loretta's an excellent attorney. Thank you for calling her for me."

"That's okay." They had been so intimate at one time, and now all she felt was a sense of awkwardness.

"Listen, I wanted to tell you again how sorry I was about everything—especially not telling you about my ex-wife." He attempted to lighten the atmosphere. "You know they say love is blind, but marriage is a real eye-opener."

Skye gave a polite snicker. "I'm sure."

"You're not going to marry me, are you?"

"No, I'm sorry. I want something different now than I did when we first met."

Luc got up and stood in front of her, taking her hands. "Just because someone doesn't love you the way you want them to doesn't mean they don't love you with all they have."

Skye got up and kissed him on the cheek. "I know. And I'll always have a spot in my heart for you."

"Chief Boyd has ordered me to stay in Scumble River. Could we at least have dinner or something?"

She steered him toward the door. "I don't think that's a good idea. When Wally gives you the deed, leave it with Charlie; he's a notary. I'll stop by the motor court and sign it."

"So this is it?"

"Yes. Good-bye, Luc. Thanks for all the good times."

"Adieu, darlin'."

After he left, she sat in the lounge chair with Bingo on her lap. For the most part, she was thinking about Luc and the fun they'd had before things turned bad, but every once in a while she wondered what Grady might mean by a grand finale.

CHAPTER 22

In Cold Blood

Thursday morning, six a.m., Skye struggled to wake up. The idea of the New Orleans mob with her name on their hit list had made falling asleep a bit difficult. She had finally propped the shotgun her father had given her next to her bed, but she still startled awake at the least little sound.

In the shower that morning she kept thinking about the knife scene from *Psycho*. This whole situation had her spooked. The only thing Skye wanted was a hot cup of tea and ten minutes of peace. Instead, the second she poured the boiling water into her cup, the phone rang. She let the answering machine pick up but snatched the receiver from the cradle when she heard Wally's voice.

"Wally, it's me. What's up?"

"Can you come to Grady Nelson's house right away?"

"Uh, it'll take me a couple of minutes. I just got out of the shower. What's wrong?"

"I don't want to talk about it over the phone. Just come as soon as you can." Wally gave her directions and abruptly hung up.

Skye threw on a pair of khaki slacks and a black twin set. She pulled her wet hair into a ponytail with an onyx barrette and slid her feet into black loafers. Grabbing her watch and her cosmetic bag, she ran for the car. Maybe she'd have time for makeup later.

220   *Denise Swanson*

The Nelsons lived in one of the new subdivisions just inside the Scumble River School District. Previously, the county sheriff's department had been responsible for that area, but it had been annexed into the city limits last summer.

It wasn't hard to find the house, what with two squad cars parked in the driveway, their lights strobing. Skye pulled the Bel Air in next to Wally's vehicle and got out.

The Nelsons lived in a large Tudor with lots of fancy windows and a three-car garage. No one could blame poverty for the way Grady had turned out.

Officer Quirk greeted Skye at the open double doors. "The chief's in the living room with Mrs. Nelson. Go straight through the entryway, and take a right at the hall. He says for you to go directly in."

"Thanks, Roy." Why was Wally with Mrs. Nelson? Where were Mr. Nelson and Grady?

Following Quirk's directions, Skye passed an impressive curving stairway and walked into a huge two-story living room with one entire wall of floor-to-ceiling windows. Whatever Mr. Nelson did for a living paid very, very well.

Mrs. Nelson and Wally were seated on a sofa in front of the fireplace. "Chief?" Skye didn't want to sneak up on them. The poor woman was sobbing into a hanky.

Wally gestured for Skye to join them. "Mrs. Nelson, Ms. Denison is here now. You wanted to talk to her."

Skye sat on the woman's other side and shot Wally a questioning glance. He shrugged.

Mrs. Nelson grabbed Skye's hand in a death grip. "You've got to save my son. Tell them. This isn't his fault. He has problems. He's got a learning disability and is emotionally disturbed. Please don't let them put him in jail."

Skye forced her face to remain passive. What had Grady done? "I'll be glad to share the results of my evaluation with anyone you and Grady give me permission to talk to." She turned to Wally. "What's going on?"

Wally spoke to the woman. "Mrs. Nelson, now that Ms. Denison is here, can you tell me what happened?"

She looked at Skye, who nodded encouragement but wondered why Mrs. Nelson wanted her opinion.

"This morning at breakfast, Grady and his father got into an argument about going to look at the alternative school. Grady said he'd never go to that retarded school. His father said he'd go wherever he was told. Then . . ." Mrs. Nelson took a deep, sobbing breath. "Then Grady pulled a gun from his pocket and shot his father in the chest."

Oh, my God! Skye felt her heart race and her stomach clench but maintained her professional calm. She patted the woman's shoulder with her free hand. "How awful for you."

"I ran to phone for the ambulance, and when I got back, Grady was gone."

"How's Mr. Nelson?" Skye asked.

"His wound is serious, but he should be okay," Wally answered.

"Please, can't I go to the hospital and see my husband now?" Mrs. Nelson begged.

"Just a couple more questions, and then Officer Quirk will take you." Wally made a note on his pad. "We have to find Grady. Do you have any idea where he might have gone?"

Before Mrs. Nelson could answer, Skye blurted out, "Nanette. What if he went to her house?"

Wally said, "Calm down. She's safe. I've got an officer with Nanette, one at the bus driver's, and a couple of deputies are patrolling the school area."

"How about that list of Grady's friends I left for you yesterday afternoon?" Skye was trying to think of everything at once. This was too serious to forget anything or anyone.

"It's being checked out."

They almost missed Mrs. Nelson's whisper. "I know where he'll be. He'll go to Ursula's. She lives in the old family farmhouse east of town. He loves it there. She always protects him when we try to discipline him."

Wally motioned Skye to follow him out into the hall. She freed her fingers from Mrs. Nelson's grasp, massaging them to restore the circulation.

"What do you think?" he asked once they were out of ear shot. "If he's at Ursula's, will he take her hostage, or will she continue to defend him?"

"That's a hard question. I'm pretty sure that if she changes her role from protector to more parentlike, she's probably in danger. And considering she is Mr. Nelson's sister, Grady's shooting him may open up her eyes to his faults. I don't suppose you have a SWAT team available."

"I can borrow one from Kankakee or Joliet, but they would take at least an hour to get here." Wally scratched his head. "What do you think of calling Ursula?"

"Good idea. You might be able to get an idea of her status."

"How did Grady get a gun, anyway?" Skye asked.

"Mrs. Nelson doesn't know. Claims he didn't have it last week. She does laundry every Friday evening, and I have the feeling she searches his room while putting away his clothes."

"That's surprising. She doesn't seem brave enough. I'll bet she's really careful to put things back exactly as she found them."

"People can fool you." Wally stepped back into the living room and asked Mrs. Nelson for Ursula's number, then guided Skye down the hall into a room lined with book-shelves. He went to the desk, picked up the receiver, and di-aled. "Ursula, Wally Boyd. I didn't know if I'd catch you at home, or if you would've already left for school."

Skye admired his neutral opening and wished she could hear the other end of the conversation.

"Oh, I see, of course. Can't let the boy go without break-fast. Is he there right now? In the shower. Well, why don't you put the phone down and go check his clothes? If he has a gun, take it and leave the house immediately." As Wally listened he scribbled a note on a piece of paper and handed it to Skye.

It read: Get Quirk!

She raced into the foyer and grabbed the startled officer, tugging him back to the library. Wally had written another note in her absence.

This one said: Grady at Ursula's. Call sheriff for backup. Meet us at West and County Line.

Wally spoke back into the phone. "Well, like I said, I'll explain when we get there, but he shot his father. Yes, on purpose. I don't know, he's in the hospital. For your own safety, get out of the house, now."

Wally hung up and ran for the door, Skye following on his heels. "Did she agree to leave?"

"I hope so. The line went dead. Listen, can you take Mrs. Nelson over to the Laurel Hospital or help her find someone who can?"

"Sure. Let me know about Grady, though."

Skye went back to the living room. Mrs. Nelson was staring out the wall of windows. "It's our fault, isn't it? We didn't raise him right."

"We don't always know what causes kids to act the way they do." Skye sat beside her and took her hand. "It may be a chemical imbalance in his brain."

"We should have let them put him on medication for the ADD."

"Maybe. But it's a hard decision to make. There's a lot of conflicting information."

"We thought of military school."

Skye shuddered, thinking of Grady trained in weaponry and hand-to-hand combat. "The chief and Officer Quirk had to leave. Is there anyone I can call for you, or would you like me to drive you to the hospital?"

"My sister lives in Clay Center. She doesn't work. I'll call her."

"Let's do that now. Then we can call the hospital for a report."

Mrs. Nelson got up and started toward the kitchen, but it was taped off with bright yellow crime scene ribbon. With a sob, she turned toward the library and used that phone. Her sister agreed to come right over.

The news from the hospital was good. Mr. Nelson was in recovery.

Skye sat with Mrs. Nelson until her sister arrived, and still it was only a little after eight when she got into her Bel Air. Hard to believe that so much had happened and she was barely late for school.

She pondered what to do next. Would the kids know what was going on? She knew Wally hadn't been using the radio, so the people with police scanners wouldn't have heard.

She decided that the best course of action would be to get to the high school and see what was going on. Homer would need her if the kids were stirred up.

Nothing seemed out of the ordinary as she drove to school, parked the car, and entered the building. There were no urgent messages in her box, and her phone was silent. Skye took a moment to use the rest room and put on some makeup before going to find Homer.

She knocked on his door and took the sound of a grunt as permission to enter.

He looked up from the paper he had been writing on. "What now?"

As she told him about her morning, the pen he had been holding slipped from his fingers. "Do they have the boy in custody?"

"Wally was supposed to let me know, but I'm sure he's busy one way or the other. We could call the police station and ask."

Homer pushed the phone toward her. "You call. All those dispatchers think they're your second mother."

She dialed. "Thea, Skye. Pretty good, considering. How about you?" She could see Homer's impatience, but there was no shortcutting the amenities. "Good, your knee's better?"

Homer snarled.

"Keep up with those exercises. Listen, have they got ahold of that Nelson boy yet? Yeah, the one who shot his dad." Skye briefly wondered how many Nelsons were currently on the wanted list. "They did? No shots fired? Excellent. Thanks. Bye."

"They got him?" Homer asked.

"Yes, Ursula took his clothes while he was in the shower and left the house. When the police arrived, he was wrapped in a towel, trying to find something to wear. Sounds like he gave himself up in exchange for his clothes."

"Good. Now we don't have to worry about Grady's doing something stupid at school."

"Not him directly, but we'd better keep an eye on his friends."

"Yeah, I suppose so."

"Should we tell the kids what's happened?" Skye had no idea of the right thing to do.

"No." Homer moaned. "This isn't a school anymore. It's hell with fluorescent lights."

"It's not that bad. Think of all the good kids." Skye left him and returned to her office.

She worked all morning on psychological reports, periodically checking the mood in the hall. At noon, she took a walk around the cafeteria. Nothing unusual.

Trixie met her at the door to the teachers' lounge. "Nanette just got to school, and she wants to see you right away."

Skye opened the fridge, grabbed a couple of cans from

her stash of Diet Coke, and followed Trixie to the library office, where Nanette sat huddled on an orange plastic chair.

Skye sat next to her in its twin. "Hi. You wanted to talk to me?" Skye offered the girl a soda.

"Grady's going to kill me next." Nanette popped the top and took a long drink. If anything, she looked worse than she had the day of the bus incident. Her hair hung in unwashed strands, and the dark circles under her eyes had grown larger.

"The police have him. You're safe now."

"I know the police got him. That's why I'm here. The cop that was with us this morning told my mom I could come to school because Grady was in custody."

"But you don't believe him?"

"They'll never hold him, and then he'll come for me." She took another swig of pop before speaking again. "I was with them last Friday night."

Skye nearly fell off her chair but managed to retain an outward pretense of calm. "I'm not sure I understand."

"Grady, Arlen, Elvis, and the rest of them hang out at the bandstand in the park. Last Friday night I ran into them at the carnival, and they took me over to the bandstand.

"There was this dead guy on the steps, and Grady made me take this leather pouch thing he had around his waist off of him. It had some papers and keys in it. Grady was real mad there wasn't any money."

"Then what happened?" Skye asked.

"Grady spray-painted his new tag on the inside of the bandstand, then picked some stuff up off the ground. He wouldn't show us what he had."

"Tag?"

"You know, like his mark, the symbol that means this is Grady's territory."

"Oh. Then what?"

"Grady figured out from the sticker on the key that it was to a rental car. He also figured the car would be parked at the motor court, so we went over there and matched the license number and took the car."

"I see."

"I didn't want to. I wanted to go home. But Grady forced me inside. It was so scary. We drove for hours around town, then out at the recreation area. Finally the gas ran out. The boys pushed the car into one of the fishing ponds, and we walked home. I told Grady I never wanted to see him again." Nanette started to cry.

"That was very brave." Skye hated this next part. "What you say to me is confidential, unless you tell me you're going to hurt yourself or someone else, but I'd like to tell the police about the car. Would that be okay?"

Nanette gasped. "No. I mean, why?"

"It may help the police find out who the murderer is, and keep Grady in jail longer."

"Does my mom have to know?"

"Yes, if we tell the police, they'll call your mom. I know right now it seems better to keep everything a secret, but it really isn't a good idea in the long run," Skye explained.

Nanette didn't answer for a while. Finally she said, "Okay. Will you tell them?"

"I can, but they'll probably want to talk to you, too. Chief Boyd is really nice. He won't yell at you, I promise."

"Okay."

"Wait here with Mrs. Frayne. I'll be right back." Skye ran back to her office and called Wally.

He asked her to bring Nanette and her mom to the station. Quirk had gone to lunch, and he didn't want to leave Grady alone with Thea. They were waiting for transport to the county juvenile facility.

When Mrs. Carroll arrived at the school, Skye filled her in and gave her Wally's instructions. Mrs. Carroll looked as bad as her daughter. She moaned when she heard Nanette had been with the boys Friday night, but otherwise she said little.

Mother and daughter followed Skye to the police station in their own car. Wally talked to the three of them in his office. Nanette told the same story she had told Skye and was able to indicate on a map where the car had been dumped.

After mother and daughter left, Wally turned to Skye. "Just when I think I've heard it all." His face was sober. "I'm beginning to think that Grady Nelson's sole purpose in life is to serve as a bad example."

"What's his demeanor like?"

"Cocky. The kid isn't at all scared or remorseful. He thinks nothing is going to happen to him."

"Is it?"

"Oh, yes. We have physical evidence. Even if his parents refuse to testify, we've got the gun." Wally shook his head. "I don't understand Ursula Nelson."

"Oh?"

"She pretty much traps the boy and protects the fingerprints on the weapon by sliding it into a plastic bag using her fountain pen, but she still hires a lawyer for the kid."

"I think I understand. She wants what's right. Grady needed to be turned in to the police, but he also has a right to an attorney." Skye chewed a nail. "Is the lawyer here yet?"

"Oh, he was Johnny-on-the-spot. Ursula must have called him before we even got the kid in custody. He's some hot shot from Laurel. Thinks this case is going to make his reputation. He's hoping to be on the six o'clock news."

"Great." Skye shook her head in disgust. "Did he let Grady talk?"

"Some. They want to trade info on the Iazetto murder for Grady being tried as a juvenile."

"You going to let him?" Skye asked.

"The county prosecutor said yes."

"I suppose it's for the best."

"Too bad Nanette didn't come forward a little sooner."

"Yeah." Skye stared at the floor. Could she have made

Nanette talk yesterday by pushing a little harder? Maybe, but that wasn't her job. She'd done the right thing for the girl, and that was what mattered. "Did Grady's story match Nanette's?"

"Pretty much. His version didn't have him forcing her to do anything, and he had some extra details."

"Like what?"

"What he found that he didn't share with the others. One of the things was the gun he used today."

Skye leaned on Wally's desk. "So, maybe it'll have Iazetto's killer's fingerprints, too."

"Maybe. He also mentioned finding a letter and pocket watch, or at least the metal back off of one."

"Where are they? What did the letter say?"

"He stashed them in the shed at his house. Claims he didn't read the letter." Wally tapped a pencil on his blotter.

"He's probably telling the truth. His reading skills are poor."

"I talked to the boys that were with him, and they back up his story. If they have the time line correct, things happened fairly quickly."

"So, Grady didn't notice anything that could help identify the killer?" Skye asked.

"He did say the pocket watch back has the letters DOC engraved on it."

"Is there anyone in town with those initials?"

"I've got Thea looking through the town tax records."

"Did you get the letter and watch yet?"

"I was waiting for Roy to get back from lunch so he can guard the prisoner." Wally looked at his own watch. "He should be here by now. Want to go on a treasure hunt?"

CHAPTER 23

Betrayal

The Nelson house looked liked a haunted castle in the twilight. No one was home, and the darkened windows almost seemed to taunt them as Skye and Wally got out of the squad car. Skye shivered and buttoned up her sweater. The day had grown progressively cooler. It was hard to believe that so recently she had been sweating and cursing the heat.

Wally led the way to a small gardening shed located at the back of the property. "Grady says he hid the stuff in here because the family doesn't use this building anymore. They hired a lawn service last year."

"They have a fifteen-year-old boy at home and need to pay someone else to cut their grass. My parents had Vince and me out on the mower the minute our legs could reach the pedals."

"I made a nice bit of pocket money cutting grass for the neighbors when I was a teenager," Wally said, and swung open the shed's metal door.

It screeched on rusty hinges, sending a shudder up Skye's spine. "How should we do this?"

"Don't touch anything in case we need to try for fingerprints." Wally pulled on a pair of thin rubber gloves he had taken from his pocket.

"Did Grady say where in here he stashed the loot?"

"In a box of grass seed." Wally swept the dark interior with his flashlight.

Skye saw an old hand mower, a couple of broken lawn chairs, and a wrecked snowmobile, all swathed in spider webs. Dust covered the contents of the shelves lining the back wall.

Wally's beam of light fell on the front of a box with a picture of an impossibly green lawn. He reached for the container and the shelves came to life with swarming insects.

Skye screamed as flies and gnats flew into her eyes and hair. Wally jumped back, swore, and shook his left leg. A mouse ran down his ankle, over the toe of his shoe, and then to freedom.

After a moment they exchanged sheepish looks. Wally took a deep breath and moved forward. Skye repositioned herself several feet to the rear. Wally snatched the box of grass seed from the shelf and hurried outdoors with it. He gently folded back the flaps, keeping his face as far from the opening as possible. He hesitated a moment, then slid his fingers inside and came out with—nothing. This time he put his whole hand in the box. Again nothing.

Skye spotted a roll of lawn and leaf bags inside the shed. She used a tissue from her pocket to tear one off and spread the black plastic on the ground. "Pour it out here."

Wally complied. All that was inside the box was seed. He searched the rest of the shed but didn't find either the watch or the letter.

"Guess I better get the fingerprint guy out here." Wally put the seed box back and closed the door. Driving back to the police station, he said, "Either Grady lied to me, or someone saw him pick the stuff up, followed him here, and stole the evidence after he hid it."

"Grady's good at lying, but what would he gain in this situation?"

"Nothing but an angry cop."

*   *   *

It was nearly seven when Skye got home. She had been gone for thirteen hours and was exhausted. All she wanted was to wash the cobwebs from her hair, have something to eat, and enjoy a little quiet time. She vowed that unless a big black car and a man carrying a violin case actually appeared on her doorstep, she was going to quit worrying about the mob tonight.

Before heading to the shower, she played her messages. Simon had to work again. He told her to phone if she was nervous about staying alone and asked what she wanted to do Friday night. It was too late to return his call; he'd already be at the funeral home. She'd talk to him tomorrow.

The water sluicing down over her head and shoulders felt wonderful. She reluctantly turned off the faucet and stepped out of the stall. After wrapping her wet hair in a towel and slipping into her favorite nightshirt, she padded barefoot into the kitchen and flung open a cupboard door.

Pasta sounded good. It was too late to make a marinara sauce, but a little olive oil and crushed garlic would do just as well. She put a pot of water on to boil and turned on the oven for garlic bread.

Twenty minutes later she was sitting in front of the TV with Bingo curled up next to her and a tray of angel hair pasta, garlic bread, and salad in front of her. She was just in time. One of her favorite old movies was about to start.

The opening scene of *And Then There Were None* started to roll as she took her first bite. All through the movie, she sifted bits and pieces of what she knew about the local murder through her mind. At the end of the two hours, she had a plan.

It was too bad they hadn't found the watch back or the letter, but she thought she had a lead on what they meant. After watching the news on TV, she rinsed her dishes, brushed her teeth, and climbed into bed. She had a good feeling about tomorrow. Miss Letitia would be home, and

Skye was pretty sure she was on the verge of identifying the killer.

Unfortunately, Friday morning Skye was scheduled to be at the junior high school.

Ursula pounced on her the minute she walked in. "Grady might have accidentally shot his father, but he didn't kill that guy in the park."

"I think you're right." Skye walked behind the counter and put her arm around the older woman. "How's your brother?"

Ursula stiffened, then sagged. "He's going to be fine. The bullet missed all the important arteries and bones. It lodged in soft tissue. They were able to remove it and sew him up without complications."

"That's wonderful." Skye eased Ursula into a chair. "Any news on Grady?"

The woman shook her head. "He refuses to see me or his parents."

"You did the right thing by helping the police arrest him." Skye patted Ursula's shoulder. "You stopped Grady from acting further on his impulses and doing something more that he would have regretted later." Skye didn't think for a minute that this kid would regret anything, but a little white lie to make Ursula feel better seemed permissible.

"Just so they don't charge him with murdering Gabriel Scumble or whoever that guy was."

"I don't think they will."

"You're still looking into it?"

"Definitely."

"Thanks," Ursula muttered, and turned quickly away.

After her talk with the secretary, Skye also spoke to Neva Llewellyn, the principal of the junior high, and brought her up to speed on Grady.

Afterward she finally got down to work at her real job. Since more special education administrative duties had been dumped in her lap, something had to give in her schedule, and unfortunately it was the tasks that weren't mandated by state and federal law that were the first to go. Which meant she had to figure out which kids to stop seeing for counseling. She sighed and started crossing out names.

They really needed a social worker. Great, another thing to bug the school board about.

Skye arrived at the high school with a mental list of things to do, but the uneasy atmosphere hit her the minute she walked through the door. Fridays usually felt different, but in a good way, with teachers smiling and the hallways buzzing with barely suppressed excitement. Freedom was only hours away.

Today the buzz sounded more like a hive of angry bees, and it was fostered by several of the teachers. She wondered what had gotten them so stirred up.

Skye had intended to grab a soda from the staff room but decided to avoid the negativity she was bound to find there and instead went straight to her office. This was a mistake. Coach and several of his cronies were waiting for her there.

She knew this group. She called it the Forgotten But Not Gone Gang. These were the teachers who no longer remembered why they had gone into teaching but for various reasons refused to leave the profession. They gave all the other good teachers a bad name.

Coach was sitting behind her desk as she entered, and from that position of power, he said, "So, you finally decided to grace us with your presence."

Skye raised an eyebrow. "Did we have an appointment?" No matter how many schedules she posted, the staff of one school remained convinced she was out shopping during the time she spent at the other schools.

A woman whose teased blond hair and polyester stirrup pants had gone out of style several decades ago was sitting on the edge of the table Skye used for testing. "We think it's outrageous that students and faculty have been put in danger without our knowledge."

"Danger?" Skye finally placed the speaker. She was an English teacher who taught mostly the accelerated courses. Skye hadn't seen her this agitated since she had been assigned a remedial reading section.

"Don't play dumb with us, Missy." Coach sputtered a fine spray of spit, coating the desktop. "Grady Nelson and his gang of thugs."

Ick. She'd have to break out the can of Lysol before she used her desk again. "No one is in any danger," she said. "All precautions have been taken." She lost her cool. "Grady's in jail, for crying out loud. What more do you want?" Time to get these bozos out of her office. She wanted to check on Nanette and the kids who really needed her.

"You tell Homer that the 'flu' is going to be hitting the faculty hard come Monday morning if he doesn't tell us what's going on and how he plans to ensure our safety." Coach finished his speech, signaled his troops, and marched out.

Trixie came in as the last one left. "What was that all about?"

Skye already had a can of disinfectant in her hand. She explained, then added, "I think it may be time to equip the faculty lounge with a Valium salt lick."

Trixie giggled. "Either that or we need to start aerial spraying of Prozac in there."

"I guess I'd better let Homer know we're about to have a mutiny," Skye said, and picked up the phone.

"He left for a lunch an hour ago."

"How convenient. No wonder I was privileged with their visit. They couldn't find Homer. I'll write him a note." Skye took a sheet of paper and pen from her drawer. "Have you seen Nanette today?"

"Yes, she seems better. Her father called last night, and she's going to go stay with him for a while."

"That's probably for the best, although I hate seeing anyone forced to leave."

"No one's forcing her. She's excited about the change." Trixie helped herself to a piece of hard candy from the jar on Skye's desk. "What happened after you took Nanette to talk to Wally?"

Skye filled Trixie in on events of the last twenty-four hours, concluding with "So, I'm going to talk to Miss Letitia after school."

"You really think the murder has something to do with what happened two hundred years ago?"

"Yes. Some skeletons just won't stay buried."

"Thank you for seeing me, Miss Letitia." Miss Letitia had answered the door of the Historical Society building wearing jeans, a plaid flannel shirt open over a T-shirt, and work boots. Skye had been surprised by the woman's appearance.

"Nonsense, I like seeing young people who are interested in history."

Skye stared at her feet. She didn't want to deceive Miss Letitia. She just hoped that once the older woman knew the true reason for Skye's visit, she would still tell her what she needed to know. "I'm not really here because of my love for history. I believe some of what's happening right now in Scumble River has to do with what happened two hundred years ago."

"I wouldn't be a bit surprised. As Thomas Carlyle wrote, 'The Present is the living sum-total of the whole Past.' "

Skye nervously held a delicate cup and saucer. Miss Letitia had insisted they sit in her parlor and have tea while they talked. "Uh, right." It wasn't often that someone in Scumble River quoted Thomas Carlyle to Skye, and she was momentarily startled. "Well, I'm sure you're aware that the man who we thought was Gabriel Scumble was murdered last Friday night." The older woman nodded, and Skye went on.

"Later we found out his real name was Snake Iazetto, and he was a part of the New Orleans mob."

"I had heard that as well." Miss Letitia took a dainty sip of tea and looked expectedly at Skye.

"This information turned police attention away from Gabriel and Pierre Scumble, and onto Snake Iazetto. But I think the killer's intended victim was Gabriel, not Snake. Snake was just in the wrong place at the wrong time."

"That has frequently happened throughout history."

"Which leaves me with the question: why would anyone want to kill Gabriel Scumble?" Skye set her cup and saucer on a nearby piecrust table.

"And you think it has something to do with what happened in the past. Why?"

"For several reasons. First, because Gabriel knew no one in town. He had some contact with Fayanne over the phone, but surely even Fayanne couldn't develop a murderous grudge through a telephone conversation."

Miss Letitia crossed her ankles. "Let's say it is highly unlikely."

"This led me to the past. I didn't realize until I saw the Living History Pageant, but both Fayanne and the mayor have ancestors who were original Scumble River settlers. The motive for the murder could have to do with a previous grudge. After all, there are family feuds that go on for generations."

"You may be on the right track there," Miss Letitia commented. "Fayanne is the last of the Emericks and the mayor's children are the last of the Clapps. Both families have just about died out. Anything else?"

"Mayor Clapp's ancestor was named Dewey, correct?"

"Yes."

"Did he have a middle name?" Skye held her breath. If Miss Letitia didn't know, who else would?

"Yes, he did. Why?"

"An article with 'DOC' engraved on it was recently connected to the murder.

Miss Letitia got up from her chair, selected a book from the shelves near the window, and opened it to a page in the middle. She handed it to Skye. It was a town census, and the mayor's ancestor had boldly signed it—Dewey Eldon Clapp.

Skye sagged back in her chair. "D, E, C. Shoot, I thought I was onto something."

"No need for bad posture, dear. If you recall from the Living History Pageant, Dewey owned the drugstore in town. Back in those days the druggist was often also the equivalent of the town doctor, even if he had never been formally trained. Dewey's nickname was 'Doc.' "

"Great." Skye perked up. "Now for the million dollar question. Was there bad blood between the Clapps and the Scumbles?"

"Not that I can immediately recall, but Pierre Scumble was not the saint he was portrayed to be at the bicentennial. I told the committee that his business dealings were not always on the up and up, but they refused to listen to me." Miss Letitia was silent for a moment. "In later years the Clapps and the Scumbles were in the coal mining business together. As was Fayanne Emerick's ancestor."

"Well, people who are in business together often end up with bad feelings toward each other."

"Sadly true. Lucan wrote, 'There is no friendship between those associated in power; he who rules will always be impatient of an associate.' "

Skye was getting used to Miss Letitia's tendency to speak in quotations. "Do you think there would be any record of the bad feelings between Clapp and Scumble?"

"Nothing in plain sight, but let me do some digging. Perhaps something will reveal itself."

"Thank you." Skye got up and moved toward the door.

"Please call me right away if you find anything. Let me give you my number."

"Certainly." Miss Letitia took the slip of paper Skye handed her. "You really ought to have calling cards, dear. They are ever so much nicer to hand to people. Have a pleasant evening."

As soon as she got back to her cottage, Skye called Wally to fill him in. He had left for the day, and she found herself talking to her mother instead.

"If it's important, you can call him at home. But he said he didn't want to be disturbed." May paused. "Lately he's been really adamant about no one bothering him at home. Have you noticed anything odd about him?"

"He seemed sort of unfocused the night I called him about the murder."

"I wonder what's going on with him," May mused.

"Who knows? Anyway, I'm not calling him at home about this. Just leave a message." Skye outlined what she had found out, and then said, "Anything new on Grady?"

"They recovered the car he stole, but so far they haven't found anything that could be called evidence in or on it."

"Darn, I was hoping the missing watch back and letter would be in it."

"Nope." May changed the subject. "What are you doing tonight?"

"Simon and I are going out."

"What about Luc?"

"I told him good-bye. He's ready to leave town as soon as Wally gives him the green light."

"Good. Maybe I'll nudge Wally a little. The sooner Luc goes back to New Orleans, the better."

"Right. Talk to you later, Mom. Bye."

"Bye."

Skye looked at the clock on the microwave. It was five thirty-seven. Simon was due in twenty minutes. She hurriedly changed clothes, freshened her makeup, and brushed her hair.

When Simon arrived, she was pacing the foyer, and flung open the door before he could knock. "Could we take Uncle Charlie with us to dinner? I really need to talk to him. He knows all the town gossip."

"Does this have anything to do with solving Iazetto's murder and getting Luc out of town?" Simon questioned.

"Yes." Skye explained what she had already figured out and what she still needed to know.

"Okay, let's go see if Charlie is free for dinner."

CHAPTER 24

True Lies

Charlie agreed to have dinner with them if they went to Rabbit's, his favorite restaurant in Laurel. It was owned by a buddy of his, and the minute they stepped inside, Charlie was thronged by old friends.

The walls were decorated with murals of a goofy-looking rabbit dressed in various costumes and posed with a selection of racecar drivers, golfers, and other sports stars.

Skye and Simon were shown to a corner booth. They ordered drinks while waiting for Charlie.

Simon tucked a curl of Skye's hair behind her ear and whispered, "Let's blow this joint and check into the Holiday Inn."

She shivered and kissed him, pulling away reluctantly. "Good idea. But I have a better one." She trailed her fingernail down his chest, stopping at his belt. "Let's clear Luc and get him out of town, then check into a nice hotel in Chicago for a whole weekend."

He captured her hand and brought it to his mouth. "One slight adjustment to your plan." He pressed light kisses into her palm. "I'm making that hotel reservation for next Saturday, whether we've solved old Luc's problems or not."

"Oh." The single syllable escaped her lips in a breath.

Before anything else could be said, Charlie slid into the

booth opposite them. "You two look flushed. Is it too hot in here? I can have Rabbit turn down the heat."

"No, we're fine." Skye felt herself getting redder.

"Then let's order. I'm starved." Charlie signaled the waitress, not bothering to ask if Skye and Simon had made up their minds. "Honey, I'd like the walleye, french fries, salad with Thousand Island, and a beer."

The server looked at Skye. "I'll have the walleye too, baked potato, and coleslaw."

"Make that two." Simon handed the woman the menu.

Charlie grabbed his water glass and took a long gulp. "So, why are you wasting your Friday night with me?"

"Besides the fact that we enjoy your company?" Skye squeezed a wedge of lime into her Diet Coke.

"Yeah, besides that."

"I needed to talk to the one person in town who knows what's happening behind all the closed doors."

"Why?" Charlie took a swig from the beer can that the waitress had just put in front of him.

"Same reason as before. I need to figure out who the real killer is because Wally won't let Luc leave town until the murderer is exposed, and I want Luc on a plane to New Orleans ASAP."

"And who do you think it is?"

"I'm acting on the assumption that the murderer thought he or she was killing Gabriel Scumble, and Snake Iazetto has nothing to do with the case." Skye paused, unsure how to proceed. Both of her suspects were old friends of Charlie's, and she wasn't sure how he would react to her accusation. She took a deep breath. "If we eliminate Iazetto from the equation, I think the murderer is either Mayor Clapp or Fayanne Emerick."

"Makes sense."

Skye nearly choked in surprise on the cracker she had just bitten into. "It does?"

"Sure. Except for Miss Letitia and me, they were the only

ones to have any contact with the man before he arrived in town. Plus, both were seen with him later that night. And one of them, Fayanne, was seen fighting with him. But . . ." Charlie gave her a sharp look. "Why don't you think that Nelson boy is the killer? After all, he shot his father."

Skye summarized all she had found out about Grady's activities that night, including the letter and watch back he had stolen. "Wally talked to the boys who were with him Friday, and they all corroborate his story." Skye twirled her straw. "The thing is, I just don't think he would have brought Nanette to the bandstand or taken the car for a joy ride if he had killed the guy. He may be emotionally disturbed, but he isn't stupid."

As the waitress served their dinners, they all fell silent. As soon as she left, Charlie asked, "Is there any physical evidence against either the mayor or Fayanne?"

"In Fayanne's case, that handkerchief that was found by the bird-watcher had both blood and her lipstick on it. And as for the mayor, the watch back could belong to his ancestor."

"How about the letter? Who was it written to?" Charlie asked between bites.

"Grady claimed he didn't read it. And considering his comprehension level, I believe him."

"Then we're back to the mayor and Fayanne." Charlie salted his fries. "And you want me to tell you if either of them had a reason to kill Gabriel Scumble."

"Right." Skye casually moved the saltshaker out of Charlie's reach. He was supposed to limit his sodium intake because of his high blood pressure.

"Well, Fayanne is greedy and mean. She'd do almost anything for a buck." Charlie paused to fork a piece of fish into his mouth. "But I don't see how she'd profit from Scumble's death."

"Could she be a woman scorned?" Skye asked. "Maybe

they carried on a flirtation over the phone, and then when he saw her he turned her down."

"She *is* mighty sensitive about her looks."

Simon had been silent throughout Charlie and Skye's exchange, but now he spoke. "I did a little checking on the mayor and Fayanne's financial situations. Fayanne is one of the wealthiest women in town, whereas Mayor Clapp is in a lot of trouble."

"I did hear his auto dealership had been running in the red for a while," Charlie added.

"Not only that, but he's borrowed money against his insurance and taken a second mortgage out on his house. If he doesn't get some money real soon, he'll have to declare bankruptcy."

"How did you find all that out?" Skye asked.

"Easy." Simon smiled. "Xavier's cousin is his book-keeper."

"Still, how does killing Scumble get him out of the hole financially?" Charlie wiped his plate with half a dinner roll and popped it into his mouth.

Skye nodded. "That's the million dollar question, all right. Let's hope Miss Letitia comes up with the final answer, because I've run out of lifelines."

Saturday was a perfect fall day—bright sunshine, crisp air, and a few reddish-gold leaves starting to color the trees. Too bad Skye couldn't enjoy it.

She put down the book she had been trying to read on her patio and stroked Bingo. The cat had been curled up on her lap and now stretched, then kneaded her leg with the tips of his claws. The pinpricks of pain were almost welcome. Her frustration level was at an all-time high. What to do?

Patience had never been her strong suit. Still, she hated to go to Wally without more evidence. If only Miss Letitia would call.

Maybe she should go talk to the mayor or Fayanne. Neither option was very appealing. The liquor store owner scared her, and she had no idea what she'd say to the mayor that would convince him to confess.

She decided to wait until noon, and if she didn't hear from Miss Letitia by then, she would go shopping. A small smile lifted her lips. After all, she did need a new nightgown for next weekend.

Meanwhile, she would finish doing laundry. The load had just started the rinse cycle when the phone rang. Skye dropped the bottle of softener and ran into the kitchen.

Her breathless hello was met with, "I'd like to speak with Miss Skye Denison, please. Miss Letitia North calling."

"This is she—her—er, I mean this is Skye Denison."

"Hello, dear. I hope I haven't called at a bad time."

"No, not at all. Did you find something?" Skye was dying to reach through the phone line and shake the information out of the older woman.

"Why, yes, I believe I have. Is it convenient to speak about it now?"

"Please." Skye ground her teeth. Was that genteel laughter in the background? Was Miss Letitia teasing her?

"I found the original records of the coal mining operation. As I mentioned yesterday, Pierre Scumble, Dewey Clapp, and Dolly Emerick were all partners, at least at the beginning."

"Did something happen later?"

"Yes. According to the papers I have here, it took a while for the mine to show a profit."

Skye tried to contain her agitation. "That sounds reasonable. You have to recoup your initial investment before you start making money."

"While that is correct, sometimes people act hastily without being fully informed."

"And in this case, that would be who—er, whom?"

"Both Dewey Clapp and Dolly Emerick sold their interest in the mine to Pierre Scumble about a week before Mr.

Scumble announced that an enormous vein of coal had been discovered," Miss Letitia answered.

Skye's heart rate speeded up. "Were you able to tell if Scumble knew about the vein, or if Clapp and Emerick had really bad timing?"

"Mr. Scumble was well aware of what he was doing. The vein had been reported to him several days before Mr. Clapp and Miss Emerick sold their shares of the mine to him."

"So, Scumble got rich, and the other two got screwed." Skye suddenly remembered whom she was talking to and felt her face redden in embarrassment.

"Exactly, my dear." Miss Letitia tittered. "And that would be a great motive for murder."

Skye thought over what she had heard. There was still one flaw. "But why wait two hundred years?"

"Perhaps the circumstances have never been right before. Also, I do remember that copies of these papers were among those given to the Scumble River Historical Committee for the bicentennial. Mayor Clapp and Miss Emerick might not have been previously aware of their ancestors' claim."

"I think I'd better take this information to Wally."

"Yes, tell Chief Boyd that I'll have copies of these records available for him by this afternoon. He may call for them at his convenience."

"Thank you so much. I really appreciate your help."

"You are very welcome, my dear. Come visit me anytime. You may be surprised at all I know about Scumble River and its citizens."

Skye hung up and stared into space. What was Miss Letitia getting at? She'd think about that later. Right now she needed to find Wally.

Wally turned out to be more difficult to locate than she had anticipated. She called the police station and his home with no luck. Finally, she asked the dispatcher to page him. Fifteen minutes passed before her phone rang, and it seemed as if Wally was having difficulty focusing again. "This is Wally, you wanted to talk to me?"

"Are you okay? You sound funny."

"I'm fine. Just tell me what you want."

"Sorry to bother you. I guess it can wait."

Wally sighed. "Go ahead."

"I think I know who the murderer is. I'm pretty sure it's the mayor."

"Pretty sure?" He sighed again. "You'd better start at the beginning."

"Well, to begin with, it looks as if Pierre Scumble cheated Dewey Clapp and Dolly Emerick out of a lot of money."

After she laid out the facts, Wally seemed a bit more interested. "That's enough for me to at least have a little chat with the mayor and the current Miss Emerick. But why do you think it's Clapp and not Fayanne?"

"Call it intuition, but I think Fayanne would have covered her tracks better. Mayor Clapp is a lot more impulsive."

"Good point."

"When are you going to talk to the mayor?" Skye asked.

"I'll call him now and have him meet me at the station in half an hour." There was a brief silence. "I'll tell him it's a town emergency. You meet us there, too."

"Really? You're letting me sit in on the interrogation?" Skye couldn't believe her luck.

"Yes. I want you to lay out the case against Clapp, just like you did for me. We need to rattle him into making some false move because there really isn't any evidence."

Wally and the mayor were sitting in the chief's office when Skye arrived. Both looked disheveled. Wally got up and met her at the door. As he guided her to the chair next to the mayor's, he whispered in her ear, "Be sweet."

She knew what he meant. Wally wanted her to act like a naïve little farmer's daughter.

Wally went back around his desk and sat down. "So, Skye, you have something you want to tell the mayor and me?"

"Well, I sure hope I'm not wasting the time of two important men like you both, but I've been thinking about poor Mr. Scumble." She forced herself to giggle. "Oh, I mean Mr. Iazetto. Anyway, the more I thought about that poor man coming to our town and getting himself killed, the worse I felt."

Mayor Clapp patted her hand. "My dear, you really don't have to worry about that sort of thing. The killer was probably some stranger here for the bicentennial and is long gone now."

"You know, that's what I thought, too." Skye widened her eyes. "Because the only ones who had any contact with Mr. Scumble before he came to town were Fayanne Emerick and you."

"Uh, how do you know that?" The mayor squirmed.

"The day of the Founder's Speech you said you originally contacted him, then turned him over to Fayanne."

"That doesn't mean someone else couldn't have talked to him."

"Well, Fayanne did say he was harder to get ahold of than the president. Do you think he would have taken just anyone's call?"

Wally spoke up. "That's a hard question to answer. What else did you find out, Skye, that you want to share with us?"

Skye knew that Wally was telling her to back off. She smiled at the mayor. "Anyway, I thought it was interesting that the last two people to be seen with Mr. Scumble were you and Fayanne."

Mayor Clapp was sweating.

". . . Though the thing that really got me thinking was the engraving on the watch back Grady Nelson found at the crime scene."

"But how did you see that? I took . . ." Mayor Clapp trailed off, realizing what he had said.

Wally leaned forward. "Yes, Mayor, you took the watch and the letter from where Grady had hid them in his shed, didn't you?"

"No—I mean—that's not what I meant." Clapp sagged in his seat. "Anyway, why would I kill Gabriel Scumble? Except for a couple of phone conversations, I'd never even met the man."

"That puzzled me too, until I had a chat with Miss Letitia." Skye watched the mayor's already pale complexion turn translucent. "She told me all about how Pierre Scumble hoodwinked Dewey Clapp and Dolly Emerick out of their rights to the coal mine."

"I don't know what you're talking about." Clapp mopped his dripping face with a handkerchief. "And even if what you say is true, that happened two hundred years ago. What could it have to do with anything now?"

She looked him in the eye and said quietly, "I understand that you are in a lot of financial trouble, Mr. Mayor. Maybe you found a way to get back some of that money Gabriel Scumble swindled your ancestor out of."

Clapp struggled to his feet. "Why are you doing this to me? I've been mayor of this town for twenty years." He lurched toward the door. "I don't have to take this kind of treatment."

The mayor disappeared down the hallway. Skye sat there, at a loss. "That went well," she said sarcastically.

"Yes, it did. Now Quirk will follow him."

It took Skye a moment before she guessed. "He'll go straight for the letter and watch. He needs to get rid of them." She frowned. "Unless he already has."

"I'm betting he kept them. At least the letter." Wally smiled. "Quirk is waiting on the corner in his mother's old Pinto. Clapp will never notice him."

"What should we do?"

"Wait in the squad car."

They didn't have to sit there for long. Quirk radioed them within ten minutes. Clapp had driven straight to the Brown Bag Liquor Store.

"Time to pay Miss Emerick a visit." Wally started the motor. "Any chance I could persuade you to stay at the station and not follow me?"

"Nope."

"Didn't think so. Then do what I tell you."

"Yes, sir."

Wally called for backup on the way over. He parked next to Quirk's Pinto at the motor court. Wally told Quirk to come with him and then turned to Skye. "Stay in the car."

She nodded. Getting in the line of fire didn't really sound like a good time to her.

Wally and Quirk had just gone inside the building when Justin came flying around the corner of the liquor store. The panic written across his face had Skye out of the squad car and heading toward the teen before he even spotted her. They met on the side of the road.

"What are you doing here?" Skye asked sharply.

Justin froze, and his face lost all expression.

She immediately realized her error. This was not a kid you could be confrontational with. He would withdraw and refuse to communicate. "Sorry. I'm a little uptight right now."

Justin mumbled, "That's okay, but . . ." He gulped. "Uh, so, why did the police go in the liquor store?"

Skye knew she probably shouldn't tell Justin what was going on, but she blurted out, "The police are following Mayor Clapp. We think he's the one who killed Mr. Iazetto."

"Shit." Justin's voice cracked. "Frannie's inside there."

"Oh my God. Why?"

"We're investigating for the school newspaper. We figure Miss Emerick is the murderer, so we're taking turns watching her. I was supposed to take over, but the police rushed in before I could." Justin shifted from one foot to the other.

Skye was afraid he was about to run into the building himself. "Do you know exactly where Frannie is?"

"The storeroom." Justin grabbed her. "We've got to do something."

"Do you know if there's an outside door to the store-room?"

He nodded. "Frannie was going to prop it open for me." He started to tug her toward the back of the building. "What are you waiting for? We have to find her."

Skye quickly considered her options. She couldn't radio Wally to let him know that the girl was there. Fayanne and the mayor might hear. She couldn't just stand here and hope Frannie was okay. Her only choice was to go inside and try to either tell Wally about Frannie or find the teen and get her out of the building.

"Okay, you stay here." She wished she could lock the boy in the squad car. "I'll go in and get Frannie." She spoke over her shoulder as she ran toward the back of the liquor store.

Justin's information had been correct. The door was propped open with a small wedge of wood. Skye eased inside, thankful the door didn't squeak. She felt as if she couldn't breathe. What if Justin followed her? What if Mayor Clapp found Frannie and held her hostage?

As her eyes adjusted from the bright sunshine to the dim light in the storage room, her gaze swept the area, but she didn't see Frannie. A thin shaft of light to the right caught Skye's attention, and she crept forward. Just as she reached the doorway, a hand snaked out and grabbed her arm.

Skye swallowed a scream and whirled around. Frannie had her finger to her lips and jerked her head toward a door between the storeroom and the interior of the liquor store. It was half-open, and they had a clear view of the mayor stand-ing at the counter and Fayanne behind it. They were arguing.

Clapp yelled, "That bitch Skye Denison knows every-thing. She sat in front of me like butter wouldn't melt in her mouth and told the chief how I killed Scumble."

Fayanne snorted. "She's guessing. They have no proof. Just sit tight and keep your yap shut. You'll be fine."

"That's right; they don't have any evidence yet. That's why we have to get rid of that letter."

"No way. That's our only proof that Scumble intended to give us the money. Now that we know he may be still alive, that letter is like cash in our pocket." Her voice softened and took on a wheedling tone. "Look, you already killed one man for this money—and we felt really bad about that—but he turned out to be a gangster who deserved to die. It's almost as if God is saying we're in the right. Don't give up now. Burning that letter would be like burning thousand-dollar bills."

"I should have never left it with you," the mayor whined. "If only my wife weren't such a snoop."

"Be a man." Fayanne's demeanor abruptly changed from cajoling to belligerent. "Keep your mouth shut, and it will all blow over."

"That's easy for you to say. You're not the one who shoved that pickax into the man's heart. You're not the one who's heading for the electric chair." Clapp stuck his hand in his pocket and withdrew a gun. He pointed it at Fayanne. "Give me the watch and the letter, right now."

"Okay," Fayanne said. "Calm down. No need to get so riled. They're in the safe."

Clapp went behind the counter and grabbed Fayanne with one hand, still pointing the gun with the other, and dragged her into the open area. "Where's the safe?"

Fayanne motioned with her chin. "In the storeroom."

Skye felt the girl beside her tense and jump back. Out of the corner of her eye, she saw Frannie bump a pile of boxes containing wine bottles. The top one teetered. Skye held her breath. It wobbled again, then crashed to the floor. The sound of glass breaking was thunderous.

As Clapp's head whipped around in response to the sudden noise, Fayanne grabbed his arm and wrestled the gun from his hand. She pointed it at him and shoved him toward the storeroom. Skye used her foot to push Frannie flat to the floor behind a stack of boxes and turned toward the liquor store owner and the mayor. Fayanne had switched on the light, and she and Clapp stood in the doorway glaring at Skye.

Skye's mind raced. She needed to get them out of the storeroom before they spotted Frannie.

Fayanne said coldly, "I should have known. You just couldn't keep your nose out of this, could you?" She motioned with the gun. "Get your big butt over here."

Skye moved toward the pair, relieved to divert their attention away from where Frannie was hiding behind the boxes. "Listen, Fayanne, I heard what you were saying. The mayor killed the guy, not you. Put down the gun, and you'll be fine."

Fayanne cast a speculative glance at Clapp. "You'll tell them what you heard? That I didn't have nothing to do with the killing? It was all him."

Skye nodded. "Just put the gun down." She had finally spotted Wally and Quirk. They had eased into positions to the right and left of the storeroom door and had their guns aimed at Fayanne.

"How should we do this? I'm not letting you go until I'm sure the police aren't going to come after me."

"Uh, well . . ." Skye wondered what she should do. It was obvious that Wally and Quirk couldn't do much while Fayanne had her gun leveled at Clapp's and Skye's heads. "Let's call Wally and have him tell you himself."

Fayanne pursed her lips. "You call him. Tell him I want it in writing."

"Where's the phone?"

"Behind the counter." Fayanne used her gun to gesture, and Wally stepped out from behind a cardboard display. He put his gun to Fayanne's temple and said, "Drop it."

She hesitated for a second but finally brought her arm to her side and let the gun slide from her fingers to the floor.

Quirk came out of his hiding place and took the mayor by

the arm. "Eldon Clapp, you are under arrest for the murder of Snake Iazetto. You have the right to remain silent . . ."

"Are you nuts or just self-destructive?" Wally yelled. Quirk and another officer had driven off with the two prisoners a few seconds before. Now the chief focused his attention on Skye. Justin and Frannie stood by her side.

"I had no choice. Justin ran up to me and told me that Frannie was in the liquor store. You had already gone inside, and there was no way to let you know. I couldn't leave her in danger."

Wally blew out a stream of air. "You could have been killed. That gun Clapp and Fayanne were waving around had real bullets in it."

Justin frowned. "You're right Chief; I should have been the one to go in, not Ms. D."

"Hey, no one had to go in to rescue me." Frannie said, "I would have been just fine. I can take care of myself. I've been studying karate."

Both adults looked at the teens. Skye raised an eyebrow at Wally. "I give up. Which would you have preferred being in danger—Justin, Frannie, or me?"

"None. None would be my first choice." Wally shook his head. "But I can see your point."

"Thank you." Skye smiled. "And I can see yours."

Wally used Quirk's Pinto to drive Skye and the teens to the police station. He went inside, and Skye drove Frannie and Justin home in her car. She spent some time letting them talk over what had just happened. Finally, she turned them over to their parents and headed back to the PD.

She found Wally in his office and threw herself in his visitor's chair. "So, anything new?"

"Plenty. Fayanne is still testifying against the mayor, and in exchange we're not filing charges against her as an accessory."

"She was a fool to cover up for him the first place."

"According to the mayor, the murder was an accident.

Gabriel Scumble had agreed to pay Clapp and Fayanne one hundred thousand dollars each to make up for Pierre's chicanery. So, after the picture-taking session at the carnival, the mayor asked for his money. Iazetto masquerading as Scumble didn't know what the mayor was talking about, but he tried to bluff it out by putting Clapp off."

"Let me guess. Clapp told Fayanne, and she confronted Iazetto/Scumble that night in the Beer Garden."

"Right." Wally nodded. "So, Clapp approached Iazetto/Scumble again, and again he was put off. Clapp went back to tell Fayanne, and she punched him in the face for being so useless."

"Which, of course, hurt his male ego."

"And made him determined to get the money he felt was rightfully his. He took Iazetto/Scumble out to the bandstand so they could be alone and demanded the money. Clapp tried to grab the pickax from Iazetto, saying he didn't deserve the honor of having it. They struggled, and Iazetto ended up dead."

"Amazing. So then, even though the mayor had already killed the man he thought was Gabriel Scumble, he and Fayanne still planned to try and get the money Scumble promised them from his estate. So they had to keep the letter in order to prove that Gabriel Scumble intended to give them the money his ancestor swindled theirs out of." Skye shook her head.

Wally took over the explanation. "And then when they found out that Mayor Clapp had killed Snake Iazetto, not Gabriel Scumble, they decided to go back to plan A and get the money from Scumble himself."

"Which meant they still thought they needed the letter," Skye added.

"Yeah, it was a little too valuable to just get rid of."

"Ironic that it will end up being the key that locks Eldon Clapp behind bars for a very long time."

Pillow Talk

It had been a tough week for the town of Scumble River. Mayor Clapp and Fayanne Emerick, while not always the most popular residents, were an integral part of the community. The disclosure of their villainy had hit everyone hard.

Skye had spent many hours tying up loose ends. One of the things on her list had been talking Homer into allowing Frannie, Justin, and their friends to start a school newspaper. At first Homer had been adamant—no newspaper. But Skye took to stopping by his office several times a day and repeating her request. She had finally worn him down with the promise that she would sponsor the activity. How much trouble could a bunch of bright kids writing stories get into?

Another item on her agenda had been finding out what was going on with Charlie. On Monday after school she had confronted him about his look of exhaustion, odd behavior, and absences. He finally confessed he was seeing a woman over in Laurel. He didn't want to tell anyone until he decided if the relationship would last. It hadn't. They had ended things the night before. Skye was relieved. The relationship had obviously been bad for his health.

The rest of her questions had to wait until Wally had time to talk to her. He had finally agreed to join her for lunch at her place on Saturday.

*   *   *

Saturday afternoon, Skye could see the weariness in Wally's posture as she guided him through her cottage and toward the chaise on the patio. "Have a seat. I'll be right back with the food."

He dropped into the chair with a sigh, put his legs up, and closed his eyes.

She hurried back inside and grabbed the tray she had prepared. It had been a long seven days since she had walked out of the police station after Fayanne's and the mayor's arrests. No way was she going to let Wally fall asleep on her. She had waited too long to find out the whole story surrounding Snake Iazetto's murder.

"Lunch is served." Skye made as much noise as possible as she put the tray on the round glass table between the two lounges.

Wally opened one eye. "Keep it down. I have a splitting headache."

"Would you like some aspirin?"

"Thanks, I have my own." He pulled a prescription bottle from his pocket, opened it, and poured a capsule into his palm. "What's for lunch?"

"Beef stew, homemade rolls, salad, and brownies. There's coffee in the carafe."

"Sounds great." Wally started to fill his plate. "You baked bread?"

"No, these are from Grandma Denison. When she heard Luc left town last Sunday, she called me over and gave them to me along with some advice. I froze the rolls until today, but I'm going to try and live the advice."

Between mouthfuls, Wally asked, "What piece of wisdom did she impart?"

"That I need to learn how to fall in love without losing myself."

"Sounds like something we all need to keep in mind." Wally continued to eat. "This is the best food I've had in quite a while, but I know that you didn't invite me to lunch just because you wanted to feed me. Go ahead and ask your questions."

"Thanks. I would like to wrap up some details, just for my own satisfaction." Skye took a sip of her Diet Coke. Where to begin? "Gabriel Scumble, the real one, what's the story with him? Why didn't he show up and why couldn't they find him in Montreal?"

"He didn't make it to the bicentennial because the poor man had a stroke while waiting at the airport to board the plane. He has no relatives, and he had given the week off to his personal assistant, so when the hospital tried to contact someone about him, it took several days to find anyone they could inform. He was unconscious until last Friday, and at that point contacting someone in Scumble River wasn't their first priority."

"Why was his penthouse all packed up and all the personal information gone?" Skye paused, a forkful of salad at her mouth.

"He's in the process of moving to France. Everything was boxed and waiting to be shipped. He'd been staying at a hotel and had all his personal items with him in his suite."

"I wonder why the building manager didn't tell the police that."

Wally finished his lunch and pushed his plate away. "Who knows? But Gabriel Scumble is extremely wealthy, and that might have something to do with it. A lot of rich people put a high price on privacy and pay the help very well not to reveal anything about them."

"So I understand."

"One good thing that has come from all of this is that Gabriel Scumble is giving the town of Scumble River a check for one hundred thousand dollars."

"Why?"

Wally smiled. "He's trying to make up for his family's long history of cheating people. He's the last of the Scumbles and wants to repair the name before he dies. Of course, he's no fool. The money comes with the condition that no one in town will try to sue him for anything Pierre may or may not have done to their ancestors."

"I wonder what the town will do with all that money." Skye got up and cleared the dishes.

"Argue."

"Too true." She came back with a fresh pot of coffee and a plate of brownies. "So Iazetto's body had no identification on it because he hid his wallet and rental car papers in the lamp, right?"

"Correct, and Grady stole the rest."

"Let's see. Grady got the keys to the rental car, the back of the mayor's watch, and the letter from Pierre Scumble to Mayor Clapp that the mayor dropped when he was struggling with Iazetto. Okay, then what were the papers Nanette mentioned, and whose gun was it?"

Wally swallowed a bite of brownie. "As far as we can tell, the gun was Iazetto's. His were the only prints on it, besides Grady's. And we think the papers were the IOU your boyfriend signed for Iazetto. They must have washed away when the car was submerged."

"When did you find out that Luc owed Iazetto money?"

"Amant told me the whole story when I returned the deed to him and told him he was free to go back to New Orleans." Wally licked his fingers. "I suppose you knew all along."

"Not until you arrested him." Skye quickly steered the conversation in another direction. "I hope Luc pays back the Iazetto family really soon. I signed the deed the day you gave it back to him. And I'd like to know that the mob isn't going to come beating down my door in search of their money."

"You're probably safe. The 'family' would have a hard time blending into Scumble River."

Skye shaded her eyes. The sun was bright today but not hot. A lot had changed in the last two weeks, including the weather. "I think I figured out how Fayanne's lipstick got on the handkerchief."

"How?"

"When Iazetto arrived at the Founder's Day Speech, Fayanne kissed him as he got out of the car. My guess is he used his hanky to rub her lipstick off his face and then again when she gave him the bloody nose at the Beer Garden."

"That's as good a guess as any." Wally leaned back and closed his eyes. "Fayanne maintains she and the victim were not intimately involved."

"There's one thing I haven't been able to figure out. I know the mayor had to have followed Grady that night in order to retrieve the watch and the letter, but how did he do it? I mean, Grady and his gang took quite a long joy ride in that stolen car."

"Clapp says he discovered that the watch and letter were missing and figured he must have dropped them at the bandstand. He went back there and arrived just in time to see Grady pick up the stuff. Since everyone had parked at the motor court, the mayor's car was right there and he could follow them. He waited behind some trees at the recreation club gate because he figured they had to come back out that way. When they came out walking, he followed Grady home on foot."

"He was lucky Grady didn't stash the watch and letter in the rec club somewhere." Skye checked her own watch. It was two-thirty. Simon was picking her up at five for their weekend in Chicago.

"The mayor decided that Grady would wait until he was alone to hide the stuff," Wally said, and crossed his legs. "Anything else, Miss Marple?"

Skye debated whether to ask this last question. It really was none of her business, but she was concerned. She shrugged mentally. He could always refuse to answer. "Wally, this isn't really about the murder, but I am worried about something."

"Yes?"

"Well, when I called you the night of the murder, you sounded funny on the phone, and then when we met at the station, you seemed a little unfocused at first. And that's happened a couple of other times. Plus, it was unusual for you not to attend the dance. Is everything alright with you?"

"I figured you had noticed." He sat up and swung his legs off the chaise lounge. "You have to keep this a secret. You can't tell May or Charlie or Trixie or anybody. Promise?"

Skye caught her breath. What was he going to confess to? "Cross my heart."

"I've been having terrible headaches and trouble sleeping for several months, so I finally went to the doctor. He's doing all these tests and has me trying all this stuff at home. Every time you've called, I've either been attached to a bunch of machinery or just fallen into a deep sleep. The night of the dance, my headache was so bad I took a pill and went to sleep at seven o'clock."

Skye covered his hand with hers. "I'm so sorry. Are you feeling any better?"

"The doc thinks it might be stress-related."

"That could do it. Has something changed in the past few months?"

Wally sighed. "Darleen's been calling." With that bombshell, he refused to say any more, claiming he had to get back to the police station. Soon afterward he said good-bye and left.

Skye cleared up the mess from their lunch and checked her watch again. Only three o'clock. She had plenty of time to pack and make herself beautiful.

Simon had reserved a suite at one of the best hotels in Chicago. They had enjoyed room service for dinner and were relaxing with a glass of champagne as they gazed at the beautiful skyline.

"So, did you sign that deed for Luc?" Simon asked.

"Yes. Charlie acted as go-between so I wouldn't have to see Luc again." Skye closed her eyes and sighed. "Just think, for a while there I was a millionaire, and I didn't even know it."

"You probably could have asked for a percentage of the money when the land is finally sold."

"No, this way it's a clean break. There's nothing to tie me to Luc. I can finally write 'the end' to that chapter in my life."

Simon clinked his glass against Skye's. "To the beginning of the next chapter."

She took a sip of the sparkling liquid. "You are a wonderful man. I'm sorry it's taken me so long to figure that out."

"You're a special woman. I'm glad I waited." He slipped his arm around her.

Skye snuggled back against him. "You really didn't have to get a suite. A regular room would have been fine."

"Ah." Simon led her through the bedroom to the bathroom. "But a regular room wouldn't have this." He swung open the door and revealed a huge circular tub in the center of the floor.

"Oh, my!" She could feel the color rising in her cheeks. "You should have told me. I didn't bring a bathing suit."

"Perfect."

Signet

Denise Swanson
The Scumble River Mysteries

When Skye Denison left Scumble River years
ago, she swore she'd never return. But after a
fight with her boyfriend and credit card
rejection, she's back to home-sweet-homicide.

Available wherever books are sold or at
penguin.com

S394

Penguin Group (USA) Online

What will you be reading tomorrow?

Tom Clancy, Patricia Cornwell, W.E.B. Griffin,
Nora Roberts, William Gibson, Robin Cook,
Brian Jacques, Catherine Coulter, Stephen King,
Dean Koontz, Ken Follett, Clive Cussler,
Eric Jerome Dickey, John Sandford,
Terry McMillan, Sue Monk Kidd, Amy Tan,
John Berendt…

You'll find them all at
penguin.com

*Read excerpts and newsletters,
find tour schedules and reading group guides,
and enter contests.*

Subscribe to Penguin Group (USA) newsletters
and get an exclusive inside look
at exciting new titles and the authors you love
long before everyone else does.

PENGUIN GROUP (USA)
us.penguingroup.com